BALLOON

ALTITUDE

Author: Christopher Keith
Title: Balloon: Altitude
www.christopherkeithauthor.com

ISBN: 9780648241423
ISBN: 0648241424

Published by Pagetrim Book Services
www.pagetrimservices.com
info@pagetrimservices.com

OTHER BOOKS
BY CHRISTOPHER KEITH

Balloon: Altitude

Balloon: Solitude

Balloon: Latitude

Lifeline

Clotho

Curse of the Travel Bug Vol. 1

Curse of the Travel Bug Vol. 2

By the Book

FACTS

In 1927, Hawthorne Gray set a high-altitude record on his first balloon flight by reaching 29,000 feet. On his second flight, he ascended to an impressive 42,000 feet, but the record was not officially recognised because he had to abandon the balloon by parachute to save his life. Undeterred, Gray attempted the feat again, successfully reaching 42,000 feet once more on his third flight. Tragically, he ran out of oxygen during the descent, lost consciousness due to hypoxia, and was later found dead in a tree.

In 1934, Americans William Kepner, Albert Stevens, and Orvil Anderson reached 60,000 feet and were the first ever humans to report seeing the Earth's curvature with their own eyes. They were compelled to parachute to reach safety when their hydrogen balloon exploded mid-flight.

In 1956, US Navy Lieutenant Commanders Malcolm Ross and Lee Lewis set a new record by flying to an altitude of 76,000 feet. Then, in October the following year, they surpassed their own achievement, reaching 85,700 feet.

In 1960, Joe Kittinger achieved remarkable fame by setting two new records: flying a balloon to the highest altitude and then performing the highest ever parachute jump from 102,800 feet; the first person to jump from the stratosphere, cementing his place in history. These astounding records, however, stood for only six years.

Lieutenant Commander Malcolm Ross embarked on another space balloon adventure in 1961, accompanied by Lieutenant Commander Vic Prather. They launched from the deck of an American aircraft carrier, soaring to a record-breaking height of 113,740 feet.

Kittinger's 1960 skydiving record was shattered in 1966 when Nicholas Piantanida, an amateur parachute jumper, skydived from a crewed balloon at 123,500 feet. His record would stand for the next forty-six years.

Austrian skydiver, Felix Baumgartner, jumped from a helium balloon in 2012 as part of the Red Bull Stratos Project. He set two world records that day: jumping from just over 128,000 feet and reaching an estimated top speed of 843.6 miles per hour, exceeding the speed of sound.

Two years later, in 2014, Alan Eustice from Google smashed Baumgartner's altitude record when he jumped from a space balloon at 135,908 feet, more than one mile higher. However, reaching a maximum speed of 822 miles per hour, he did not break Baumgartner's fastest skydive record.

BALLOON

ALTITUDE

CHRISTOPHER KEITH

PAGETRIM
BOOK EDIT &
DESIGN SERVICES

ONE

It was supposed to be the peak of his career, a day of jubilation and recognition. Many years of hard work, sleepless nights, and relentless perseverance had led him to this point. It would've heralded as a revolutionary step forward, propelling humanity into a new era of tourism.

Yet, in a devastating twist, it had all gone catastrophically wrong, and hundreds of thousands of people, if not millions, had just lost their lives.

In a guarded crouch amid scattered debris, Will put his fist to the floor as the dust dispersed and settled around him. His spacesuit, forty-five kilos of engineering brilliance, had been custom-made using a complex system of equipment and layers designed to keep him warm, comfortable, and safe from cosmic threats. But his breathing was rapid, and he had to focus on slowing it. Panic was more taxing than physical exertion and would drain his oxygen tanks. The more he allowed his pulse to quicken and his mind to race, the less time he would live.

He rose cautiously and switched on the EVA headlamps mounted on the sides of his helmet. The twin lights speared through the dust and smoke as he swung his head around the office, observing the carnage. Damaged computer hardware and a tangled nest of cables and wires littered the floor. He looked up towards the steel beams hanging precariously above him. The roof had been ripped off, revealing a rust-coloured sky filled with thick, black smoke that had turned daytime into night.

Without warning, the unstable floor gave way, and Will dropped like a brick, surfing concrete for three storeys when it came tumbling and crashing down to the ground in a deluge of debris.

As the dust resettled and his heart resumed a steady beat, he wiped his visor and looked down to find himself swinging six feet above the floor, his legs treading the air. His parachute was hopelessly snagged on a twisted steel strut above, leaving him suspended as he was still strapped into the harness. His red nylon canopy was now a ragged, torn mess, smeared with soot, dust, and grime. Against the dark orange sky, it looked almost camouflaged, leaving the Fable Sky insignia obscured and indecipherable. The frayed edges of the canopy fluttered weakly in the noxious breeze while the badly buckled steel strut groaned beneath the strain. He twisted himself to assess his surroundings from his trapped position. The office was a scene of broken furniture, shattered glass, chunks of concrete, and electronic equipment scattered like discarded toys. To his left, through the dense haze of smoke and dust, he glimpsed flames licking at the remnants of the building's outer walls, fractured and jagged like broken teeth. The flames could easily migrate in his direction and consume the entire structure.

The parachute's quick-release buckles were supposed to be his salvation, but one was jammed tight, leaving him stuck like a moth caught in a spider's web. Panic briefly flirted with his consciousness, but his focus remained on the problem. One of the many facets of his training. After all he had been through that day, this was no time to lose his cool.

He spotted a shard of glass within reach, embedded in a pile of rubble. As more smoke poured in through gaping holes in the wall, choking the office and reducing visibility to one metre, he stretched his arm to its fullest extent but struggled to grip the piece of glass with his gloved hand. The suit, designed for the vacuum of space, was a cumbersome burden on Earth, testing his patience and precision.

Ariane's words from earlier that day played in his mind: "Have you ever tried tying shoelaces while wearing boxing gloves?"

Fumbling and finally clutching the glass shard between his thumb and first finger, he used the sharp edge as a makeshift knife and sawed through the harness strap, his arm aching and his breathing heavy in his helmet. Passing the glass through the thick webbing required painstaking effort, but finally, with a frayed snap, the strap split in half, and he fell the remaining distance, landing awkwardly on top of the debris. Pain rippled through his weaker leg and hip, but he pushed himself upright, ignoring the pain. The immediate danger of hanging strapped to his parachute with fires raging nearby was over, though the threat remained. The building could topple at any moment, burying him alive, and who knew what hazards waited outside its ruined walls.

Needing a moment to catch his breath, he leaned heavily against a damaged metal cabinet. The sound of his breathing echoed loudly inside his helmet, a constant reminder of his dwindling oxygen supply. He almost gagged but managed to avoid throwing up. It was not as though he could flip his visor unless he wanted a slow, agonising death, so his options were to keep his stomach contents down or bathe his visor and put up with the trapped stench.

He had to keep moving, had to find a way out of this death trap and locate his crewmates. Despite the pain in his leg and hip, intensified by the crash-landing and heavy suit weighing him down, he crossed the room through the thickening smoke. Glass fragments and plaster crunched beneath his boots as he approached the next room, its double doors hanging off their hinges. Beyond them, a collapsed wall formed a steep incline. He paused to assess his options, realising the slope was his only escape route. The brief stop brought him the half-moment he needed to compose himself.

He climbed the slope carefully, but the loose rubble shifted underfoot, dislodging fragments of brick and concrete that clattered noisily as they tumbled down the incline.

At the summit, the full extent of the town's devastation unfolded before him. Out-of-control fires blazed, turning the sky into a hellish orange-and-black panorama. Most buildings were reduced to skeletal remains, their doorways and blown-out windows spewing toxic smoke into the already darkened sky.

On the fringe of the town, fires raced through woodland, leaping from tree to tree. They would burn for hours, days, perhaps even weeks. This morning, none of this would have seemed possible. How had it turned out like this? Dazed by the unreality of it all, the horror too awful to grasp, he clenched his teeth so hard his jaw ached.

He glanced upward again, hoping for signs of his crew in the disturbed sky. "This is Will. Do you copy? Where are you? Did you make it back safely?"

His voice, raw with emotion, cut through the static. The silence that followed was deafening, interrupted only by the sound of his breathing.

"Jefferson, it's Will. Do you copy?" He waited, desperate to hear a familiar voice. "Donavon? Lloyd? Peta? Ariane? Can anyone hear me? Do you copy?"

His message went unanswered.

"Listen, I'm in a town. I don't know where. I don't even know if it's still England. The damage here is catastrophic. I hope you can hear me. I'm going to try to head to the edge of the town."

Scanning the scene again, left to right, right to left, above, then ahead, he saw no signs of life. No one crawled out of the ruins. The death toll would take months to tally up and would shock the world.

Where was his crew? Their radio silence sent another wave of dread through him.

Were they even alive?

Jefferson would know from the flat or fluctuating bio-signs on his monitor.

If he was still alive himself.

Checking the readouts on his solar-rechargeable computer built into his wrist, he noted the time was two minutes past three. His oxygen had dropped to ninety-four per cent, giving him less than eight hours to find his crewmates, find shelter, and find hope within this nightmare.

Drawing a steadying breath, he moved forward, battling against the frightening realisation that what should have been a moment of triumph had become a day of unimaginable terror.

TWO

Earlier that day…

The lighthouse stood proudly at the precipice of a sheer cliff overlooking the vast, tumultuous Celtic Sea, a sentinel against the harsh elements and treacherous waters below. It had first lit in 1837 and became automated one hundred and fifty years later. But major advances in satellite technology meant ships were less likely to get lost or caught in stormy weather because they relied on VHF radio *and* hi-tech navigation for guidance, making the whole lighthouse concept redundant in the modern world.

Located in St. Ives, Cornwall, the lighthouse was one of the oldest in the country, a monument to maritime history, and tallest in the region, rising an impressive forty-four metres into the sky. Despite its rich, historical significance, the lighthouse was often described as architecturally unremarkable, even ugly by some locals. The white exterior walls with a navy-blue band around its middle was heavily marked by its weather-beaten, utilitarian concrete, showing signs of the relentless assault by decades of salt-laden winds and rain. The cylindrical tower lacked the ornate embellishments or picturesque charm found in other lighthouses of its time. Instead, it stood as a sombre, stoic figure, its austere appearance and single-minded purpose to guide and warn mariners with its elevated light source and distinctive daymark.

At the top, the lantern room housed a powerful beacon, which, in its heyday, could be seen from miles away, piercing through the thick fog and violent storms that frequently lashed the Cornish coast. Encased in protective glass and crowned with a functional dome, the lantern room was accessible via a narrow, spiral staircase that wound its way up from the watch room below.

The base of the lighthouse was solid and broad, anchored firmly to the rocky ground of the cliff with an entrance defined by an arched doorway. Nearby, remnants of the old keeper's house and auxiliary buildings could still be found, their stone walls and slate roofs crumbling under the weight of time and neglect. While considered an eyesore by modern architectural standards, the lighthouse had fulfilled its mission with untiring dedication. It had saved countless lives by guiding ships safely around the jagged peninsular, warning them of the dangerous rocks hidden beneath the waves. Its lamps, with a decent range of twenty-two nautical miles, occulting every nine seconds, had provided a modicum of safety for maritime pilots along the South West Peninsula, proving consistent reliability in nature's tumult.

Owned by Jefferson's family for several generations, the lighthouse now served as his heirloom and a tourist icon to the rest of the country since its decommission. While no longer providing navigational aid to mariners, it had been repurposed to offer navigational support to Fable Sky, the world's largest helium balloon, tethered to the cliff just two hundred metres away, ready for its inaugural launch into space a few hours from now.

Jefferson had amassed a hefty fortune out of his property management and an impressive investment portfolio. Instead of investing in overdue lighthouse maintenance, he had sold off his assets and poured all his money into the balloon project, converting the watch room into a flight control room and the basement into a preparation hub for the crew. For the most part, its anatomy was kept in its original condition. The interior walls were cylindrical bare brick and the wooden floorboards and window frames had never been replaced.

While the flight control room was compact, fitting snugly into its rounded space, Jefferson cherished the solitude and autonomy it offered. This small sanctuary was his domain, a place where he could immerse himself in his work without anyone overseeing his every move. The walls were lined with state-of-the-art tech, giving the room an almost futuristic feel. Dominating the space was a long, curved desk, its surface a tangle of technology and high-definition screens that displayed complex data visualisations and lit up the room, casting a bluish glow that blended with natural light streaming through the surrounding row of windows. Various Ethernet and power cables snaked across the floor, connecting computers to the navigational instruments that communicated directly with the balloon. As the core of Jefferson's operation, these computers were well-equipped with the latest meteorological forecasting software. Capable of processing massive amounts of data in real time, they provided critical information on wind patterns, temperature variations, and atmospheric pressure. Algorithms crunched high-value numbers at lightning speed, generating forecasts both detailed and reliable, essential for navigating the balloon safely and efficiently and ensuring it stayed on course through the turbulent skies.

Todd's terminal on the opposite side of the room was far smaller, less personalised, and certainly messier, covered in all manner of computer hardware and an empty coke can that had been partially crushed. A series of sleek panels were filled with tiny lights, indicating the flow of data between the control room and the balloon's on board systems.

Despite the room's technical assembly, personal touches reflected Jefferson's character. Photos of family and friends were pinned to a corkboard along with old postcards from the places he had visited. Two potted plants in full bloom sat on the windowsill, adding a touch of green to the otherwise metallic and digital environment.

The flight control room would oversee the journey to the edge of space—a kind of mission control base. And Jefferson, once head keeper of the lighthouse, responsible for entering the names of passing ships in the logbook, repainting all the wooden structures, and keeping the area clean right down to the coastline, was now the flight director. He handled all the administration, from IT to book-keeping. Should the flight succeed, he anticipated it would kick-start space tourism and replace the heavy losses incurred from owning an obsolete lighthouse. That money would feed back into its upkeep and replenish his retirement savings.

Plain and simple business strategy.

Inside the lighthouse tower, wearing a freshly dry-cleaned suit, a blue so dark it seemed almost black, the fifty-five-year-old stared at the screens, deep in thought. He'd always been a reliable sleeper, but in recent weeks, with the launch growing nearer, he had not slept well, some nights staring out of his bedroom window until dawn crawled across the glass. Reading before bed, cups of herbal tea, and soothing meditation apps hadn't helped. Last night, he had managed no sleep at all.

Jefferson's day had begun at three in the morning in total darkness. By half four, he had showered and dressed in his best suit to show respect for the occasion and was sitting inside his Range Rover, towing the gondola from a garage up to the cliff, where two helium trucks, gleaming under the first rays of the sun, had arrived and positioned themselves strategically round the deflated zero-pressure helium balloon to begin inflation. The trucks, each adorned with safety warnings and complex piping systems, were the lifeblood of this operation, carrying the precious gas that would give life to the enormous balloon.

The envelope, an engineering marvel, lay spread out on the ground, an enormous, shimmering fabric that seemed almost ethereal in the morning light. The engineers and technicians in high-visibility vests and hard hats moved with choreographed perfection between the helium trucks and the balloon.

Thick hoses connected the helium trucks to the balloon's intake valves, and the atmosphere was filled with the low hum of the trucks' engines and occasional hiss of gas being carefully released. The process of inflating a helium balloon of this size required attention to detail. Technicians monitored pressure gauges and flow meters so the helium entered the balloon at the correct rate to avoid any mishaps.

With the helium now flowing, the balloon slowly came to life, rising and swelling, its translucent skin catching the light and reflecting a spectrum of colours. The transformation was gradual but mesmerising, hinting at the helium's sheer power and the balloon's design ingenuity. The entire operation was overseen by a senior engineer who stood slightly away from all the activity, clipboard in hand. She communicated via a radio, coordinating the team and ensuring every step was executed flawlessly.

Jefferson's eyes never left the balloon for the entire hour, watching nervously for an indication of trouble as the massive structure took shape, towering above the ground and planting an upside-down pear-shaped shadow. This marvel of modern aeronautical engineering was designed to reach stratospheric heights, where it would collect valuable data from the upper regions of the atmosphere.

With the inflation process completed, final checks were made with the engineers inspecting the balloon for any signs of leaks or stress points while Jefferson retreated to the flight control room. Despite his fatigue, he looked his best, his short, grey hair neatly held in place with spray and his moustache and goatee neatly clipped and shaped. A demon for details and a prodigious capacity for hard work, Jefferson had everything organised perfectly, and was ready to send the zero-pressure helium balloon on its mission.

THREE

At half past six, Todd came bounding up the steep and narrow wooden staircase, flanked by sturdy railings polished smooth by years of use. He pushed open the heavy, wooden door that led into flight control room, arriving breathless and sweating.

Todd was both Jefferson's nephew and his subordinate, a fresh-faced young man with foppish gold hair in a ponytail and a left earlobe punctured with a series of black studs at regular intervals. Genetics had screwed him in two ways, giving him the acne of a teenager and the build of a twelve-year-old.

"Someone needs to get themselves in shape," said Jefferson. "How old are you?"

Todd bent over, puffing and panting, and looked up at his uncle. "Twenty-two."

"Your grandfather used to run up those steps in his sixties without breaking a sweat."

"He must have been… bionic… or something."

"If they tire you that much, why not take the lift? That's why it was installed. So everyone in the family could come up and enjoy the view."

"That old thing?" He inhaled a deep breath and pointed in the general direction of the lift, which stopped one floor below. "It scares the crap… out of me."

"Why?"

"It makes funny noises."

Jefferson shook his head and folded his arms. "*You're* the one who makes funny noises."

Todd leaned out of the window for some fresh air, staring across the clifftop. Jefferson joined him, resting his elbows against the frame. The pre-dawn sky was streaked in orange and mauve shades with the sun teasing the horizon. It lit up a small flotilla of boats just off the coast, ready to witness the launch. Fable Sky, basking in the orange dawn, swayed gently against its ropes. The helium trucks had already gone and had been replaced by the technicians, who conducted final checks.

Taller than the Eiffel Tower, standing at 1,300 feet, the zero-pressure balloon dwarfed the lighthouse. The measured helium blob pumped into the ultra-thin polyethylene material, twenty microns thick, had accumulated at its crown, vertically stretching the balloon in the shape of an inverted teardrop. At high altitude, the helium would expand, filling it to roughly 3,000,000 cubic feet.

The balloon had already attracted the public's attention, drawing curious onlookers from nearby towns and villages. A few families, amateur photographers, and tourists had staked out temporary spots, eagerly awaiting the imminent spectacle. Kids pointed excitedly at the balloon standing as the centrepiece, and adults murmured in admiration and curiosity. News vans from local media outlets were parked along the perimeter, their logos brightly emblazoned on the sides, confirming the media interest in this morning's flight. Reporters bustled about, preparing their segments, and setting up equipment, ready to broadcast the event. Even a local radio station had set up a temporary booth, broadcasting live updates and interviewing visitors who shared their thoughts and their excitement about the event. The atmosphere was festive, with a few food trucks and vendors setting up shop, selling hot drinks, snacks, and souvenirs to the gathering crowd, carrying with it the hopes and aspirations of everyone who had gathered to witness this extraordinary event.

"You said there would be huge crowds this morning," said Todd, wiping his sweaty brow with the back of his hand. "I'm counting less than one hundred people down there. Where is everyone?"

"I expected a lot more by now."

"Maybe they'll turn up in time for launch."

Jefferson glanced at the time. "That's less than two hours away."

Todd spotted three technicians circling the balloon. They climbed aboard the red gondola, which resembled a circular raft, measuring three by three metres with a seating capacity of six. Made from the highest-grade aluminium, the seats featured engineered foam and fabric, making them more robust. Equally spaced around the open deck, wide enough to accommodate spacesuit-wearing individuals, they came with swivelling and reclining capabilities, allowing passengers to adjust their views. Securely mounted on the frame sitting above the gondola was a high-gain antenna, while special reflective tape affixed to the envelope ensured it was easily detectable by commercial planes on radar.

The technicians secured spare oxygen tanks with a bungee net inside a hexagonal storage cage, positioned centrally among the six recliner seats, providing easy access from all sides. The cage also housed the solar wing camera and Akroid balloon, critical elements of their mission that were tied down firmly by the bungee nets and straps. One of the technicians activated the batteries, providing the essential power for the balloon's electronic systems, vital for maintaining its technology during the flight. A second technician approached the main control panel with a complex array of switches, dials, and readouts that formed the technological heart of the balloon. She flipped a series of power switches, activating the electronics.

With the power now flowing steadily, the first technician ran diagnostics on the transponder's signal output, a critical component responsible for sending and receiving signals that would allow the ground team to track the balloon's position and status in real time.

Off in the distance, Todd spotted a line of military trucks speeding along the country lane, their rugged, camouflaged exteriors blending with the verdant countryside. The convoy moved quickly, their engines roaring as they sped along the winding road, leaving behind a cloud of smoke that hung in the air. As the trucks raced to the horizon, they seemed almost to disappear into the sunrise, so Todd turned from the window and faced his uncle, now back at his computer. "What do you want me to do?"

Before taking on the Fable Sky project, Jefferson had spent twenty-five years at the Met Office, specialising in atmospheric and oceanic administration that served civil aviation and the shipping industry. Todd, on the other hand, was gifted with computers. In fact, he was knowledgeable about engines and most technology, expert at sniffing out issues and doggedly resourceful in his ways to repair them, though there were some power tools with which he should never be trusted. He had inherited his technical prowess from his father, Jefferson's brother, a self-taught mechanic and IT specialist. But Todd's lack of expertise in deciphering complex meteorological charts and navigating sophisticated software used to predict weather patterns limited the scope of his duties, so he was assigned to more straightforward, less demanding roles.

"Why don't you go downstairs and check on the crew, see if they need anything?"

"I just came from there."

Jefferson wheeled his chair back, stood, and took off his suit jacket. "How are they doing?"

Todd tightened his ponytail. "Tense doesn't even begin to describe it."

FOUR

Underneath the lighthouse was the basement, nicknamed the white room, where the Fable Sky crew prepared for what the local media had once dubbed: *A giant leap for space tourism.*

With its white tile flooring, white sandstone walls, and the multiple spotlights dotted across the ceiling, it was a changing room cum storage space cum strategy hub. The circular room was divided into two hemispheres by a row of concrete pillars that supported the ceiling, wide enough for someone to stand behind and not be seen, with a wooden bench curving around one side of the cylindrical walls, lined with clothes hooks.

The white room had recently been cleaned, and everything gleamed with a sanitary sparkle, leaving a disinfectant odour in the air that masked the smell of salt, oil, and mildew. An open stepladder stood beneath a spotlight hanging out of the socket by its wires, still awaiting repair after the electrician had left to deal with a sudden home emergency two days ago and hadn't yet returned.

Dressed in a shirt, tie, blazer jacket, and dark skinny jeans that accentuated his long legs and trendy plimsolls, Will sat down on the bench, nervously tapping his feet and checking his watch every few minutes. His laptop was still on, so he switched it off, folded down the top, and slipped it inside its case. He opened the newspaper to continue a political story he'd started earlier that morning, a distraction from his nerves.

Eyewitness accounts from Spanish naval ships and a US submarine confirmed the uranium on board the North Korean naval ship heading towards Yemen was indeed bomb-grade, enriched uranium, contradicting vehement denials from both the North Korean military and government. The Spanish naval ships, part of an international coalition monitoring maritime activity in the region, reported suspicious behaviour and the unusual configuration of the vessel. Meanwhile, the US submarine, covertly tracking the ship's movements, provided detailed surveillance and analysis, confirming the nature of the cargo.

Reading the paragraph twice without absorbing a word, he discarded the newspaper and stared up at the domed ceiling, wondering how many people had arrived to see the balloon. Anthony, his son, had promised to attend. Had he kept his promise?

Will strolled over to the toilets on the other side of the room, passing the brick-lined containment block that fed water into the two cubicles. Anxious and excited in equal measures, he relieved himself for the fifth time that morning. As founder of the Fable Sky mission to the edge of space, he was under considerable pressure. Not once had he declared himself the captain because he held the title of flight operator. Yet, it was clear everyone viewed him as the de facto captain, seeing him as both an inspirational and well-respected leader. Despite this perception, he doubted whether he truly lived up to this esteemed mantle. He didn't like being regarded as the captain because he valued the collaborative nature of their mission. To him, leadership was a shared responsibility, and he believed every member of the crew played a crucial role in their success. Elevating one person above others undermined this collective effort and piled undue pressure on him. Moreover, he was uncomfortable with the spotlight and preferred to work quietly behind the scenes, focusing solely on his specific tasks without the added weight of being the key figurehead. He respected the expertise and contributions of colleagues and recognising their efforts equally was fundamental to maintaining morale and a cooperative environment.

Opening the bathroom cabinet, he found an assortment of pills for common ailments, including heartburn. His stomach was hideously writhing with nerves, with acid reflux rising in his chest, so he chewed an antacid tablet.

Back in the changing area, Will saw two technicians had just arrived to conduct spot checks on their spacesuits and life support equipment, ensuring all the seals were airtight, the communication systems were fully functional, and the mobility joints operated smoothly. They also checked the integrity of the life support systems, confirming the oxygen supply, carbon dioxide scrubbers, and temperature controls worked perfectly. These checks were critical to the safety and success of their mission, as any malfunction in their spacesuits or life support equipment could pose a serious risk to the crew in the harsh environment of space. Their detailed assessments and rigorous testing protocols provided an additional layer of security and confidence for the crew prior to launch.

Peta sauntered across the room, carrying a Nora Roberts novel the size of a cinderblock with a bookmark poking out of the pages. She showed no trace of nerves. The thirty-one-year-old was petite with the tightly packed muscle of a runner and an athletic build that moved with fluid, casual grace. Without its customary patina of thick foundation and powder, her baby face looked even younger than usual.

"Where's Donavon?" asked Will.

Peta shrugged as she sat on the bench. "My cousin's never been good at timekeeping. You know that."

Ariane was on her knees repacking her grey duffle bag on the floor. Finally satisfied, she pulled its drawstring tight. "Why don't you call him?"

"He tends not to answer his phone, and then never calls back. What about Lloyd? Where's he?"

Ariane stood, hanging her bag over the hook above the bench. "Lloyd went out for another cigarette."

"He knows we launch in ninety minutes, right?"

Peta lowered her book, peering over the rim of her reading glasses. "I still can't believe you let a chain-smoker join the crew."

"Lloyd designed the balloon. It was a condition."

"Let's hope his lungs survive the atmospheric pressures, then."

"That's what the spacesuits are for. Speaking of which, we should start changing into them."

Ariane gave Will a playful salute. "Yes, boss."

Peta shook her head at Ariane and drew back her lips to bare gritted teeth. "Brave. He doesn't like being called that."

Ariane's eyebrows went up. "What's wrong with being the boss?"

Will put his hands in his pockets. "Let's just be clear here," he said with a slight smirk, "I'm not the only one in charge. Jefferson is the flight director, and Donavon is chief navigator. We all call the shots. I just despise the word *boss*, that's all. It... how can I put it? It insinuates superiority and arrogance. Now, make me a cup of tea!" His smirk morphed into a smile.

Ariane tipped her head to one side questioningly, and Will saw the gold hoops in her ears with a backdrop of such straight, dark hair. But he was far more interested in her eyes, the green that blurred in the faintest hint of blue. By eye and skin colour alone, she looked Mediterranean.

Will turned and knocked his shin on the stepladder, not hard but enough for his skin to shine red.

Peta laughed. "Way to not act like the boss, *boss*."

Will looked at his feet, blushing under his hipster beard, and laughed. Bringing his eyes back towards the girls, he said, "Start getting changed! There, that *bossy* enough for you?"

He glanced at his watch for probably the umpteenth time that morning. 06:33. The launch was scheduled for 08:00.

The pressure on the crew, especially Will, was immense. He knew the stakes. Aside from the obvious, the consequences of failure would be two-fold. One, that they had failed to reach the stratosphere. Two, that they would not try something like this again. It was expensive, time-consuming, and fraught with danger. In life, if you missed that one chance, that one defining moment, it could be lost for all time.

FIVE

Stored inside a large locker fitted with toughened glass and a solid lock were five custom-fit, British-made spacesuits, each one modelled on those worn by Air Force pilots flying high-altitude missions. Name badges were sewn into the upper arms of each suit. Tailored to build, Will and Ariane had both got standard-sized suits. Donavon, likewise, while Lloyd and Peta had required smaller suits. The full assembly featured several layers, including its polyester structural restraints with folded and pleated joints and the anti-abrasion outer layers. A beige liquid-cooling ventilation garment – a one-piece mesh made of spandex with zippered front entry – would be worn beneath the spacesuit.

Bolted to the front of the spacesuits were the primary life support packs, incorporating the air-cooling ventilation fans, batteries, a pair of fitted oxygen tanks, and the extravehicular communicators. These components ensured steady air supply, temperature control, and enabled the crew to communicate effectively during their missions. It also had a carbon dioxide removal feature, four and a half kilos of cooling water, and various warning systems.

Will opened a steel door and entered the walk-in, climate-controlled vault at the back of the white room to check the thermostat. The air inside was cool and crisp, maintaining the perfect conditions for the sensitive equipment stored within. Dominating the compact space was a large compressor tank, an imposing piece of machinery designed to refill the crew's oxygen tanks multiple times over. Its metallic surface gleamed beneath the overhead light. Along the side wall, three reserve oxygen tanks were stowed on a sturdy rack, each one ready to be deployed at a moment's notice. The hum of the compressor provided a steady noise in the background, underscoring the importance of this hi-tech vault in ensuring the crew's safety and mission preparedness. Will checked the readings on the thermostat, confirming the room remained optimally cooled for the storage and maintenance of these essential supplies.

"You're anxious," said Ariane, standing off his shoulder and speaking in her mild Illinoisan accent.

Will spun around. "Yes, I am, a little. You? How are you feeling?"

"I'm a NASA research pilot. I guess pioneer flights are in my blood."

"You're used to flying untested aircraft to the stratosphere. Do you still get nervous?"

"The fear of God is the foundation of wisdom."

To drive that message home, understand the risks, and accept them, he had to think about his own possible demise in granular detail. Not only of death itself but the effects on his family, friends, and the ballooning community.

Will rechecked the time on his old diver's watch, a gift from his father, once a scuba-diving enthusiast who had used the watch for thirty-odd years during more than eight hundred dives, including some of the world's most famous shipwrecks. The markers and hands had faded over time, but its black face had hardly aged and remained vivid.

07:00 had arrived.

Will returned to the changing area to find only two of his four crew members, Peta and Ariane, resting on the bench. "I'm going upstairs to look for Lloyd and Donavon. Seriously, you two should start getting changed."

He stepped out into the small foyer between the main door and the lift. Even on this bright, sunny day, the foyer was dark and gloomy, the single bulb with a dome-shaped cover lacking sufficient brightness. He pressed the button and waited a full two minutes for the lift's arrival, checking his watch once more. He ran his hand over his head, shaved almost to the skin, and smoothed his beard.

The lift doors rolled open, and Will stepped forward onto the ugliest maroon-and-green-patterned carpet. The upper half of the lift consisted of mirrors, their edges rusted and surfaces pocked with age. Almost half-a-century old, the frail lift had once malfunctioned at the midway point of the lighthouse with Will inside, slowing and bouncing to a stop and leaving him trapped for an hour. That was seven months ago, but it still bothered him.

Scraping and squeaking on its rusty runners, Will barely detected whether the lift carried him up or down until the sudden shudder announced its arrival at lobby level.

Will found Lloyd and Donavon talking and smoking in front of Lloyd's retro duck-egg-blue camper with *Greenpeace* and *Save the Whale* stickers all over the windows.

Parked beside Lloyd's old van was Donavon's motorcycle, enhanced with a few not-quite-legal speed modifications. His helmet hung on one handle grip; his backpack hung from the other.

Two local girls half Donovan's age walked by arm in arm, heading towards the balloon a short distance away. The taller and slimmer of the two wore purple hot pants and a tight top, her friend a more conservative yellow skirt that stopped above her knees.

Donavon whistled, tilted his head, and ran his eyes down their legs.

The girl in hot pants turned and smiled.

Donavon slapped Lloyd hard on his back, knocking him forward. "You see that? Still got it!"

"We need to get a move on," said Will, tapping his watch, distracted by the balloon dominating the skyline behind them, a striking and otherworldly sight against the backdrop of clear, blue sky. Its vast, silvery surface shimmered in the sunlight, creating a dazzling spectacle that drew the eye. The balloon's unique shape and the way it caught the light made it look like a floating diamond suspended on a long, delicate piece of string. Designed to ascend to the edge of space, it hovered gracefully above with impressive size and grandeur, capturing the imagination of all who saw it. Its gentle sway added to the surreal beauty of the scene, emphasising both its fragility and strength.

Lloyd trampled his cigarette with his heel and wiped his hands on his T-shirt. "Coming."

Donavon, wearing dark jeans and a tucked-in white shirt with the sleeves rolled up to his elbows, continued to smoke, even though he was a self-proclaimed non-smoker and a gym fanatic. As he took his last drag, he casually exhaled the smoke through his nose and flicked the remaining cigarette away.

Hiking his backpack onto his broad shoulder, he walked slowly towards Will. "What are we waiting for?"

SIX

Slipping into her one-piece spandex suit, careful not to disrupt her stuck-on biomed sensors, Ariane stretched her arms and legs and adjusted the adult-fit diaper around her crotch.

Peta was already dressed in her spandex suit. She tucked her cropped, brown hair behind her cute, pointed ears.

"Is your cousin's head in this?" asked Ariane.

Peta turned. "Of course. Why do you ask?"

"I get the impression that he doesn't take things seriously in life, which worries me considering what we are about to do today."

"That's Donavon for you. He'll be fine. He used to work for the RAF. He knows what he's doing."

"I hope so."

The lift doors opened; the boys came in through the main door and broke off in different directions.

Will strolled to his space on the bench with the subtlest limp. He undid his tie, hung it over the hook, then slipped off his plimsolls, his socks. He looked like someone who captained a cruise ship, not a high-altitude helium balloon, though Ariane had faith in his flying expertise.

She turned her attention to Lloyd, the oldest on the crew at almost fifty years of age. He didn't blink, lost in thought, or drowning in fear. She could see the tension in his eyes. A look she had grown accustomed to over time, witnessing hopeful NASA pilots come and go, unable to cope with the pressures of the job and the risks it posed. She studied the balloon designer with increasing suspicion as he fetched a handkerchief from his bag and wiped his large forehead. He then put on his spandex suit but struggled with the heavy spacesuit until he remembered how its hard and soft components fitted together after a few missteps. It was the first time she'd had her doubts about Lloyd. And if Ariane could count on anything, it was reading people, one of her most reliable virtues.

Which was why she'd questioned Peta about Donavon and his commitment to the flight. It had come as a surprise when Will had said he never answered calls or rang back because he was always on his mobile. It was never out of his hand. From Donavon's overconfidence to Lloyd's nervous, stiff gait, she believed her concerns about the pair were justified.

The crew had been put on a strict forty-eight-hour diet. It didn't stop Donavon from reaching into his backpack for a ham salad roll. He took two large bites, his muscly jaw moving like a grinding machine, then closed the foil packaging and shoved it back inside his bag. As if summoned, he turned and disappeared behind the concrete pillars, pulling his mobile from his pocket.

On an impulse, Ariane followed him to the other side of the room with her water bottle.

Donavon had his back to her and spoke quietly into his mobile. "Can hardly hear you. Signal's shit. Who's this?"

Hesitant to call out his name, Ariane listened instead to his conversation.

"You'll get the fucking money, all right?"

He cut off the caller, scrawled a quick message, and hit send.

"Are you getting changed?" she asked.

Donavon spun around and palmed back his choppy, black hair, shaved close at the sides as if groomed for prime-time television. A good-looking man in the middle of his life, he was in excellent health and was packed with weightlifter's muscle. He had a solidity and strength in his physical shape, enough to indicate he was more than capable of looking after himself.

He closed the distance between them until they were just centimetres apart. His sharp, blue eyes drew Ariane in and held her gaze captive.

"Why? You want to watch me undress?"

"Not particularly."

His eyes widened, then narrowed, and a lazy grin appeared. "We both know you're lying."

Taking her time to respond, she covered the pause by sipping her water, reading his dare for a reaction. She didn't rise to the bait. "It's important that we stay focussed today. Agree?"

Looking down at the message that beeped on his mobile, he started typing using both thumbs. "I'll get changed in just a minute."

Rolling her eyes, Ariane turned and marched back to the bench.

The crew took their time getting changed. No one spoke. They folded their clothes in silence and neatly placed them on the benches or hung them on the hooks. They clamped down and connected two oxygen tanks to their life support systems. They put on their spacesuits and slipped on their parachute packs. And still, it was done in silence.

Ariane's first time at the lighthouse four months ago had been a sobering visit, and she had been quick to draw her conclusions. The crew was underprepared for the uncertainties of travel into the upper atmosphere because they hadn't yet been there. She had. Was this mismatched crew capable of flying to the edge of space? On balance, she believed so. But Donavon and Lloyd concerned her. There was no room for error, zero tolerance for incompetent behaviour.

A month before her first England visit in early February, Derek, her director, had called her into his office inside the Armstrong Flight Research Centre in California, NASA's core for aeronautic research and atmospheric operations. Nestled within the vast Mojave Desert, the cutting-edge facility boasted state-of-the-art laboratories, wind tunnels, flight simulators, hangars, testing facilities, tools, and technologies that aided in aeronautic research and development and enabled scientists, engineers, and research pilots to collaborate on groundbreaking projects.

Ariane had remained mute as she listened to the details of her next assignment. "Why me?"

Derek clasped his hands together. "Because you, my sweet rocketeer, are the most qualified."

"Yeah, to pilot supersonic aircraft, Derek! If I *am* the most qualified, why send me to England to fly in a balloon? It makes no sense."

"As I said, your objective is to launch the Akroid payload successfully at high altitude."

"I'm not happy about this."

"View it as another string to your proverbial bow. Listen, if Akroid can collect enough space dust, it will look great on your portfolio."

"That's bull and you know it!" She stormed out, slamming the door behind her.

Dedicated to her work, always putting in overtime, and establishing herself as one of the best NASA research pilots in the facility, she knew this had nothing to do with professional development. She had passed the space physical, equivalent to a military or civilian flight physical, held more than the one thousand hours of minimum flight time in a jet aircraft as the pilot in command, and had flown some of the most advanced and sophisticated aircraft ever built. No, this reeked of internal politics, not professional *fricking* development. At work, she had everyone vying to be her partner, even Derek. She had turned him down. Three times. In no uncertain terms, she had told him she was taken and not looking for anyone else. Was this the real reason he was posting her to southern England on a futile mission?

Ariane donned the one-piece lower torso assembly unit, incorporating a body seal closure, waist bearing, and slip-on boots. Before attaching it to the upper torso, she untucked her St. Christopher, the patron saint of travellers, and kissed the lucky charm necklace. She switched on her life support and confirmed her oxygen, giving her eight hours. Reserve tanks for each crew member were already stowed on the balloon, providing up to sixteen hours for a return flight. The additional tanks were just for emergency purposes. All in all, they were expected to fly up and back on a single pair of tanks. Upon reaching the stratosphere, their suits would be pressurised at 3.5 psi, and the gas inside would be one hundred per cent oxygen, twenty per cent more than on the ground.

Ariane watched Donavon on his return, trying to decide if he could be trusted. His body language suddenly changed. He quickly caught up with the crew, slipping into his spandex with ease, then putting on his spacesuit. Lastly, he put on his gloves. That's when Ariane noticed Donavon's little finger missing from his right hand. His suit glove had been tailored without the fifth digit, so no empty finger hung loose.

"Make sure your glove couplings are fastened properly," he said, flexing his fingers inside both gloves. "We don't want anyone imploding up there."

What Ariane had seen of his personality up to this point – punctuated by a self-absorbed narcissism – underwent a swift and dramatic change. A man who had been so preoccupied with himself and his mobile suddenly adopted a professional attitude, displaying a level of competence and seriousness that she hadn't expected.

Before fitting their helmets, which had EVA headlamps mounted on both sides, Ariane handed the crew an anti-fog compound to spray on the inside of their visors to prevent condensation build-up.

"The visors are heated," said Donavon.

"Heaters have been known to fail in the past," Ariane said. "You wouldn't want to reach target altitude and not see the view."

Donavon applied two sprays to his visor and passed the bottle around before rechecking his glove fastenings.

Will faced the crew. "This is it. Just remember–"

Lloyd started frisking himself as though searching for his wallet. "Have these suits been pressure tested?"

"Yes, an hour ago," said Will.

"When you were still outside smoking like a chimney," said Peta.

Lloyd pushed back a strand of thinning grey hair that had drifted above his eyes. "Did they check them properly?"

"Just put your helmet on!" said Donavon.

Will repositioned his communication cap fitted with an audio headset and dual microphones. He slipped his helmet over the top, twisting it into a locking position.

Miked up and equipped with all the technology, he lifted his visor and finished his speech. "Remember, we've all trained for this. We accepted this project knowing the risks, so let's respect the training, practice what we've learned, and have faith in ourselves and the mission. Today, we make history."

SEVEN

The door leading to the stairs burst open. Todd was breathless, panting and sweating when he charged into the white room, probably at Jefferson's behest.

"Are you ready? Are your oxygen tanks installed? Did the technicians check your life supports?"

"Yes," said Will, turning on the solar-charged computer built into his sleeve. "Why are you so hot and bothered?"

"I just ran down from the flight control room to see if you were ready."

"We are, and we're on time. Where's Jefferson?"

"He's coming down in just a minute. Said he had to double-check something."

"Why did you use the stairs?" asked Ariane. "Why not just take the elevator?"

"The booby trap? No thanks."

"Booby trap?" said Peta, trying not to laugh. "It's perfectly safe."

"You use it then. I'm going nowhere near it."

Peta handed Todd her digital camera with its wide-angle lens attachment extended. "Here, make yourself useful please and take our photograph."

Todd reached out for the camera.

"The button is sensitive, so just lightly tap it or you'll end up taking loads of the same picture."

The crew lined up side by side and huddled in close.

Todd framed a shot. "How many shall I take? Just one? Is the flash on?"

"Man, this guy asks lots of questions," said Donavon. "Just take the picture!"

"Okay, say *moon cheese*."

The crew sniggered just as the flash went off. Todd smiled, seemingly proud that his quip had made the group laugh.

Peta took back the camera, checked the picture quality in the review mode, and returned it to her bag.

Jefferson followed by the medic entered the room through the main door. "Good to go?"

The crew traded looks and nodded, indicating they were primed and ready to carry out the flight. While they all bore the appearance of seasoned aeronautical pilots, only Ariane embodied the essence of true piloting with such an impressive resume. Donavon alike, with his extensive experience flying helicopters for the RAF. Both possessed remarkable skill, but there was something more distinctive about Ariane's approach to aviation.

Contrary to Ariane and Donavon, Will's identity was firmly rooted in the art of business rather than aviation. For Will, genuine piloting transcended mere navigation through the air; it entailed a complete mastery and control over the vessel in question, unbound by the capricious tendencies of the wind or the elements of chance. In his view, reliance on pure luck was antithetical to the skill of piloting, which demanded precision, foresight, and an unyielding determination to chart one's own course in the boundless skies.

"You all look dashing," said Jefferson. "This is one proud moment for me."

Peta cocked her head. "Don't cry."

That garnered some more laughs.

"I'll try my best to hold it until you've left."

Jefferson conducted a briefing with the crew, his idea of an inspirational speech with a few critical reminders thrown in.

"Regulate your breathing as shifts in altitude can affect the oxygen levels, clarity of mind, and physical well-being."

"Report changes in physical state, no matter how minor they may seem. Early detection of symptoms like dizziness or nausea can prevent potential complications and ensures the safety of everyone on board."

"Keep a close eye on the instruments and readings, paying attention to altitude, pressure, temperature, and all other vital metrics to navigate the balloon safely up high."

"Ensure helmet cameras are rolling at all times, not only for the historical archives but also as a valuable resource for analysis and troubleshooting."

"Always keep your belts fastened. Unexpected turbulence or sudden manoeuvres can pose risks if not properly secured."

"Look out for one another as this flight is a collaborative endeavour, reliant on your collective efforts and vigilance of every crew member."

"Above all, enjoy the experience. It's your time to shine and for all your hard work to pay off."

Then Jefferson handed the crew over to the medic, a well-spoken gentleman in his sixties wearing a brown tweed suit with a clipboard under his arm. He asked if anyone had any last-minute medical complaints and, if so, to speak up now.

Silence confirmed there were no issues.

"And how are our pressure cookers today?" he asked. "I trust they are fine?"

Ariane looked at her crewmates. "Our what?"

"He means stomachs," said Jefferson.

"Hungry," said Peta. "We all are."

Thursday and Friday's meal plan had involved a strict, low-residue, low-fibre affair, enforced by the medic to prevent any uncomfortable bloating and to reduce the urge to defecate in their diapers. From this point on, the only consumable at their disposal was the in-suit drink pouch filled with two litres of water. A small tube near their mouths sat inside their helmets to draw water from.

"Has anyone here experienced any bowel movements this morning?"

"I unleashed a baby's arm earlier," said Donavon.

"Disgusting!" Peta shook her head. "Please."

The medic drew his wrinkled hands together. "Anyone else evacuated any infant-sized appendages this morning?"

No one raised their hands.

"I trust you all went to bed at eight o'clock sharp and had a splendid sleep."

"I don't think any of us got a full night," said Will. "I was awake three hours before my alarm, which I set for four this morning."

"Understandable," said the medic. "Well, do take it slowly up there. If you do need to… shed some pounds in the upper regions, try not to strain. You must try to keep your bowel muscles relaxed."

Will grinned. "I'm just waiting for one of Jefferson's toilet jokes. It seems due."

Jefferson crossed his arms. "I'll have you know that poo jokes are not my favourite. But they are a solid number two."

Peta pinched the bridge of her nose through her open visor. "Can we stop talking about babies' arms and number twos, please?"

It took twelve more minutes to clear them through medical and debriefing.

After that, there was nothing left to do: no pre-flight safety pantomime, no more lectures, and no last-minute spot checks.

Will exchanged a nervous smile with Jefferson before he led the crew into the foyer. It was time.

EIGHT

The lift doors rolled slowly open, and the crew shuffled out in single file. Jefferson, Todd, and the medic climbed the stairs, regrouping in the lighthouse lobby.

"You stay safe," said Jefferson.

"It's finally happening," said Will, speaking through his open visor.

Jefferson grinned. "I've got high hopes."

Will rolled his eyes at the pun.

"Seriously, though, no messing about up there. Come back in one piece."

Jefferson had put a lot of work into making everything run smoothly and within timeframes. To Will, that was no surprise. His old friend was a perfectionist; punctuality was an ingrained discipline. The only time Will had known him to be unpunctual was when it almost cost his life.

For a moment, Will was somewhere else, years ago, at Headcorn Airfield in Faversham, leaning on the reinforced wicker of his balloon, necking red wine while he waited for Jefferson to show up. If Will was the talented balloonist, then Jefferson was the driving force behind all the legalities such as licences, insurance, and flight clearance approval. Will was lousy at administration.

Daylight was fading, and Jefferson was an hour late. If he didn't arrive shortly, the flight would have to be postponed. Flying solo increased the workload and decreased the margin for error. Without the support of a co-pilot or crew, there was the heightened risk of overlooking critical tasks, misjudging weather conditions, or encountering difficulties during take-off or landing. Attempting to fly in the dark posed significant risks, including limited visibility of obstacles, difficulties with assessing altitude and terrain, and maintaining orientation. And flying under alcoholic influence was not only illegal but also highly dangerous. In any case, the balloon was only certified for daytime flights, so he would no longer be insured once the sun had gone down.

Over the past decade, numerous accidents involving hot-air balloons had taken place, ranging from minor mishaps to catastrophic outcomes, painting a troubling picture of the risks associated with this adventurous flight mode. Reports detailed a variety of causes, including sudden changes in the weather, mechanical failures, and human error. Each accident had left a mark on the industry, leading to increased scrutiny and calls for stricter safety regulations. The allure of floating high above the Earth in a colourful balloon was undeniable, but so too were the potential dangers lurking beneath the surface of this seemingly serene experience.

He tried Jefferson on his mobile once more but made no contact. Surface winds were below ten miles per hour, and it was a glorious, tranquil evening, the blue sky laced with pink-orange streaks, so Will unpegged the pickets tying the balloon down and climbed inside the basket. He turned on the burner. The pilot light ignited the propane. Upon pressing the thrust lever, flames shot into the envelope's mouth and the balloon rose, 700 feet per minute, into the blue yonder. In no time, the air grew cooler, cleaner, and thinner. Squinting to view his instruments in the fading daylight, dismissing the readings on the temperature gauge and compass, he steadied his drunken focus just long enough to obtain the altimeter and variometer readouts.

Will looked at the purple sky and admired nature's patterns in the tableau below. Building lights appeared as pinpricks in the darkening backdrop to the east. He engaged the burner, giving the balloon more elevation.

"Congratulations!" he yelled, raising his bottle of red wine as if proposing a toast. "You win! You don't even care about him. But fair is fair. The court has ruled; the judge is never wrong. Never!"

Swigging more wine, Will stared at the stars sprinkled like diamond dust across the sky as if he had crossed into space. What would it be like in the cosmos? He would need to wear a spacesuit to protect himself from the harsh temperatures, UV radiation, and lack of oxygen. Absorbed by the starry ceiling, he pushed the burner lever for max thrust, and the balloon surged even higher, reaching for space because he did not fear death, and he could not accept his ex-wife was the fitter parent. Up high, isolated from everyone, no one could bother you, not even yourself. Except today. The day he lost his son. The day the civil court, her lawyer, and justice robbed him of shared custody.

Banishing his negative thoughts and the harsh courtroom memories, he thought about his career. Life as a balloonist had yet to bring in the kind of earnings it had once promised. His financial instability had worked against him in the courtroom showdown for custody. Business was too slow. Weather too unreliable. Too much local competition. Regulation was too strict. Licencing and insurance were too expensive. The main problem was ballooning only appealed to the minority. The public needed something different, audacious, and high profile. Like flights into space. They would come from afar and pay a fortune for such a rarefied experience and a godlike view of the Earth's curvature. Bound by gravity and biology, venturing into the stratosphere wasn't easy, but space flights had been carried out as far back as the sixties, and since then, altitude records had been challenged and broken. Was it so unrealistic in the twenty-first century?

"Flights to the edge of space." He knocked back more red wine and pulled the thrust lever. "Space flights. Yeah."

Like a powerfully thrown spear, the idea was stuck in his mind, overriding the self-destructive gloom engulfing him. His pulse ticked up a beat and his breathing grew rapid to the point of hyperventilation. Drunk and drowsy, his arms and legs grew suddenly numb. His vision blurred, and light-headedness stole up on him. The wine bottle fell from his loosened grip.

Bending to assess the altimeter, he knew instantly what was wrong. At 16,400 feet, the balloon was too high. Having logged thousands of flights for both business and pleasure combined, he had erroneously exceeded an altitude capable of biological function. He had little time to revive himself by descending so hypoxia didn't have him foaming bloody bubbles at the mouth, leading to an unpleasant death.

Despite his hypoxically impaired state, he barely managed to reach up and pull the cord that opened the valves at the envelope's pole. Hot air was instantly vented, and the balloon began to dip.

Will collapsed, groping drunkenly for bottled oxygen, but found none in the basket's sewn-in pockets.

The balloon sank to 12,000 feet.

At 7,000, he still lacked muscle functionality in his limbs, and his judgment and coordination were severely affected.

6,000 feet.

Feeling the descent only speed up, Will realised he had over vented. Too weak to stand up, all he could do was watch the dial on the altimeter spin down, faster and faster, and await the inevitable.

5,300.

4,800.

3,900.

The wind grew louder, the descent faster.

Will almost threw up.

1,000 feet.

He gripped one of the pockets when the balloon started spinning.

500 feet.

Dizzy and nauseous, disabled by the twin effects of the alcohol and hypoxia, he blacked out right before the balloon crash-landed in a field.

Will was unconscious when the paramedics found him the next morning, twelve hours after the crash, when a dog-walker spotted the pancaked balloon and called emergency services.

He was still unconscious when the ambulance drove into the casualty bay.

He woke up alone in a bed with little recollection. That was alcohol for you. He could still taste the red wine on his tongue. A monitor beside him registered his heartbeat, and the doctor explained he would be taken for surgery on his broken leg and busted hip.

What occurred next was a combination of rough carpentry and micro-surgery. He was knocked out cold throughout the night post-operation with his right leg in traction, plastered from foot to thigh and suspended in a sling. Cuts and bruises marred his face and body.

Jefferson was standing beside his bed, holding a get-well card and a box of expensive chocolates when he came around. "How many times have I told you about flying in the dark?"

Will's voice was dry and raspy. "How many times have I told you I don't like chocolate?"

Jefferson smiled. "How's this for a coincidence? I recently watched a movie about a man with two broken legs. The cast was terrible."

Will shook his head. "As terrible as your jokes?"

Jefferson lowered his eyes. "I'm sorry."

Will coughed into his fist, forcing him to arch forward. "You've told worse jokes."

"I'm an ageing father. I'm entitled. But you know what I mean. If I hadn't been caught up at the lighthouse…."

"Don't beat yourself up."

"No, I let you down."

Will looked at his left hand. It was so swollen he couldn't find his knuckles. "I let myself down."

Jefferson's bottom lip jutted. "Is that a pun? Not bad."

Will did not see the funny side.

Jefferson placed his hand on Will's shoulder. "I heard what happened. At the court."

Will looked up and wiped the tear in his eye with the back of his right hand. He had arrived at a crossroads, both in his career and his personal life, and he was finally thinking clearly. "I have a business proposition I want to run by you."

Inspired by the idea of space tourism, he spent his time in the hospital performing exhaustive research on his laptop and making enquiries. He did a cost analysis and searched for a designer who possessed the right skillset.

After his release, he sought advice and scientific validation from ballooning professionals and industry experts, and even attended a college, albeit just once. He soon realised he needed a crew, a support team, investors, and most importantly, time.

Their first proper meeting was one of the most productive. He and Jefferson had devised a mission that would see them trial their first flight to the edge of space in a balloon, one day targeting adventurists unable to resist the magnetic pull of the great wide world. The mission was too enormous to be figured out at a single sitting, but they did set their sights on a summer launch in three years. To meet the target date, they had to find an affordable design engineer and a reputable company that could manufacture the world's first passenger-carrying space balloon.

NINE

The early morning burned so June-hot that a cool breeze was needed to take the edge off. June in England was always a nice time of year, but this was not a temperature the locals were used to.

The balloon was a statue. Seabirds circled the crown, just as intrigued as the spectators gathered around the bright red gondola, suitably attired in light clothing with bared legs.

And the numbers kept rising.

Eight hundred.

Nine hundred.

A thousand.

And then well over a thousand.

Mostly locals from the nearby towns and villages, out to enjoy the spectacle on this bright Saturday morning. Some had arrived in the early hours to snag prime viewing positions.

Out on the sea was an armada of sailboats and fishing trawlers, their colourful hulls bobbing gently on the almost flat surface. The owners and crews of these vessels had anchored their boats in anticipation of the upcoming event and were now gathered on deck.

The early morning sun beat down on the Fable Sky crew's visors as they threaded their way towards the balloon in twos, with Donavon at the front leading the way.

"I expected more people," said Donavon. "Like before."

"You just love being centre of attention," said Peta.

He turned, walked backwards, and flung open his arms. "I'm a big deal."

"A big *what?*"

Donavon stuck up his thumb. "Funny."

Will stared mostly out towards the sea, not at the balloon or spectators held back by rope to form a path. Despite the crowds and hysteria, his sole focus was getting off the ground. In truth, he would have preferred a private event without the fanfare, fearing another failed launch, disappointing the crowd again, causing epic personal and professional embarrassment. The last six years had been building up to the next six hours, and it was a key moment in his life.

Since the sixties, there had been so many achievements in space exploration. The International Space Station and Hubble Telescope, satellite communication technology, Sputnik, the Apollo missions, the famous moon-landing, and space probes to Mars. Aeronautic records were constantly being challenged, both vertically and horizontally. If the flight proved successful and indeed shattered records, the question lingered: would it be regarded with the same reverence and acclaim as the other monumental achievements in space exploration? The answer, perhaps, seemed doubtful. Balloon flights, while undeniably impressive, occupied a different domain of human ingenuity compared to the monumental milestones of space travel. Still, despite the uncertainty surrounding its place in the history of space exploration, optimism permeated his thoughts. Success could pave the way for recognition and opportunities. Perhaps there would be documentary deals, interviews, and published articles chronicling their historic flight. The allure of potential acclaim tantalised his imagination.

As he contemplated the possibilities, he wondered what headlines would grace the front pages of local newspapers the next day, if at all. Would they capture the magnitude of their achievement, or would their feat be relegated to a footnote in the annals of history? Whatever the outcome, Will remained assertive in his belief that their daring adventure would leave an indelible mark on the population's consciousness, inspiring future generations to reach for the stars, whether by balloon or supersonic rocket.

While the launch had been downplayed by the media this time around, satellite vans clustered across the clifftop were already streaming live images onto the Internet. Half a dozen reporters, all local media and well-known to one another, had their cameras raised and started filming when the crew walked by. When had any other British venture dragged on with such drama and nationwide publicity?

It suddenly struck Will how big the occasion actually was. All this greatness. It was strange, not feeling it so much but knowing it. He wasn't the type who enjoyed such spectacles or basked in the limelight. This was neither a flight of fancy, the outcome of some drunken bet, nor some rich man's haphazard enterprise. Nor was it an orchestrated media event to boost a corporate image, although it did promote a service they soon planned to offer to the public. This was, primarily, a business venture that involved research, assessment, and above all, a passion for flying. It was a debut mission, an opportunity to observe and report. To analyse the key data. Once they had collected enough information in the upper atmosphere, their sights would be set on refining their technology behind the space balloon, streamlining its design, and then optimising its performance to make future missions not only more feasible but economically viable in their quest to offer revolutionary space trips and tourism. However, if no business opportunities arose from it, a view of the Earth's curvature would provide some consolation, capturing the true essence of a balloonist's passion.

Arriving at the red gondola, the cacophony of whistles and cheers that had greeted them from the excited crowd morphed seamlessly into thunderous applause and exuberant shouts of admiration. For the Fable Sky crew, it was more than a show of support; it validated their tireless efforts, determination, and pursuit of the extraordinary.

TEN

"Fable Sky, do you copy?"

Will glanced up at the flight control room in the lighthouse, where Todd was standing at the window. Audio was adequate at best, the sound a touch metallic. His spacesuit was equipped with an open mic system, meaning he didn't have to press any buttons to transmit, allowing the crew to communicate hands-free throughout the flight.

"Will here. Go ahead."

A burst of static crackled in his headset before Jefferson's voice came through, clear and confident. *"All systems are up and running smoothly,"* he announced. *"The weather conditions are perfect. Honestly, you couldn't have chosen a better day for a sightseeing trip in space. The skies are clear; the views will be spectacular."* His words carried a reassuring tone, filling Will with a sense of readiness and excitement for the upcoming adventure.

"Is Anthony up there with you?"

"*I haven't seen him. Sorry.*"

Will sighed. "His mum probably had other plans."

"*I'm sure he'll turn up in time for launch. How's the spacesuit?*"

"Feels good."

"*Our sponsors will be glad to hear it. You've got about eleven minutes to launch. Strap in and get comfortable.*"

Once Donavon had finished pandering to the surrounding crowd, pumping his fists and generally acting up, he claimed the navigator's seat with access to the altimeter, anemometer, dynamometer, barometer, and GPS screens.

The thrill of the grand occasion produced a heartbeat Will could feel even in the pads of his thumbs as he cradled himself into the flight operator's seat, outfitted with the command post joystick, giving him full control over the winch cable and their ascent speed. The real challenge was knowing when to operate it. The variometer gauge was also mounted in front of his seat so he could monitor the climb rate.

The crew fastened their shoulder restraints and their waist belts, aided by the technicians, who checked the sub-straps and rotary buckles were wedged precisely where they belonged.

Will tucked his heels under the seat and settled his hands on the joystick.

"*We've just passed the five-minute mark,*" said Jefferson. "*On approach for launch.*"

While final safety checks took place, the crowd began to break up into smaller knots of conversation, their voices a mix of excitement and curiosity. Their mobile cameras were up and ready, their eager faces behind them prepared to capture every moment and share the spectacle as it unfolded. Eyes remained fixed upon the Fable Sky crew and technicians, who bustled around making last-minute adjustments, ensuring everything was in place.

Will waved back at a group of young boys holding onto white balloons and waving at the crew, their round-cheeked faces bearing wide smiles.

Ariane, seated next to Will, joined in with the waving.

"Four minutes and counting."

When the technicians turned their backs, a group of well-wishers ducked under the safety ropes to get a close-up shot with their cameras. The technicians jumped down and rapidly ushered them back behind the ropes.

One technician broke off to inspect the steel tether cable. Engineered to rigorous military specifications, the high-tensile cable could extend as high as twenty-eight miles, anchoring the balloon at its intended float altitude. It would guarantee the balloon remained within vertical proximity of the launch site, preventing it from drifting miles away. At the balloon end, the cable was secured in a sealed conical socket basket mounted underneath the gondola, and included a load-bearing swivel, allowing the balloon to rotate freely while in flight. On the ground, the cable was bolted securely to a winch drum the size of a fuel tanker that held the twisting cables, wound together to form a thick, metallic rope. It was the critical link connecting the balloon to the Earth, enduring the strain of strong lateral winds while maintaining a steady vertical position, ensuring both the stability and manoeuvrability of the balloon, making it a marvel of engineering designed for the most demanding conditions. It had cost them a small fortune and was based on the same principles as deep ocean cables connected to tsunami and seismic monitoring buoys, designed with a high degree of reliability and strength to withstand immense environmental stresses. Jefferson had overcome several bureaucratic hurdles to secure flight clearance so no air traffic would intersect the balloon's vertical path.

"How long do we have?" asked Will.

"*Two minutes and fifteen seconds*," said Jefferson. "*We are set for lift-off at eight o'clock, as planned.*"

Will watched Lloyd tighten his waist belt and restraints. His eyes widened behind his visor; his hands drew in like tensing claws around the seat arms.

The technicians, carrying pre-flight checklists, moved into position, ready to orchestrate the launch by firing the squibs that would separate the gondola from a steel frame mounted in the ground.

"*One minute to launch. Counting.*"

Donavon made one final assessment of his instruments. Everything looked in order.

The crew shifted and settled in their recliner seats, feeling secure in their padding and restraints.

"*On behalf of Todd and me and all the people watching around the world, good luck, enjoy the ride, and see you back here safe and sound in about six hours.*"

"Thanks," said Will. "Same to you."

Jefferson began the final countdown. "*20… 19… 18… 17…*"

The sound from the spectators had ebbed, transitioning from an anticipatory buzz to a more subdued, almost reverent hush. Some were on their mobiles, fingers texting or tweeting or reading their screens while others had phone conversations through earbud, connected to people nationwide, sharing their screens for a live broadcast. Most held up their mobile cameras in front of them, either filming or photographing.

Will glimpsed the familiar heavy metal T-shirt emblazoned with the iconic logo in the crowd. It belonged to his son, now filming the crew on his mobile. A smile crept across Will's face. Anthony had got his hair cut short with a spiked top. He was fifteen now, on the cusp of sexual maturity, and looked taller and leaner than when he last saw him a year ago. He was the one great thing to come out of a bad marriage. But that was old news. Not the sort of memory he wanted on a special day like today.

Smiling behind his visor, Will waved his son goodbye.

Anthony smiled and waved back while still filming.

"*3… 2… 1… go for launch.*"

The ground fell away with suddenness as if the balloon had been tied to a bungee cord, then released, flinging them into the air while the cord retracted to its natural size.

Computers lit up, their screens flickering with data. Gauges sprang into life, needles twitching with accurate measurements. The gondola swayed gently, a subtle indication of the massive forces at play, while equipment vibrated with energy coursing through the launch systems.

With a smooth but powerful lift, the balloon soared into the sky, ascending at the rapid rate of 1,340 feet per minute, below the maximum aerodynamic pressure the envelope could comfortably endure.

The terrain below swiftly transformed. Everything shrank down, becoming miniature versions of themselves. Buildings in St. Ives turned into tiny blocks, roads into thin ribbons. The hustle and bustle of life on the ground seemed to freeze, as if the entire world had gone still in awe of the ascent. Spectators, animated with excitement just moments ago, stopped moving, their eyes glued to the balloon as it climbed higher and higher.

Birds that had been fluttering nearby vanished from view, their forms blending into the landscape. One horizon stretched out in all directions, an unbroken line where the Earth met the sky. The gentle ocean waves, visible before launch, froze into a flat, blue blanket, serene and motionless.

As the balloon continued its upward journey, towing the crew towards the stratosphere, the land receded into a distant memory, and the infinite sky beckoned with the promise of new discoveries.

ELEVEN

Jefferson and Todd stood at the window, watching Fable Sky lift off the ground and rise into the air.

A group of aeronautical enthusiasts? Or daredevils about to make history with success or headlines with failure?

Time would tell.

If Will was nervous, he hadn't shown it. Mannerisms and the functioning of his senses had been conducted with calm, professional economy. His natural way had shone through at the final press conference four months ago, fielding questions, expert in his replies, admitting there had been setback after setback but that it was normal in ventures as audacious as flying to the edge of space. A few cynics had been present in the conference room, claiming the Fable Sky dream was merely that—a dream. Some reporters had picked holes in the project, calling the gondola a gimcrack contraption, the crew deluded, the flight a fantasy, and the launch some pathetic attempt to entertain local crowds, fooled into an infectious, carnival-like event.

One had brought up Will's accident and accused him of drunken recklessness, but Will had been quick to shut her down, clarifying that he had simply misjudged the altitude and crashed because of hypoxia, which was no lie. The fact he had not been picked up by paramedics until the morning when the alcohol had dispersed from his system spared him his career, despite the empty red wine bottle discovered in the wreckage, prompting media speculation. He never would have got the project up and running with a revoked pilot's licence.

Still, the reporters had been adamant the balloon would never see the stratosphere. And their doubts had substance.

"This is your third attempt in just as many years," said the female reporter. "What makes you sure this time will be any different from the last?"

Seated alongside his crew at the table, adjusting the mic on his blue tie and perfecting his professional smile, Will leaned forward onto his elbows. "Three years ago, we had to cancel at the last minute because of a twist in the balloon's envelope. As a result, the seam split when the helium inside came under pressure. Although we managed to fix that, we had problems getting our hands on more helium and, consequently, lost the optimal window because of low-pressure that built up in the atmosphere."

"What about two years ago?" a male reporter called out, sitting about eight rows back.

"Again, envelope problems."

"Envelope problems? You mean the material split open again?"

"There was a rupture, yes, not in the seam but the envelope itself, and the balloon deflated."

Jefferson would never forget the humiliating moment the balloon keeled over in front of thousands of spectators that included the local media, broadcasting to people worldwide. Before the launch, the helium had started leaking from the envelope. It was refilled. It leaked again. The flight had to be postponed, and rapid diagnostic testing was performed to locate and repair the tear. But it was too late. The flight window passed, and they had to reschedule for the following year. The failed launch had been a miserable time for them all, a real low point. Their lack of financial resources and willing investors signalled the end of the project.

The country had lost interest.

The crew had lost motivation.

With funding and enthusiasm dwindling, both Jefferson and Will had considered calling it quits.

"Either you've been unlucky, or you just aren't cut out for space flights. I think we can all agree it's the latter."

Jefferson had wanted to punch the smug reporter in the throat for his snide comment. Behind the scenes, the crew had worked tirelessly to bring the flight to fruition, often reaching breaking point. Despite Donavon and Will investing all they had, the ongoing lack of funding hindered further progress.

Enduring intense media scrutiny, they had acquiesced to numerous concessions while dealing with the burden of public perception. Their fortunes took an unexpected turn, though, when NASA reached out. The crew soon found themselves in discussions with NASA directors, exploring the potential of a joint venture and its ramifications for both the Fable Sky crew and the renowned space agency.

In a momentous development, NASA agreed to subsidise the balloon mission, establishing an unlikely partnership. This collaboration aimed not only to advance scientific endeavours but also to foster global participation in space exploration and related disciplines. Promoting various science and astronomy projects and encouraging people worldwide, not just within the United States, to take part, NASA sought to ignite curiosity and engagement, uniting diverse communities in the shared pursuit of knowledge and discovery.

A male reporter chewing gum rose and aimed a finger at Ariane. "Who's the hot, new addition, and what's her phone number?"

The reporter, despite his impertinence, had posed a good question. Who was she? Jefferson knew little about her and was still curious as to why NASA had insisted she join the Fable Sky crew. Early thirties with long, black hair and a natural tan, Ariane was an experienced research pilot, the best of the best, but it occurred to Jefferson the highly acclaimed research institute she represented wanted to steal the limelight.

A camera flash left a white smudge on Jefferson's vision. When it passed, he turned to the American. "I'll let Ariane answer that."

Ariane slanted her microphone. "I'm here to oversee the successful launch of Akroid."

Still chewing gum madly, the reporter shrugged. "Sorry, love, I don't know what Akroid is."

"That's because I haven't finished speaking."

Laughter filled the room and even drew an applause from some reporters.

"So, Akroid is a cosmic dust collector designed to capture cosmic meteoroids found in the upper stratospheric region. It includes several silica aerogel cushions, which are capable of absorbing the microscopic meteoroid particles. Akroid will be remotely controlled through radio frequencies by operators at the NASA Marshall Space Flight Centre in Alabama. NASA wants to expand opportunities for people, not just Americans, to learn about and participate in NASA's aeronautics and space programs by supporting and enhancing science, engineering, data, and research. We want to integrate that research with education to build a diverse and scientifically literate and global workforce."

The pre-flight press conference lasted a further half hour. Most reporters asked legitimate, relevant questions. The usual cynics wanted to stir the pot and elicit reactions. Even so, Will and Ariane answered carefully, always with dignity and respect. Will's replies never wavered, and he never lost his composure, always dictating the discussion's momentum and tone.

"How do you feel about this year's launch?"

Will met eyes with Ariane, smiled, and then faced the small crowd. "Confident, actually. The balloon is twice as strong. We have a very talented crew, and having a NASA research pilot gives us an advantage we haven't had before."

Jefferson closed his eyes and drew a deep lungful of salty air. To his right, the Celtic Sea was a glittery, smooth surface. According to the weather bulleting announcers, it would be a calm, cloudless day.

More vehicles had arrived, driving onto the grass to join the other vehicles in the makeshift lot. An ice-cream van had taken up residence beside an enormous boulder, away from the cluster of vendors selling foods and cold drinks. The words *Yippee Whippy* were printed above the serving window in bright pink letters, and an ice-cream prop sat atop the roof like a cannon. It had a long queue already.

Jefferson could hear the crowd still cheering, filling him with a swell of pride and gratitude. Thanks to their pioneering efforts, ballooning had once again caught the imagination of a nation. Will deserved all the credit. He had made this happen, an idea spawned from his reckless behaviour, leading to a tragic event. Jefferson's guilt would never wane. A rat invasion in the white room had caused him to lose track of time, making him miss their scheduled balloon flight. For months, he'd dreamed nightmares of Will spiralling to the ground and plunging into that field, shattering his right leg, and leaving his face cut and bloody and his body rattled by the nasty effects of hypoxia.

Perhaps that was why he found it difficult to match Will's confidence. Outwardly, he exhibited an aura of composure and self-assurance. Internally, his optimism had gradually seeped away, as he worried something would go wrong. After all the trials and setbacks, today was the last shot. The future of his lighthouse depended on it.

Jefferson returned to his terminal and placed his headset over his ears, adjusting it until he had a snug and comfortable fit. As he settled into his chair, his focus sharpened. Taking a deep breath, he immersed himself in his role, ready to tackle any challenges that might arise. He reviewed his contingency plans, mentally rehearsed his responses, and braced himself for the unexpected. Yet, despite these preparations, nothing could have truly prepared him for the trials that were about to unfold.

TWELVE

"10,000 feet," said Donavon, eyeing the altimeter, atmospheric pressure gauge, and flashing GPS dot on his navigation screen. The computers diligently recorded valuable data: air pressure, temperature, atmospheric composition, wind speed, infrared and ultraviolet radiation, altitude, coordinates, and drag. Each parameter was accurately logged, creating a comprehensive dataset for further analysis on the ground.

For Lloyd, every foot in climb added a notch of anxiety. He hadn't dared to take in the view even once. But every time Donavon called out the altitude readings, it served as a harsh reminder of his vertigo. His space helmet only intensified his isolation and fear.

He swallowed hard, tasting the tobacco still in his mouth. Sipping some water through his straw, he glanced across at the empty seat between Donavon and Will, glimpsing the dark sky background. His stomach dropped as precipitously as though he were plummeting back to the ground.

Chosen as the space balloon's designer, he was relieved to see Fable Sky living up to expectation, streaming through the sky with the perfect combination of elements. The computers delivered vital information; the gondola travelled effortlessly. The envelope continued to expand, and once it reached full capacity, the ducts at the sides would vent any excess helium.

Lloyd's career had started with a company called Mitchell Harding, specialising in yachts and, later, superyachts that were not only aesthetically stunning but technologically advanced and highly functional. He had spent most of his career in the marine field, working all over the country. His dual master's degree in boat science and engineering and his natural flair had brought him success and recognition, allowing him to branch out independently.

He was self-taught when it came to designing balloons, and he had freelanced for some of the industry's top players. His prolific output included successful limited editions such as Aspire, a racer style balloon designed to take part in global competitions, and the Bronze Series, most popular among the ballooning community for its lightweight and fuel economy. With his increased recognition, he began to network, rubbing shoulders with the right people.

His life was turned upside down when he got caught for tax evasion and was handed a six-month prison sentence. His network collapsed, his reputation was flushed down the toilet, and he lost all credibility in the industry. It was utterly unfair. Granted, he had done a lousy job of keeping his tax records. Underreporting his earnings had been a careless, costly mistake, deserving, in his mind, of a fine and a caution at most. He had always fought against injustice and had been a tireless advocate for animal rights. If there was a petition to sign, he would sign it. If there was a protest taking place, he would be there. Who would fight against his injustice?

The days were long during his imprisonment, giving him ample time to reflect on his life. In the monotony of his cell, he often found himself lost in thought, replaying past events and decisions leading to this point. He pondered his neglected relationships, squandered opportunities, and the principles he had compromised in vivid detail. He received no visitors in the six months he spent there, forgotten and abandoned until, out of the blue and to his shock surprise, the warden announced he had a visitor just a few weeks before his release.

Lloyd was escorted to the visitor's room, where a young man in trendy clothes waited patiently for him. He introduced himself as Will and declared he was hunting for someone to design Fable Sky, a new type of tourist balloon.

"Do you think you've got what it takes?" asked Will after explaining the mission and the type of balloon he required.

"Design the world's largest zero-pressure helium balloon that is resistant to the harsh conditions of the stratosphere? That's a new one. But yeah, I can."

"Great."

Incapable of holding eye contact, Lloyd broke from Will's stare, delaying his response. "On one condition."

Lloyd could tell by the way Will cocked an eyebrow that he expected to hear a request for exorbitant sums of money. To claim full or joint ownership of the balloon. To christen the vessel *Lloyd. The Lloyd Space Balloon Series.* Or something cooler that honoured his work. He dipped his head, staring down at the table as he spoke. "I want to join you on one of the flights.

Once it's been built. Only the maiden flight. Not, you know, permanently or anything. Only one time. It's just that I like to experience my balloons in action. You know, for validation and assessment."

He *liked to experience his balloons in action*. Where did that come from? It was true he liked to test out his boats, as sailing was a hobby, but not balloons, for he had a crippling fear of heights. Will intended to fly the balloon into the stratosphere, targeting twenty-eight miles above the Earth. But Lloyd knew exactly what he was doing. He'd always been a nobody. Flying a balloon to the edge of space could make him a somebody. His career teetered on non-existence, with burned bridges and a *severely* burned bank balance. Perhaps this was an opportunity to revive his career and earn back his credibility. It could lead to bigger and better opportunities, repair his finances, salvage his reputation, and bring him some happiness. Furthermore, it was a chance to live a little. Life for Lloyd had been all work and no play for several years. There were certain things he was not cut out for. One involved flying. It would never be easy, but he knew that avoiding his fear would only make it grow stronger, and the best way to recover was to face it once more.

"I need to discuss it with my business partners," said Will. "I'll be in touch."

Will returned one week later to confirm that Donavon and Jefferson had agreed to his request, pending an interview once he got out of prison. Fitness drills, space training, and skydiving lessons would be the next step, and his payment for designing the balloon would have to be renegotiated. Lloyd agreed with no hesitation.

Eighteen months down the track, Fable Sky was ready for manufacture, a milestone marking the culmination of careful planning, innovative design, and rigorous testing. The vision was finally transitioning into reality. The gondola, the heart of this ambitious project, was to be constructed using the latest advances in yacht-building composite technology: a blend of strength, durability, and lightweight efficiency. Lloyd opted for custom-moulded fiberglass, chosen for its superior resilience and versatility, forming the gondola's outer shell and providing a sleek, aerodynamic surface capable of withstanding the harsh conditions encountered at high altitudes. Inside, a honeycomb construct would add an extra layer of strength while keeping the overall weight to a minimum. The design not only enhanced its structural integrity but also improved its thermal insulation, crucial for maintaining the stable internal temperatures during flight.

Supporting this advanced composite structure, a network of aluminium ribs would provide the fundamental framework, precisely engineered and positioned to distribute stress evenly across the gondola, enhancing both its stability and safety. The use of aluminium, known for its strength-to-weight ratio and corrosion resistance, meant the gondola could withstand the demanding environmental stresses it would face.

Fable Sky was not just ready for manufacture; it was poised to set new standards in aerospace innovation, bringing a dream closer to reality with each passing day.

There was Aspire and the Bronze Series, but nothing quite measured up to Fable Sky.

"13,000 feet," Donavon called out.

Lloyd took deep breaths as he came back to reality. His chest constricted, as if an enormous snake had wrapped itself around his upper body, crushing him. He tried to exhale, but hardly any air escaped his lungs. He loathed himself for not remaining strong, letting fear and the pressure of the situation overwhelm him. But it felt like more than just fear and pressure; it seemed as though forces beyond their control were gathering, preparing to upheave the world.

THIRTEEN

Air temperature had dropped to minus eight degrees while the altimeter read 16,000 feet.

"What's the current rate of climb?" asked Donavon.

Will, gripping the joystick, checking the variometer, said, "990 per minute."

He moved the joystick forward, increasing the thrust at the winch drum, and pushed the climb rate to the maximum he felt comfortable with at this stage of the flight, and that was 1,100 feet per minute.

Will admired the rugged hills that undulated and stretched towards the horizon. As the sun climbed higher, its golden rays illuminated the jagged peaks and valleys, casting a warm glow over a patchwork quilt of forests and fields, interspersed with occasional towns—small dots of civilisation in the sprawling wilderness. Dense forests appeared as dark, verdant patches among the green countryside, neatly divided by hedgerows and narrow country lanes. It provided an overview of nature's raw, unbridled power blemished by human hands.

To the west, the countryside abruptly ended, giving way to the vast, shimmering expanse of the Atlantic Ocean. The deep blue waters stretched to the horizon, their surface dotted with white caps as waves bucked and broke. Beyond the horizon lay the American continent, separated from Britain by thousands of miles of ocean. The thought of this distant land, so far but connected by the very ocean glimmering below in the morning sun, lit Will's imagination.

From his high-altitude vantage point, the planet seemed vast and intimately connected. Altitude brought symmetry to the chaotic, bustling world, making more sense to him. Land was divided into neat patterns, with farmland and meadows checkerboarding the country, winding roads disappearing to the horizon, and villages and towns and farms nestled in valleys. Rivers meandering, lakes sparkling like wires lit by electrical current. Rocky outcrops jutted from the ground, remnants of ancient geological upheavals. Along the jagged coastline, cliffs dropped dramatically into the sea, and sandy beaches formed gentle crescents.

Normally, though, Will viewed the landscape as a series of good and bad landing sites.

"20,000 feet," said Donavon.

"What's that in miles?" asked Peta.

"Almost four."

"So, twenty-four to go."

"You're really *good* at maths."

"Shut up, Donavon!"

Donavon let out a small huff. Not quite a laugh, but close.

"What's the air temperature?" asked Will.

Donavon leaned towards his screens. "It has dropped to minus fifteen degrees. And atmospheric pressure is now at six hundred HPA."

The polyethylene envelope was holding up well within the harsh environment. Above, the sky was an intense indigo blue. Below, away from all the boats scattered along the coast and docked in the St. Ives Bay area, an oil tanker cut a white swathe on its path. Will's eyes circled back to the launch site. The spectators had shrunk down to a tiny, organic mass at the other end of the cable, unravelling on the cliff at high speed. His son was among them. Seeing him at the launch had given Will an extra boost.

He missed Anthony all the time. Jacqueline, his ex-wife, went out of her way to make sure they had limited contact. She was vengeful, cold-hearted, and just plain wicked. She was the type who would spit in your coffee if she didn't like you. Why had he fallen in love with such a meddlesome, spiteful woman? Their marriage hadn't always been so strained. Will had always felt the proximity of a sympathetic son or daughter would help resolve their differences. During pregnancy, their relationship had been comfortable, perhaps convenient. But she had given birth, not because she wanted a child, but because she could find no motivation to terminate the pregnancy. They'd named their newborn son Anthony after Jacqueline's brother, who had drunk himself into an early grave. From the outset, she had difficulty with breastfeeding, getting Anthony to latch on. It made her angry, and once she slapped his face.

On the weekend of Anthony's ninth birthday, Jaqueline walked out on Will and took their son with her. She had been proposing divorce for some time, but he had tried to stick it out for Anthony's sake. It didn't work out, and Will wound up in court, trying to prove he was a good father while her lawyer tried to discredit him and raised difficult questions, helping the judge reach her decision. Anger didn't suit Will. He never felt comfortable with himself on the rare occasions he ever lost his temper. Whenever confronted, he always held back and let the challenger have their say, then responded carefully in an affable way. He had completely lost it at the custody hearing, letting his emotions prevail with an outburst both unnecessary and uncharacteristic. And, as anticipated, with the support of a top lawyer, Jaqueline claimed victory.

Will was a good father, but the judge considered him unfit. Unlike Jacqueline, a top consultant optometrist on a six-figure salary, he could not offer adequate financial support for his child because his job as a balloonist did not provide a steady income. Still, he believed he had been discriminated against because he was male, and the courts often tended to favour maternal care. They didn't know Jacqueline like he did. Still, if she hadn't left him when she did, he wouldn't have flown a balloon while intoxicated and conceived the idea that had now become a reality. On the other hand, he would also have a fully functioning knee, free of the metal plates and screws holding it together, and a hip that didn't ache in cold weather.

Donavon looked at his screens. "29,000 feet."

"The height of Mount Everest," said Peta.

"Also close to where the ozone begins," said Ariane.

Without the variometer confirming a climb rate of 1,040 feet per minute, it would be difficult to judge if they were still rising. The sensation of ascent was subtle, often imperceptible to the human senses, especially at such high altitudes where visual cues on the ground were less distinct. The variometer's precise measurements provided the critical information and offered a reliable gauge as to their vertical speed when other indicators were ambiguous.

"Did anyone check the parachutes?" asked Lloyd.

A long silence filled their helmets.

"Who even packed them?" That was his second question, spoken with a hint of panic.

Will, still thinking about Anthony, snapped back. "The technicians packed them and ran extra checks."

"Are you sure? Did you see them do it?"

"I saw them pack ours, but not yours," said Donavon.

"Stop it!" said Peta. "Don't listen to Donavon; he's being a dick, as usual. I saw them pack the chutes, including yours. There's nothing to worry about."

A male voice crackled across the airwaves, cutting through the static with pressing immediacy. "*Fable Sky, do you copy? This is Jefferson. We have a problem.*"

FOURTEEN

"This is Will. What's happening?"

When he got nothing back, he repeated his transmission. "Jefferson, do you copy? What's the problem?"

Jefferson's radio silence had Will worried until his voice bellowed through their helmet speakers. *"We've been experiencing long communication blackouts. I've been trying to reach you for the last fifteen minutes or so. No one heard me, right?"*

"We haven't heard from you since take-off. It seems fine now."

"Todd got it working. Something to do with the site grounding on the duplexer, or something. We're monitoring it carefully. How's everything up there?"

"Fine," said Donavon. He reported that the balloon was travelling well and read off data from the computers.

"Living the high life."

"Very funny," said Peta.

"*Would love to be up there, but I hear the cost is astronomical.*"

"Okay, stop now!" she said.

"*How's the view?*"

Donavon glanced down. "Nothing we haven't seen from a plane window before."

"*I have to say I'm envious.*"

"Get on a plane, then."

"You'll get your turn," said Will.

"*You bet. We will continue to monitor the duplexer. If you can't reach me or don't hear from me for a while, you know why. Speak shortly. Out.*"

Will turned to his co-pilot. "Where are we at?"

Donavon leaned forward. "We're approaching 37,000 feet. Atmospheric pressure is four hundred and fifty HPA, and the temperature at the balloon's pole is minus thirty-four degrees."

"How long have we been airborne?" asked Ariane, who had stayed largely quiet until now.

Will smiled, intrigued by her still and watchful silence. "About forty minutes. Is the flight what you expected?"

"It's pleasant enough."

"You sound unimpressed," said Donavon.

Will was aware of Ariane's career history because he had asked, and she had explained. She had worked in zero-gravity conditions, had practiced high angle-of-attack manoeuvring, complex landing techniques, and had flown under adverse environmental pressures. With such accomplishments and the aura with which she carried herself, he had to ask himself if this project was beneath her.

"I'm used to G-force that will make your eyes leave their sockets," she said. "But this is a nice change, I have to say."

"What's the highest you've flown in a plane?" asked Peta.

"Twenty-two miles in a rocket-powered jet."

"Sounds terrifying," said Lloyd.

"There isn't time to be scared. If you're prone to fear, you are probably in the wrong job." She left her eyes on Lloyd for several seconds before facing the view.

Will sighted a plane on the horizon, sunlight twinkling on its fuselage. It left a white scratch across the sky as it cruised slowly and silently to the north, its passengers almost certainly oblivious to the space balloon floating outside their portside windows.

He visualised the passenger experience he could soon be offering. Quick and reasonably affordable access to the fringe of space. Potential tourists would need to undertake skydiving lessons, intensive fitness training, team-bonding activities, and two days of pre-flight preparation, which included a medical examination—insurance prerequisites. Jefferson had already shortlisted a handful of companies to facilitate each element.

Very little was known about the stratosphere. In fact, the further regions of space were more explored. To understand space flights better, atmospheric conditions to assist with their forecast models had to be recorded and measured. A greater comprehension of aerodynamics and meteorology, physics, geology, and weather patterns would help the team embark on new and improved equipment, technologies, and tools.

Fable Sky was a sound vessel and officially classified as a spacecraft by the Civil Aviation Authority, but believing that it couldn't be improved was negligent and dangerous. Balloons had far fewer working parts than a rocket or plane to go wrong. However, the one-of-its-kind canopy, made from a transparent polyethylene material, making the balloon more manoeuvrable and less susceptible to elemental forces, was a fragile vessel, and the mission posed a multitude of dangers. The envelope could tear open. One of the thousands of fragile seams could split open. The ropes could become twisted and tangled. The gondola could detach and plummet. The parachutes could fail. They could ditch in the sea. Their oxygen tanks could leak. They could lose communication again. The winch cable had not been put to the test yet. Whether its components might buckle under the strain and cease to function was still a grave possibility. Their spacesuits, regulating their body temperatures and protecting them from cosmic radiation bombardment, could rupture. One simple misstep could end their mission quickly and catastrophically. The stratosphere was a hostile environment, devoid of breathable air and the atmospheric pressures necessary to prevent haemorrhaging. Without their spacesuits, their blood would be trying to squeeze out of their veins.

Banishing these morbid scenarios from his mind, Will kept his focus on task, thinking only positive thoughts. Bad pilots were pessimistic and succumbed to the pressure. Good pilots believed in their vessels, their flight crew, and themselves.

"50,000 feet," said Donavon. "Temperature has dropped to minus thirty-nine degrees."

Will squinted at the sun and pulled down his gold-coated visor, the world's most expensive sunglasses, designed to deal with changing light conditions and to protect him from eye-damaging solar radiation at high altitude. He asked the crew to do the same, and their faces vanished behind gold mirrors. He would not see them again for about the next five hours.

Will drew his attention to the first glimpse of the Earth's curvature, as impressive as he had anticipated.

"Is everyone doing all right?" asked Donavon. "Is anyone feeling unwell?"

Peta and Lloyd replied *no*, and Ariane remained still and silent.

"*Looking awesome Fable Sky,*" said Jefferson. "*You might be interested to know you have completed thirty-two revolutions.*"

"That many?" Peta asked.

"*I thought that might get your heads spinning. Flight activity in the area is limited and at a safe enough distance. Do you know how many people I had to sleep with to get flight clearance?*"

Peta sniggered. "Now we *know* you're lying."

"*I'm looking forward to seeing the solar wing images. We all are down here.*"

"We'll release the bird as soon as we can," said Peta. "Are the crowds still there?"

"*I haven't seen anyone leave. The launch was quite the show. How was it for you?*"

"Incredible," she said. "Literally took my breath away. It was like nothing I've ever experienced."

"I agree," said Will. "Better than I imagined."

"*I also looked at the live feed on the Internet. You've racked up quite a following.*"

"How many?" Peta asked.

"*Last I checked, it was over 15,000 viewers.*"

"Not bad."

"Could be better," said Donavon.

"I believe that we're making good time," said Will. "Please confirm."

"*At this rate, you should reach float altitude in less than two hours.*"

"Do us all a favour," said Donavon. "Flip the critics the middle finger, tell them *up yours* from all of us."

"*I'm sure that will go down like a lead balloon. Pun intended. I'm going to sign out, leave you to it. Stay alert. I'll contact you again when you reach float altitude. Out.*"

FIFTEEN

Todd sat in front of his computer console, elbows on the desk and chin resting in his hands, staring at his screen with a look of boredom. He swigged some Coke from a can and stretched out his legs, still aching from all the stair-climbing earlier.

Needing to keep his hands occupied, he reached under the desk and picked up his skateboard. He had hit a tree root on his way to the lighthouse early that morning, buckling the front wheel, and wanted to repair it before the day's end.

Office workers normally adorned their desks with family pictures, souvenirs, and professional awards. A large stack of paperwork and Post-it notes dominated Jefferson's terminal, with full in- and out-trays surrounded by blinking server lights. No personal mementoes other than a framed picture of his wife took up residence on his desk. Todd, by comparison, had mini toolkits, cables, and computer components in a box, just waiting to be used. And Dell, his laptop. He spent hours on there, playing video games, musing over beautiful, naked ladies, and occasionally hacking into commercial software, unlocking confidential information and wreaking havoc on any industry that fell into his line of sight. Endowed with hacking skills that had frustrated some of the world's cyber-security experts, he had gained anonymous notoriety within the web's dark corners. The Net was a trove within a virtual reality, holding endless possibilities and, with the right moves, infinite power.

Jefferson knew all about his computer capabilities and had taken him on for three reasons: his technical brilliance, a family favour, and to keep him out of mischief, deterring him from hacking large corporations. He had never been able to hold down jobs for longer than six months and had recently signed on for unemployment benefit after he got caught with his hand in the petty cash tin by the company executive of a small tech firm. Todd disagreed that stealing fifty quid had warranted the sack when he had exposed a major gap in the organisation's cybersecurity governance, saving it thousands in legal fees.

Under Jefferson's supervision, Todd was responsible for tracking data and overseeing technical anomalies when they arose. Jefferson was a competent user of technology but not savvy enough to solve a tech problem alone. Data Analyst was Todd's title. A permanent position was available if he proved himself because Jefferson wanted to run ongoing civilian space flights.

New alerts sounded on Todd's monitor, but he didn't hear them.

Jefferson had just hung up on the crew and glanced over at Todd. "Can you give me an update on the crew's physical readouts?"

Todd was busy unscrewing his skateboard wheel and didn't hear his uncle.

"Earth to Todd!"

Todd swivelled on his chair. "What?"

"Pay attention! Your computer alerts are going off. I need the clinical data for each of the crew."

"My bad." He threw his skateboard under the desk. His headset was dangling around his neck, so he slipped it on and looked at his monitors.

"Donavon's pulse is normal. Respiration, normal. Blood pressure... also normal. Body temperature, fine. Same goes for Ariane, Peta, and Will. Lloyd's body temperature is normal. Oh, um, his pulse rate is a bit high at a hundred and ten beats per minute. His blood pressure is pretty high, too. Respiration is normal."

"All right, keep an eye on him. On all of them."

Among many, Jefferson's duties involved collecting and formatting telemetry and radar data to monitor navigation and transmit commands. Fable Sky had already crossed six and a half miles—airline cruising altitude. The nearest aircraft had flown fifteen miles south and on a northwest trajectory. Heavy flight activity had been observed further east and over the Atlantic Ocean. Now the balloon was on course to reach the ten-mile mark.

Todd approached the window, his curiosity piqued by the commotion coming from outside. The spectators had their heads raised and eyes fixed on the sky. He traced the path of the steel cable unwinding from the winch drum at high speed. His eyes finally settled on the Fable Sky balloon, now a tiny dot high above. A stream of thick, black smoke poured from it, trailing ominously against the otherwise clear blue sky. The sight filled him with dread. The thick, inky plume twisted and curled as the balloon continued its upward journey, spreading out like a dark, unfurling ribbon. The smoke seemed to cause growing concern among the onlookers, who watched in silent alarm as the situation unfolded, thinking the same thing as him: was the balloon on fire? Todd was about to inform Jefferson of the impending disaster when he realised what it was.

"I think the crew has just lit the smoke identifiers. Is that right?"

Jefferson faced Todd. "Correct. Right on cue."

Triggered by several cylinders mounted onto the gondola's undercarriage, the smoke identifiers signalled that Fable Sky had achieved 58,000 feet, reaching another crucial milestone—the tropopause, the coldest layer of the atmosphere, marking the boundary between the troposphere and stratosphere. The smoke was meant to keep the media and spectators engaged, guiding their line of sight in the sky as the balloon had nearly disappeared from view.

"Do the people down there know that it's planned?" asked Todd. "What if they think the balloon has caught fire? Shall I go down and tell them?"

"We have shared everything with the media about how the flight will go today. They should know."

Todd looked up at the dissipating smoke once more, his relief shown on his face. His frayed nerves made him need the toilet suddenly, so he turned and crossed the room, but didn't see the champagne crate on the floor until it was too late. He tripped and went down hard on his knees.

Jefferson wheeled round on his chair. "Can you get those put away in the fridge downstairs? They're for the crew when they return."

Todd rubbed his knees. "I need the toilet."

"Then you're heading in the right direction." Jefferson held out his red cup. "Make me another coffee while you're down there, will you?"

Champagne crate cradled in his arms, Todd set off for the staircase, snatching the cup in passing. A silver helium balloon was tied to the crate with Fable Sky written across its middle in blue ink. It kept rebounding off his face as he descended the steep steps. The bathroom was one level down, next to the kitchen, and when he passed it, he almost lost his footing on the wet floor. Setting down the crate, he opened the bathroom door to find a powerful jet of water gushing from a split pipe beneath the sink.

Todd ran back up the steps two at a time, his aching legs working like mechanical pistons, his thick keychain swinging on his belt as he rushed into the flight control room. "There's like a huge leak in the bathroom. Can you look at it?"

Fable Sky had just cleared the tropopause, crossing into the stratosphere, where all weather stopped. As anticipated, the balloon strayed approximately 1,000 metres east of the launch site. However, Jefferson had lost contact with the balloon once more, enduring another prolonged blackout. "Fable Sky, do you copy?"

No reply.

"Fable Sky, do you copy? This is Jefferson."

With communication terminated, Jefferson removed his headset. "Radio's down again. I need you to take a second look at the duplexer, see what's going on."

"I thought it was the site grounding connections," said Todd. "Maybe it's the antenna feedline. Let me take another look at it."

Todd placed a wattmeter between the bandpass filter and duplexer and checked the reading, realising the selectivity was too low. "There it is!"

"You've found the problem?"

"I think so. The duplexer's screwed, either from damaged components or contamination, at a guess. Do we have another one?"

Jefferson pointed to some equipment near the door. "In one of those boxes."

Locating the spare, Todd switched the duplexers over and connected the newer model to the transmitter, antenna, and receiver. "How's that? Is it working now?"

Jefferson stuck up his thumb.

Pinching his crotch, Todd asked, "What about the leak? There's water everywhere. Do you want to take a look at it? Or should I call someone?"

"You'll have to sort it out. I can't leave my terminal."

Without protest, Todd turned and swiftly left the flight control room.

"And what about that coffee?" Jefferson asked out to the space Todd had just vacated, unaware he would never see his nephew again.

SIXTEEN

One hour forty-five minutes into the flight. They had crossed the halfway point. Lloyd was satisfied with Fable Sky's progress and his own performance. The avionics and electronics, critical components of their mission into space, functioned flawlessly, demonstrating remarkable reliability and exactness. Sensing his accomplishment, that his efforts had finally paid off, boosted his confidence and reinforced his belief in the success of the mission. He breathed steadily to conserve his oxygen, feeling more relaxed than at take-off. It would be a story to tell people and whatever interviews he might be invited to do. Maybe he could write a book. He smiled, trying to reassure himself that he had everything under control. For a moment, he almost convinced himself until a sudden jolt of turbulence shook the gondola, rattling his confidence. He gasped and instinctively tightened his grip on the seat arms.

All this risk, all this danger, like a roulette player choosing whether to slide their pile of chips onto red or black. Red, you live. Black, you die. The only difference was the length of time it took to learn the outcome. On a roulette table, it was about half a minute. On Fable Sky, half a day. But the tension in between was essentially the same. All to become a household name with celebrity status. To feel important and relevant and be recognised for doing something brave. Not to overcome his fear but to learn how to manage it.

The one time he had flown in a balloon to help with his research, it had been a disaster. Upon lift-off, the 90,000 cubic-foot balloon gracefully ascended, quickly gaining altitude as it sailed over a forest with two other passengers on board. Lloyd, initially hesitant, opened his eyes to find them skimming the treetops, the ground rapidly receding as they soared into the sky. The initial exhilaration of the flight filled him with pride and awe. Forty-five minutes into the flight, the wind suddenly dropped. The balloon hung eerily still and was enveloped in a thick, suffocating fog that reduced visibility to almost nothing. The world outside the balloon became a blank, grey screen, unsettling him. Suspended in time, they were going nowhere. The dense fog made discerning whatever lay below impossible, rendering any attempts to descend dangerous. Despite calm and reassuring words from the pilot, everything in him tensed and clenched. His muscles went taut with anxiety, and blood drained from his face. The uncertainty and eerie stillness of the fog-bound balloon turned the adventure into a nerve-wracking ordeal.

"How much longer?" asked Lloyd.

Donavon looked his way. "Until what?"

"We get there."

"Get there? Are you being serious?"

"Why?"

"It's not a fucking bus ride!"

"I'm just asking."

"We should reach float altitude within the next hour or so," said Will.

"That long?"

Donavon shook his head and laughed mockingly. "Build a rocket next time if you're in such a rush to *get there*."

Eyes closed, Lloyd retreated to a safe space in his mind to help manage his fears. His imagination carried him into the heart of a forest. Dawn and dusk were his favourite times of the day when all the wildlife appeared. People needed nature. Nature didn't need people. He'd read that on a drink's coaster once. A lover of all wildlife, he had turned vegan at an early age and had visited every nature park in Britain, even taking part in a practical conservation project for CSV Action Earth. Truth be told, it was for community service after doing time for tax evasion. It had been the hardest six months of his life, boxed in by concrete and steel with no windows to natural surroundings. If he didn't get a frequent dose of the outdoors, he would struggle to keep a sane mind. Fortunately, out of cell time had been generous, with plenty of recreational activities to help him assimilate and settle, enough to prevent him from losing it.

Jefferson's voice broke Lloyd's reverie. "*Fable Sky, do you copy?*"

"Peta speaking, go ahead."

"*Sorry about that. We lost the duplexer again. Should be fine now. We've replaced it.*"

"We didn't expect to hear from you until float altitude."

"I wanted to report back on your health status. Nothing to worry about. Everyone is showing perfect readings. Lloyd, your pulse rate is high. One hundred and ten beats per minute. How are you feeling?"

Lloyd knew his decision to keep his fear of heights quiet was a hundred per cent correct.

"I'm fine."

"Blood pressure is high, too."

"Noted, but I'm fine."

"Watch him, please. You've still got around 40,000 feet to go. Lloyd, keep us informed if anything changes."

"I said I'm fine!"

Lloyd glanced at Donavon, busy monitoring the uplinks from a weather beacon attached to the gondola, feeding into his monitor and giving him the geographic coordinates. He then craned his neck to view the rounded envelope in the black sky. Because of the pressure drop, it had expanded to more than several hundred times its volume at sea level. Above the envelope hung the white sun, partially eclipsed by the balloon's enormous bulk.

Air temperature at the crown, according to Donavon, read minus forty degrees. "100,000 feet and still climbing."

They were on the verge of accomplishing phase one: target altitude.

"That's roughly a third of the Earth's total atmosphere," said Ariane.

Peta pumped her fists. "Yeah? Go us."

But during the celebration, Lloyd's reaction was markedly different. As the reality of their achieved milestone sank in, a surge of anxiety gripped him, and he felt a sudden, involuntary release. The humiliating warmth at his crotch made his heart sink; a visceral manifestation of his fears and apprehension, reminding him of the immense risks they faced on their high-altitude quest.

SEVENTEEN

Fable Sky's envelope had swollen to a giant pumpkin-shaped ball, cruising towards the edge of space. There was no precise definition of where the atmosphere ended and space began, nor any official international law, but the Karman Line, sixty-two miles above sea level, was widely regarded as the closest attempt at defining the boundary. Fable Sky's claim to target the *edge of space* was more a metaphor for providing a view from the top of the sky.

Mesmerised by these darker surroundings and views she could only have dreamed about, Peta pictured the first moon-landing and recited the famous giant-leap statement in her mind. Reaching space had been achieved by fewer than six hundred individuals, and while this was not space, it was an extraordinary moment she would remember forever. It would go down as one of her greatest life achievements.

Before discovering such a thirst for extreme sports, what her counsellor called her *outlet* and *taking back control*, she had endured horrific abuse. Born to a family constrained by a lack of money and raised by working-class parents who had never completed their education, Peta had attended a low-ranking public school, worn hand-me-downs, and had lived within an impoverished council estate in Bristol in one of three identical high-rise tower blocks, shared by thugs and drug dealers.

Her mother had been strict about most things but was an evil mad dictator when it came to obedience. As a result, they had shared a complicated love. Peta came to despise her after losing her father when she was just eight, an early acquaintance with love and loss. There had been moments of empathy and care up until then. She had soothed Peta when she bumped or grazed herself and when frightened by the night. Following the funeral, her mother needed a coping mechanism and turned to alcohol and illicit drugs. A lethal combination.

The first time it happened, her mother called her into the living room one afternoon, formally and fierce. Peta expected a telling off for no apparent reason. Her mother beat her with a broom handle, leaving her with black eyes and a sprained wrist that took weeks to heal.

Every week was a struggle for the next seven years, a fight for harmony behind a polite smile that stifled her scream. Her mother beat her for any reason she could find and often no reason at all. She would then apologise and be pleasant once more. Peta had to shapeshift to please her and prove herself, always prepared in case she was on another drunken warpath. She learned to avoid her mother while strengthening her resolve. All the frustration she built up, she threw into track running. Reading also became an important diversion, living alternative lives through the characters in worlds other than her own as she was sick of wallowing in self-pity and always crying. Until one day, when she was fifteen, everything changed.

"Get up here!" her mother shouted from the second floor of their new council house, her tone demanding immediacy.

Peta ran up the stairs and stopped on the landing.

Her mother had a bottle of gin gripped in her hand and a pencil behind her ear. "I saw you with that girl!"

Peta frowned. "What girl? I have lots of girlfriends."

"And do you stick your tongue down all their throats?"

Peta folded her arms in a show of defiance. "Not all, only Dani's!"

Her mother frowned so hard, the skin on her forehead looked corrugated. "You don't deny it, then!"

"No!"

A sharp pain forced Peta to use both hands to clutch her stomach, where the rubber-tipped end of a pencil protruded from her flesh, causing blood to stream between her fingers.

The pencil's sharp tip had nicked a vein, and she had to endure two operations to repair it. She lost a lot of blood, and the doctors gave her a slim chance of fertility in the future.

"So, you want to tell me what happened?" asked the female police officer sitting at her bedside when she was well enough to speak.

Delirious, beyond sentience, Peta rolled her head the other way to avoid the question. A cardiac monitor blipped her heart rate in long green waves across a black screen. Her mother was standing at the observation window, her tattooed arms by her side with a police officer over her left shoulder.

"I don't remember."

"You can tell me. I'm here to help you."

What was there to gain from throwing her mother under the bus? She would only end up in care, no better off than an orphan. She also believed no jury would convict, and no judge would pass sentence, and she'd only have to face her mother's wrath for speaking the truth.

After seven days, she left the hospital, fearful, angry, and frustrated. A taxi driver dropped her at home, and she headed straight to her bedroom, meeting her mother on the landing where their previous encounter had ended in her bloodshed.

Though heavily built, her mother moved with the dignity and posture of someone who had received physical training, even intoxicated.

"What did you tell the police?"

Peta shook her head quickly. "Nothing."

"Don't lie to me!"

"I'm telling the truth."

Her mum just looked at her.

Peta knew what that meant and what was coming.

True to form, she grabbed Peta one-handed by the throat, crushing her windpipe.

Peta freed herself. "Don't touch me!"

She grabbed Peta again and their scuffle took a sudden turn. Her mother fell down the stairs doing the backstroke with wide, stunned eyes. When she reached the bottom, a tremendous silence descended over the house. The night ended, and her mother never woke again.

Police officers questioned Peta about the friction at home and the amphetamine drugs found on her mother's dressing table. She understood these questions had to be asked, but she put her blinkers on to shield herself from anything resembling unwelcome emotions.

Her mother's death left three indelible marks on her life. For one, an unwillingness to ever return to Bristol, so the Isle of Wight, a small island off the southern coast, became her home. Isolated, peaceful, but with plenty of recreation for like-minded adrenaline addicts. The second was a strong desire to advocate against domestic violence, having people understand not only men committed such offences. She'd campaigned to local councils and had written strongly worded letters to the government. And third, the abuse had not broken her. It had made her stronger. To look at her, no one would know what she had grown up with.

When she finished her secondary education, she trained as a nurse, inspired by the gracious staff who had saved her life at the hospital. She lasted five years, conflicted by the busy nature of hospitals and the emotional demands put upon her because the system was badly underfunded and devastated by underemployment. She became an industrial window cleaner instead, trained to Industrial Rope Access Trade Association standards, earning a living abseiling down some of the tallest buildings in the country. It was the ideal job, far removed from human encounters.

Though small in stature, her appetite for adventure was unmatched, and when it came to hot-air balloons, she had an impressive resume that included tightrope walking between two balloons at 10,000 feet and jumping from 40,000 feet using breathing apparatus. She strived to attend one balloon festival per year to participate in races. The Albuquerque International Balloon Fiesta, the largest global hot-air balloon festival, was her favourite, where more than seven hundred professional balloonists represented twenty-two countries. It was renowned not only for its impressive scale but also for the vibrant display of colours and designs filling the sky, creating a breathtaking panorama of floating artistry.

The opportunity to join the Fable Sky crew for a single test flight mission was not to be refused. And Donavon had raised her hopes about attending flights in the future if the project proved successful. He'd waited in the kitchen while Jefferson and Will met with her inside the watch room at the lighthouse.

She stuck up both thumbs joyfully following the two-hour interview. Both Will and Jefferson had sensed Peta's genuine passion for flying. Coupled with her experience, knowhow, and grit, and taking her medical background into account, they had been confident she would be a suitable reserve pilot and their fourth and final crew member. Piloting a giant balloon to the edge of space was just the type of adventure she craved. She was also a photographer and videographer by chance, so documenting the maiden flight was included in her contract.

At training sessions, Peta was always first in the gym and often last out. She had run the London Marathon four times and had finished in the top one hundred in the Paris Marathon, so the morning runs that constituted their fitness regimen were too easy. The crew would arrive at the end of an eight-mile run to find her stretching down with barely any sweat.

Peta traced the Earth's curvature with her eyes, contemplating the constraints daily life posed. Climate change was escalating, pollution choked the air, poverty and famine plagued entire nations, overpopulation strained natural resources, and disease spread unchecked. From her lofty perch, these pressing issues were obscured. Murders, massacres, military conflicts were all hidden from sight, as though no one was trapped in untenable situations. Perhaps it was one of the greatest ever illusions: the distance that provided the perception of peace and detachment was the same distance masking the relentless struggles of life on the ground. From high altitude, the world seemed serene and untroubled, a beautiful but deceptive façade that was soon about to change forever.

EIGHTEEN

The crew were a mix of personalities, each bringing different skillsets to the team, eager to use them to achieve greatness. Everyone shared a rudimentary set of social skills; whether outgoing or introvert by nature, they had established a bond. They hadn't known each other for long but had quickly formed a kinship through mutual interest. Will was humbled by this since no one was compensated for the maiden flight, and it would be the only time they flew together.

In the future, Donavon and Will would pilot the balloon, while the remaining four seats would be occupied by paying clients.

Jefferson and Todd, like family to Will, would continue their roles in the flight control room. The medic and the three technicians would also remain on the payroll. Everyone else would return to their regular lives.

Lloyd was only involved because he had negotiated iron-clad terms but had agreed he would play no part in any future flights. He was a curious individual. A recluse. You wouldn't peg him as a balloon designer. High school teacher, maybe. Civil servant, definitely. He had low self-esteem, and Will was convinced he had no friends. He lived and worked alone. He spoke infrequently and often avoided eye contact, compelled to look away during conversations. He was smart and talented, nonetheless, and not to be underestimated.

Peta would continue with her window-cleaning work, but she would also be the reserve pilot if Donavon or Will couldn't attend a scheduled flight through sickness or emergency. She was passionate, enthusiastic, in touch with her emotions, and had a big heart and caring nature. Her difficult childhood was no secret, but if there was any serious psychological damage, she kept it buried.

Ariane would fly back to the States to her career at NASA. Will liked Ariane. Not in a romantic sense, though he would be open to something with her. She possessed an exquisite charm, effortlessly mixing natural grace with authenticity. Her grounded nature made her remarkably easy to talk to, drawing people in with her genuineness. What you saw was what you got; there was no pretence or façade with her. Her beauty was the kind that stood out even more in plain clothes, a natural elegance that didn't rely on embellishment. Despite her allure, Ariane could be quite serious, often absorbed in her thoughts or focussed on her tasks. She had a contemplative manner, and her smiles were rare but radiant, making them more treasured whenever they appeared. Her seriousness sometimes made her come across as distant, yet Will appreciated her depth and the quiet strength she exuded. She was a person with substance, whose inner qualities shone equally as bright as her outward beauty.

Will saw his oxygen was reading sixty-five per cent. "Can you call out your O_2 status?"

"Mine's at sixty-three per cent," said Peta.

"Same," said Ariane.

"Sixty-one," said Donavon.

"Lloyd, what's yours?" asked Will.

Lloyd slowly looked up. "My what?"

"Your oxygen reading?"

He glanced at his wrist. "Fifty-six per cent."

"Okay, that's lower than everyone else's. Are you having breathing trouble?"

"What do you mean exactly?" he replied, a hint of irritation creeping into his voice.

"Are you breathing too fast?" asked Will, his tone gentle but persistent. "Sometimes, if we're anxious or under stress, we might not even realise it."

"Why does everyone keep worrying about me? I said I'm fine!"

"Fine, bordering schizophrenic!" said Donavon.

"We just want to make sure that you're okay," said Peta. "Sometimes it's hard to tell if something is wrong, especially if you're used to pushing through it. Can you humour us and take a few slow, deep breaths?"

Lloyd glanced around the gondola, feeling the weight of their concern on him. He exhaled with a sharp sigh. "Fine!" he muttered, and reluctantly took slow, deep breaths, one after another.

"You'd tell us if something was bothering you, wouldn't you?" asked Will.

"Can we just concentrate on the mission, please? We must be there by now."

Will looked at the variometer, which showed a climb rate of three feet per minute. "What's our altitude?"

The altimeter read 138,145 feet, the balloon coasting the final distance like a surfer riding a wave all the way to the shore.

"About twenty-six miles high," said Donavon. "Two miles short of our target, but I'm going to call it and say that's float altitude."

Will sat forward, hands clasped together. "Congratulations, everyone! We made it! We've just set a new world record, the highest ever altitude by a crewed balloon! Brilliant! Well done! Give yourselves a nice little pat on the back."

For the next five minutes, not a single word was spoken. The crew enjoyed the panoramic views and a moment of self-satisfaction.

NINETEEN

Settled at float altitude, the helium weighing the same as the atmosphere around the balloon, Will checked the time on his sleeve computer. 11:09. The flight had taken just over three hours, about forty minutes longer than anticipated.

Will listened for the next status update from Jefferson. He chalked up the long silence to more duplexer issues. Todd was on hand, and that put Will's mind at ease. He was an expert when it came to probing technology and putting faults right.

"We don't have much time up here," said Donavon. "As much as we'd love to spend it sightseeing, we've got jobs to do, so let's move on with phase two. Ariane, phase two is you. Can you launch that dust buster thing?"

"I assume you're referring to Akroid? The sophisticated multi-million-dollar cosmic dust collector?"

"Lloyd will help you set the dust buster up," he said.

Ariane scowled at Donavon behind her visor.

Using the safety tether latched to an iron ring mount on the cage, Lloyd connected the other end to his spacesuit. He unbuckled his waist belt and slowly wriggled his arms out of the restraints. Standing carefully, he gripped the seat arm to steady his balance, shuffled forward, and snagged his thigh on the edge of the cage. "Shit!"

"Show me!" said Ariane, also tethered to the cage and out of her seat.

Lloyd slowly raised his leg.

Ariane arched over to inspect the suit. "You're fine. No breach."

During training, Russian space coordinators had warned the crew that if the spacesuit fabric were to tear at an altitude greater than 50,000 feet, the oxygen would escape, leaving the occupant no more than seven seconds until their blood boiled and turned to vapour.

"My heart's pounding," said Lloyd.

"You're lucky it hasn't cooked like an egg!"

Lloyd had difficulty wrapping his shaky fingers around the cage's locking mechanism. Every time he tried to grasp the small latch, it seemed to slip through his gloves, as if mocking his efforts.

Ariane pushed his hands aside and unlocked it for him. "Have you actually trained in a spacesuit?"

"We trained in Russia," Lloyd said.

The crew had flown to Moscow to train as space tourists, taking part in specialised training on ground-based, complex space simulators. They'd also spent time at the Yuri Gagarin Cosmonaut Training Centre, thirty-seven miles northeast of Moscow, using the same simulators as cosmonauts to prepare for space travel, and had even performed a work session in the hydrolab underwater facility.

"How long for?"

"A few days."

"That's it? A few days? Have you ever tried tying shoelaces while wearing boxing gloves?"

"What do you mean?"

"That's what doing anything in a spacesuit is like. You're basically inside an inflexible, pressurised balloon. Before your next flight, I suggest you train in one for longer. That goes for everyone."

Will paused, thinking that Ariane had made a valid point. A single mistake could cost their mission, their credibility, their careers, or their lives. "Noted," he said, before turning to Peta. "While Ariane and Lloyd prepare the Akroid payload, can you launch the solar wing? We want everyone on the ground to see this."

Moving to implement Will's command, Peta latched the safety tether to her spacesuit and rose. She didn't have her balance reflexes yet and was wobbly on her feet at first.

Meanwhile, Ariane and Lloyd lifted Akroid out of the cage. The lightweight aluminium alloy payload was fitted with a self-inflating balloon using a high-pressured helium gas cylinder.

"What exactly will this thing do?" asked Lloyd.

"Approximately 10,000 tons of micrometeorites fall to the Earth every year. Akroid will unfold at its target altitude and collect the meteoric dust in the upper stratosphere on silica aerogel mounted in modular aluminium cells, acting like mini cushions. The collected samples will then be sent back to the NASA Marshall Space Flight Centre to be analysed."

"How long will the balloon stay afloat for?"

"Up to three months, but the collection will likely be done before then. When NASA is satisfied enough samples have been collected, it will make the controlled descent, and the balloon will be retrieved and retired. Akroid will be biopsied and analysed so that improvements can be made for future missions further afield."

Lloyd and Ariane swung the payload off the gondola as if returning a large fish to the ocean. They watched it plummet. Set on a timer, the gas canister valve opened and instantly filled the balloon with helium. Looking upon the balloon's crown, they watched it rise until it drew level with Fable Sky. It sailed by, climbing rapidly, exceeding their altitude by hundreds of feet as a jellyfish would swim up to the ocean surface.

"NASA could have just launched the dust buster from the ground," said Donavon.

Ariane inclined her head slightly. "Pardon me?"

"It didn't need to piggyback our balloon. If you want my opinion, I'd say NASA just wanted to steal the headlines."

"No thanks!" Ariane strapped herself into her seat and sat back.

"What?"

"I *don't* want your opinion!"

Donavon persisted. "It's also obvious to me that NASA is jealous we got our spacesuits custom-made in Britain."

He phrased it as fact, but she was quick to shut him down. "NASA has much larger science projects to worry about. It's not concerned about who takes tourism to the stratosphere on a balloon first or where anyone gets their spacesuits made."

"I don't believe you!"

"Believe what you like! NASA is simply trying to provide more opportunities for space exploration projects outside of the US. And anyway, the reason you're up here right now is because of NASA, so I think it has the right to look out for its own interests."

"There's looking out for interests and blatantly stealing the limelight."

She let her silence speak for her.

When she refused to reply, Donavon continued. "It's not only me who thinks it." He looked at the rest of the crew, who remained quiet, any expressions of discomfort and uncertainty fortunately masked behind their visors.

"Come on, back me up here!" Donavon said, hoping to break the silence.

The crew members exchanged uneasy glances, but no one spoke up. The tension was palpable, and Will grew increasingly uncomfortable with their collective hesitation.

"It's not just my imagination," said Donavon.

Still the crew remained silent.

Donavon's shoulders slumped slightly, but he wasn't ready to give up. "Look, we all want what's best for this mission," he said, his tone softening to appeal to their responsible nature. "Maybe it's time we all had an open discussion about NASA's involvement."

Ariane crossed her arms in the prolonged silence, broken only when Will knew it was time to intervene. "Let's talk about this on the ground. Now is not the time. Can we focus on the mission?"

TWENTY

With the wings unfolded and twisted into flight positions, Peta launched the solar wing from the deck. It operated on solar panels linked to a regenerative fuel cell that could produce enough power to its four rocket motors to remain in flight for days. The seven-foot solar wing immediately swooped into a nosedive. Fingers on the remote control's joystick, she guided it on an outbound trajectory before expertly steering it back to capture the entire Fable Sky balloon, the kind of footage the media would salivate over and a memento she could hang on her wall.

Her back had started to ache, no matter how many times she shifted position or adjusted the recliner seat. Now she was standing, buckled to the cage, and playing with a toy airplane in space, equipped with a hi-tech camera. Provided the signal was emitted adequately, the live footage would be conveyed to the Internet and flight control. The solar wing also performed important atmospheric research tasks for NASA, so it played a more significant role than just capturing their holiday snaps.

Peta spaced her legs apart to stretch the seated posture out of her lower body as she circled the solar wing back towards the balloon. She checked the live feed again on the remote-control monitor. Fable Sky showed as a small, white ball in a black abyss.

Will tried the flight control room again. "Jefferson, do you copy?"

Their receivers were all programmed at the correct wave-length, so what was causing the delay?

"Jefferson, do you copy?"

"*Loud and clear. Incredible images we're getting down here. How are you all holding up?*"

"We're doing fine," said Will.

"What the fuck's going on with the communication link?" asked Donavon.

"*The new duplexer is working fine. Touch wood. We had a major leak in the bathroom one level down. I've lost Todd, cannot find him.*"

"Is he all right?" asked Peta, strapping back in her seat.

"*I sent him away to repair the bathroom, haven't seen him since. He's probably just waiting for a plumber, but I couldn't find him when I went looking. Anyway, tell me what you see.*"

Will peered down over their homeland. "We can see for hundreds of miles. I'm looking at the southern coastline and the entire South West Peninsula."

"*The footage looks amazing, from the solar wing and your helmet cams. I have you on my screen. You're still live on the Net with more than 22,000 viewers. Great publicity. I trust you all brushed your hair and cleaned your teeth?*"

"Is my son still there?" asked Will. "Have you seen him? He was in the crowd when we launched."

"He hasn't been up to the lighthouse. I don't think. I'll let you know if I see him."

"Thanks. He was wearing that heavy-metal T-shirt I got him for Christmas."

"I'll keep an eye out. I'm looking at my television screen. It's black. Is the solar wing still filming?"

"That's because I'm flying it away from the balloon," said Peta. "That's space you're seeing. You should spot us in just a minute when it returns."

Peta circled the solar wing like a vulture swooping in for a kill. The low-light digital camera had a video-audio microwave transmitting device installed in a custom-made cradle attached to a Futaba servo with remote-controlled 180-degree pan-tilt view.

"Could you get some footage of Akroid?" asked Ariane. "I want NASA to see it."

Peta enjoyed a long sip of water before responding. "Sure thing." She manoeuvred the solar wing into a vertical ascent, panning the camera to capture the Akroid payload suspended beneath its balloon. Whatever she saw on her monitor, flight control saw. NASA would also see the images and anyone online watching the televised stream.

A bright flash on the horizon suddenly drew Donavon's attention.

As much as Peta tried to keep her focus on the solar wing, her eyes were drawn to the view, but the flash in her periphery distracted her momentarily. "Did anyone else see that?"

"Might be some metal debris from an old satellite," said Donavon. "Or a meteor, which can be large pieces of space debris or the size of a pebble but are normally no bigger than a grain of sand and can travel at speeds of around forty-five miles per second."

"Hope one doesn't hit the balloon," she said, guiding the solar wing back towards Fable Sky.

"If you understood basic astronomy, you would know that most meteors burn up in the mesosphere, also known as the meteoric region. Around fifty to seventy-five miles above the Earth's surface. Don't worry, Peta, you've got more chance of winning a beauty contest than being hit by a meteor."

"Get lost, Donavon! I was just saying."

"*I'm* just saying get your facts right!"

Peta shook her head. This was neither the place nor the time for another petty squabble with Donavon. They were fine together when no one else was around, their bond genuine and comfortable. During social settings, a troubling dynamic often emerged. He seemed to take pleasure in persecuting her, his behaviour shifting from playful banter to something more malicious. It was as if the presence of others provided him with an audience for his cruelty, and he relished in the power it gave him over her. Whether consciously or not, he often twisted his words, delivering them with belittling undertones to whomever he spoke. *The Express* was his newspaper of choice, stoking his right-wing views. He believed in anarchism, technocracy, and eco-futurism, thinking traditional government structures were inherently flawed, and wanted decentralised, community-based governance supported by advanced technology.

Swivelling her seat at an angle that blocked the view of her cousin, she admired the view, appreciating time was limited. Overcome by physical and emotional ecstasy, she could see, touch, and feel the universe. On either side of the balloon, she studied the vibrant colours of the planet glowing against the backdrop of space.

"Hit by a meteor!" said Donavon, subjecting everyone to his fake laughter.

Peta twisted round. "Would you shut the hell up?"

She sent the solar wing on another long jaunt, buying her another few minutes to soak up the breathtaking view of the Earth's curvature.

Suddenly, a crackly connection pierced their headsets. A distorted voice broke in, barely recognisable through the static. "*Some-thing's happ-en-ing!*" it stuttered, the words strained and fragmented. It sounded like Jefferson, but the output quality was so poor it was hard to ascertain. Unease settled in their stomachs.

From that point, things escalated quickly.

The equipment around them flashed and blinked out, all at once. The GPS navigation system faltered, its reliable signals replaced by a blank screen. The radio transmitter emitted only static, silencing their colleagues on the ground. The wireless networking technologies connecting them to mission control went dark, cutting off external communication and guidance and severing their only lifeline to the outside world.

The sensors collecting data on temperature, altitude, UV levels, and air pressure ceased their operation, leaving them blind to the environmental conditions around them.

In the blink of an eye, they were left in a void of silence and darkness.

Donavon looked at the dead computer screens. "What the fuck just happened?"

TWENTY-ONE

From the early pioneering flights of the late 18th century to the technologically sophisticated endeavours of the modern day, ballooning had captivated the human imagination for over two centuries. The sight of these majestic vessels soaring through the sky had been romanticised in literature, art, and popular culture, symbolising adventure, exploration, freedom, and the unquenchable human spirit of discovery. Early aeronauts like the Montgolfier brothers, who launched the first crewed hot-air balloon in 1783, ignited a fascination with the skies that had endured and evolved.

Balloon ventures were based on three acts. Act one: the launch, which came with an element of drama and excitement. Act two: the flight, an adventure filled with discoveries and constant dangers. The final act involved the landing, providing a disastrous or victorious conclusion to the flight.

The mission was only into its second act and had gone to plan, but that couldn't be a seed for complacency. There was still a long way to go. All the same, Jefferson's tension had abated upon Fable Sky reaching float altitude. After all the planning, preparation, setbacks, and cynicism, the Fable Sky crew had finally fulfilled the long-held dream of reaching the edge of space. He had them on his computer screen, divided into five tessellated rectangles, each sharing slightly different perspectives from their helmet cameras in addition to the live solar wing images streaming onto his television. One of the crew waved when the solar wing passed the balloon, and the screen went black momentarily. A thick blue wedge appeared as the Earth rolled by the lens.

Jefferson stroked his goatee, then rubbed his eyes. He tried to add up the hours of sleep he had missed in the past week alone. Calculating the number of coffees he had consumed so far that day also took some deep thought. His energy draining from his body with such suddenness, the last coffee giving him only deceptive surface alertness, he climbed the ladder to the lantern room for some fresh air.

He paused mid-step, looking back to see if Todd was about, listening for footsteps or his heavy-handedness in the kitchen. He'd been gone a while now. And where was that coffee?

"Todd?"

When no reply was forthcoming, he stepped outside onto a narrow balcony surrounding the lantern room and breathed in deeply. His lungs were bad. Not that he could complain. He knew he was fortunate to come away with nothing more than shoddy lungs following three decades of nicotine abuse.

Leaning on the rail, he admired a view he would never grow tired of. He could smell the sea and hear the waves slapping on the shore at the foot of the cliffs. Fond memories watching the ships sail by and the searchlight's heat soothing on his back filled his mind. He missed the old days when the lighthouse was still operational.

Out of nowhere, several British jet fighters roared low overhead, causing the lighthouse to tremble. Jefferson felt the iron rail vibrate underneath his palms. It frightened him. He watched the jets until they disappeared over the hills.

By heart, Jefferson knew the exact route that the sun took across the sky. Long before the lighthouse became automated, his parents had sold their house and moved in permanently to save money. Jefferson had slept on a futon in the watch room as a child and woken many mornings inside it. The sun came through the east window, baking his feet in warm light. It soon reached his face and made him too hot to stay in bed. At this time of day, the room lay in shade as the sun hung directly overhead. So, what was the blinding globe of white light out to sea?

Jefferson turned his head and shielded his eyes from the artificial light, burying his face in the crook of his elbow. When the light faded, he heard screaming and shouting from the cliff. Something was happening.

Observing the crowd with growing curiosity and concern, he saw it was absolute bedlam down there. People rushed to their vehicles. Mothers and fathers scooped up their children. Cyclists swung their bicycles around and pedalled frantically away. It took a moment for his brain to translate the noise now filtering up. They were not the screams of aggravation or pain. They were the screams of panic.

Jefferson's phones rang. Two landline phones were inside the tower and a mobile was in his pocket. They all rang.

When he saw several missed calls on his mobile, his first thought was of Fable Sky. Was the crew in trouble? He rushed down the ladder to the flight control room. He checked the television, devoted exclusively to a delayed Internet feed from the solar wing camera. Fable Sky remained buoyant within the stratosphere, the crew still waving to the solar wing camera, perfectly normal, perfectly safe.

His mobile rang again. It was his brother. *"Have you heard the news?"*

"What's going on?" asked Jefferson, his face turning pale.

"Turn on your television."

Jefferson grabbed the controller. "What channel?"

"Any of them."

A lump formed in his throat as if he had dry-swallowed a powdery pill that had lodged in his airway.

He held his mobile at his side and switched the Fable Sky crew across to BBC1: *"… ballistic missiles, but at this stage, it's unknown what triggered the attack."*

He changed to Channel 4: *"As for retaliation, I think it's safe to assume it would occur once the outcome is clearer."*

Then Sky News: *"… Minister has been speaking with his security advisors. What is being discussed is anyone's guess. They could be going over protocols to intercept the missi–"*

The television turned black, and the words *Emergency Alert System* appeared on the screen. It flashed five times.

The same announcement popped on his mobile.

A second message appeared on both television and mobile screens: *A British Government Emergency Notification.*

A voice recording played, accompanied by subtitles: *"We interrupt our service. This is a State of National Emergency. Standby for important instructions."*

A long beep followed. Then another automated recording.

"*A nuclear attack is occurring against the United Kingdom. Nuclear missiles have been launched from unknown locations and are expected to strike the UK within the next ten minutes. Due to the unknown facts of these missiles and their intended targets, all UK residents should seek shelter and prepare for impact. If you have access to fallout shelters, go there now. Otherwise, stay indoors and head to a secure room. Block all windows and doors. Place as many objects between you and the outside as possible. Cover your head and keep your eyes closed. Have a radio nearby and wait for news updates before going outside. Please stay calm.*"

Jefferson ran to his computer and slipped his headset on. "Fable Sky, do you copy?"

The connection was fraught with static and kept breaking up. "Something's happening..." The radio fell silent, and its comforting hum abruptly cut off.

The voice message on the television, looping in a relentless cycle, suddenly ceased as the screen went black.

Every computer monitor flickered before going dark.

His mobile phone was unresponsive, refusing to switch on no matter how many times he pressed the power button.

Outside, car alarms shrieked, a piercing sound that added to the mayhem, but they too fell silent.

Horns blared in a desperate symphony of frustration and panic, only to stop abruptly.

In the eerie silence that followed, the only persistent sound was the heart-wrenching screams coming from the spectators, which reached a crescendo.

Jefferson ran to the top of the staircase. "Todd? You down there? Todd? ... Todd?"

Turning, he paced to his desk and picked up the framed photograph of his wife. Her arms and face were nicely tanned, but at some point during the Mediterranean holiday, her skin had peeled, he remembered. It had been a day of sangria and slapping mosquitoes and had finished off in style when he had serenaded her at the waterfront, much to her embarrassment.

A dull rumble filled the air, like distant thunder.

Jefferson hurried up the ladder to the lantern room and crashed out onto the balcony, still clutching the photo.

Inland, a second sphere of light appeared, and the sky was bleached into a blurry fog of white. It quickly transformed into an orange fireball. Fiery tendrils corkscrewed from the canopy as flames rose and darkened to a purple-hued column of black smoke, turning in on itself.

Jefferson knew what he was seeing. He just didn't want to believe it.

The sudden change in air pressure struck him first, even before the shockwave—thousands of pounds of pressure that deadened the air and pulled all noise surrounding the lighthouse, hurting Jefferson's eardrums.

A tremendous blast wave struck across the clifftop. It blew people off their feet and scattered vehicles like toys.

Jefferson gripped the rail. His knuckles turned white, and his lungs felt crushed by the surge of dense air.

The glass windows of the lantern room blew.

All his reflexes kicked in: a huge spike in adrenalin, a tight clench in his jaw, a racing pulse.

A gigantic wall of fire containing a toxic mix of bomb-grade chemicals and Earth's elements bore down on the cliff, throwing projectiles of burning shrapnel and turning the sea bronze. Jefferson faced the hot tsunami as it rolled across the land at frightening speed, melting cars and structures, burning everything in its path to dust.

He held the photo of his wife to his face. The glass melted, and the skin on his hand started to blister.

He screamed and writhed, pushing against the air that had become thick and heavy like water as the intense heat flowed through him.

Then it was all over.

TWENTY-TWO

When it happened, none of the crew recognised it for what it was. Power had been lost, possibly due to overloaded junctions blowing out simultaneously.

Donavon tried the radio again. "Jefferson? Do you copy? Did you say something's happening? We've lost all power up here."

It took him three broadcast attempts to establish that no connection was being made. "This is fucked!"

"What's going on?" asked Peta.

Will breathed out heavily through his nose with a growing level of concern. "The duplexer must be playing up still."

Donavon tapped the screens with his palm and shook his head. "No, this is different. It's not only our communication. It's everything. Flight control is no longer receiving our GPS coordinates. This is turning into a fucking nightmare!"

A deafening squawk sounded in their headsets, startling the crew.

When it passed, Will said, "I'm sure Todd is working to fix it already. If anyone can get the power restored, it's Todd."

"Lucky that this isn't a tourist flight," said Donavon. "The passengers will be freaking out about now."

"Instead, it's only *you* freaking out," said Peta.

"*I'm* not freaking out. I'm pissed off."

"It can't be helped."

"Say that to our clients after they've paid us thousands of pounds to be here. I'm sure they'll appreciate your reassuring analysis."

With the highest-ever altitude in the crew's pockets, Will looked at the time, starting to think about wrapping things up and reversing the winch cable to pull them home. They had fulfilled their mission. They had collected all the data needed. Akroid had been launched successfully. The solar wing had captured epic images. The balloon and their spacesuits had survived the ascent and float altitude. No more boxes were left to tick. If he could get Jefferson back on the radio, he could relay they were ready to begin their descent.

Peta wiggled the joystick on her controller. "Even the solar wing's stopped working. How can that be? It has no connection to the on board instruments. I don't understand."

Without the interference of glaring screens, Earth's glow seemed much brighter, a breathtaking orb of blues and greens set against the infinite blackness of space. Will was gradually acclimating to the darkness surrounding the balloon. Despite anticipating the view would be the highlight of his journey, he struggled to savour this extraordinary moment. The mounting issues took precedence, reminding him of the precariousness of space flight. As the minutes ticked by without an update, his concerns deepened. They needed real-time information to help them make some critical decisions. Were they dealing with a technical glitch, a broader systems failure, or something more sinister?

"I can't get the balloon back online," said Donavon, "but I can trigger the emergency transponder beacon so Jefferson can triangulate our position from the transmitting signal. At least he'll know where we are."

"Do it!" said Will. "What do you think caused it?"

The gondola shook suddenly and violently, and the balloon was pulled down several feet, as if sucked out of the sky.

Ariane lurched forward, and her helmet collided with the headrest on its way back.

Lloyd groaned with fear and Peta almost swore, gripping the seat arms.

"Okay, I'm starting to freak out myself now!" Peta said. "What the hell is going on?"

The balloon was left rocking side to side for almost twenty seconds before it finally settled.

A hush descended over the crew, with no one daring to speak. Will's body stiffened in anticipation, as though expecting something more to happen. He glanced at each member of his crew. He couldn't see their faces, but their tensed shoulders and the fragile silence told him they were as fearful as him right then.

They remained quiet until Peta shrieked, startling everyone again. She pointed to the ground. "Look!"

Swivelling his recliner seat, Will followed her finger and lunged forward into his shoulder straps, peering over the edge of the gondola.

A giant bubble of dust and earth erupted, expanding into an enormous cloud atop a wide, towering trunk, engulfing the landscape in its wake. Moments later, a brilliant white light flashed some distance away, its intensity slicing laterally across the countryside, and the horizon lit up like a sudden dawn. Despite the protection of his tinted visor, the dazzle from the flash forced him to squint against the glare.

Following the flash, another enormous ball of milky brown material ascended, with plumes of black and orange slowly morphing into monstrous, tree-like shapes.

"Over there!" Peta shouted, pointing at another flash. The intensity was so great it seemed to light up the entire country for several seconds.

The Fable Sky crew glanced at one another as if they had just dodged a bolt of lightning.

Towards the east, a band of dark, menacing cloud emerged, interwoven with shimmering streaks of intense white light that periodically burst from the billowing smoke, creating an eerie, pulsating glow reminiscent of storm clouds. While separated by miles of sky, they were inexorably drawn towards each other, moving with frightening speeds. As they scudded across the horizon, their edges merged, forming a singular front stretching as far as the eye could see. Their unimaginable power was a hauntingly beautiful yet terrifying sight as the sky itself writhed and convulsed.

Jefferson's last words lingered: *Something's happening.*

To that, Will already had something of an answer.

A nuclear attack?

He didn't want to believe it, and his reluctance prevented him from making up his mind. Things like this did not happen in the modern world. They just didn't.

The Fable Sky crew didn't have a doomsday plan. And the speed with which the attack had unfolded, it was unlikely the government did either.

TWENTY-THREE

The crew had remained still and silent for several minutes, their eyes wide and unblinking as they watched on.

Peta's hands on the seat arms clenched in some reflexive death grip. The explosions continued relentlessly, painting the countryside with terrifying beauty, illuminating the sky in an almost continuous strobe of destruction. It had Peta transfixed, watching this silent desecration of land and life as sheets of fire blazed and darkness smothered the South West Peninsula. The world below was rapidly changing, the normalcy of everyday life obliterated by the overwhelming force of the explosions, and all she could do was watch. How many had there been? Six? Seven? More? And in those frozen few minutes, she tried to fathom a cause. Was this a ground attack by terrorists? Had power stations gone into critical meltdown? Had the country been struck by asteroids or some other space rock? Donavon had told her not five minutes ago that meteors could be large pieces of space debris.

Then the penny dropped.

Was it a nuclear airstrike? Was this deadly surprise attack a declaration of war? Was the UK under sudden siege by some consummate evil? Just the previous year, the Russian president had threatened to aim nuclear missiles at various European cities, including London, for the first time since the Cold War. The former Soviet Union owned approximately 6,000 nuclear warheads stored in hundreds of launch installations, more than any other country in the world. Were the Russians behind this catastrophe?

She closed her eyes, but it only drew her attention to her laboured breathing. Inhaling deeply to overcome the panic channelling through her had little effect. When she opened her eyes, she sighted the solar wing in the distance, its sleek form gradually receding as it soared further away. Its rockets would continue to burn fiercely until the fuel cells were depleted, at which point the device would lose power and control. As the last of the fuel was exhausted, the solar wing would inevitably nosedive towards the ground, its trajectory no longer guided by thrust but instead dictated by gravity. The monitor on her controller showed a blank screen. With a despondent sigh, she let it slip from her grasp, the device clattering softly onto the deck.

"Jefferson, it's Will. Do you copy?"

They waited, everyone straining to hear a distinctive voice within the white noise.

"Jefferson, it's Will. Do you copy?"

"He can't hear you," said Donavon. "You're wasting your time."

"Jefferson, Will here. Do you copy? Are you getting this?" He read the time on his computer, noting it was half-twelve. "Jefferson, are you there? Answer me!"

Thirty minutes had elapsed since the last radio transmission. There wasn't much to do in the face of the unthinkable but think about it obsessively.

If Jefferson couldn't get through, Ariane believed NASA would find a way to dial into their frequency and update them on the developing situation. To remain cut off could have disastrous outcomes. What only moments ago had still been a thrilling, serene mission had now transformed into a life-or-death situation. With advanced communication technologies at its disposal, NASA was their best hope. If anyone could breach the silence, it was the renowned space agency. It had contingencies for almost every scenario, and she trusted their engineers and scientists would be working around the clock to re-establish contact.

The onslaught below had subsided and receded. Was the worst over? Every inch of land had disappeared beneath the brown columns and canopies that appeared to be propping up the sky. Sunlight poured over the destructive scene, giving the dark mass laden with its stew of volatile chemicals a defining texture.

Ariane glimpsed Akroid up high, a tiny cube attached to a sphere. It hadn't unfolded yet since it hadn't reached its target altitude. The situation on the ground had crippled its mission, but that was the least of anyone's concerns. These explosions, however frightening, were likely a preamble of far worse to follow. An attack of this scale would undoubtedly provoke a formidable response from her country, a staunch ally of the

United Kingdom. The repercussions could ripple across the entire globe, sparking a chain reaction of military and political manoeuvres.

She estimated the first canopy now at somewhere between sixty and seventy miles across. Contemporary missiles were thousands of times more powerful and destructive than the atomic bombs dropped on Japan, reaching a new pinnacle of sophistication. Fallout fragments from thermonuclear fusion bombs could be propelled 100,000 feet high, and radioactive particles, consisting of a mixture of fission products, non-fission nuclear material, and neutron-activated debris, could be carried by wind currents, transcending national borders with ease.

Normally one to await the facts and assess them credibly and objectively, she kept her thoughts to herself. Whatever her opinions, there had been an attack, there would be catastrophic damage and loss of life, and they were alone, suspended in the stratosphere with no means of communication or navigation.

TWENTY-FOUR

One hour since the explosions...

"So, what now?" asked Lloyd. "We do we do?"

Will was asking himself the same question with an awful perception of sand draining from the hourglass. Their mission no longer had merit or purpose. They had to abort the flight.

The mushroom clouds stretched as far as they could see, looming over the southwest corner of England and beyond. The balloon might not survive a controlled descent with lethal fragments zipping about the air, possibly tearing the envelope to rags.

As a father, an overwhelming terror gripped him as he thought of his son caught up in the explosions. As the alleged captain, he had to remain calm and be assertive. The urgency of the situation heightened his anxiety, but he needed to steady his hands and focus if he wanted to survive this ordeal, so he switched off his headset to stifle the voices and the incessant background noise, needing a minute to think clearly and assess the situation without distractions. There could have been less damage than he first imagined, fewer casualties, and survivors banding together executing tactical rescues. The bombs might have been non-nuclear. Without communication, they crew knew little other than what they had witnessed first-hand from above. But the odds of it not being a nuclear attack were slim. And he could find no other explanation for it.

Over the years, he had learned to be flexible in his thought processes in a potential crisis, knowing when to rely on gut feelings: *the balloon won't clear those power lines without dropping ballast; surface winds have exceeded ten miles per hour; descend now, issues with the burners.*

On board Fable Sky, he had all the gut instincts but little control. The situation he now found himself in threw these thoughts and instincts into disarray. He needed time, which he did not have, to carefully think this through and make the right decision.

Switching his headset on again, his awareness clicked into gear as he tuned into the discussion. Hearing their voices gave him a small measure of company.

Peta and Donavon debated over what action to take.

Donavon was willing to run the risk and return.

Peta thought it was a bad idea and stated the best thing to do was wait it out and let the dust settle.

Lloyd chimed in and agreed the smart play was to wait for their communication systems to be restored so a rescue could be coordinated for their return.

What rescue? Donavon argued.

Ariane advised that they disconnect the gondola from the envelope, relying on the multiple chutes to deploy and carry them back to the ground. Quick, easy, and safer than a slow descent via cable. She explained that robust aircraft would have difficulty flying through bomb clouds with all the debris in the air. A fragile balloon would have no chance.

Will tried to add his voice to the mix but couldn't find a suitable gap to make himself heard. Instead, waiting for the right opportunity, he listened to all opinions patiently.

In the end, he was forced to use his voice at full volume to get a word in, hoping his focussed input might anaesthetise the panic. "We're faced with a dilemma, and none of our options come without danger and risk. The way I see it, we have four options, and we need to choose one. Option one, we open the vents and begin our descent since we no longer have power in the winch cable to pull us back. It will take a few hours to get down, by which time the clouds may have dispersed a bit. We can probably expect a bumpy ride, and the balloon may get damaged in the process. If it does, and we plummet, we will not be able to escape the gondola in time, and we will most certainly be killed. Option two, we detach the gondola from the envelope, freefall, and deploy the chutes. Option three, we abandon Fable Sky and take our chances individually. If we decide to jump, we can wait for the clouds to thin out before we go. We'll then be in control of our own fates, at least. Our parachutes have all been programmed to open automatically at 8,000 feet."

Again, the debate heated up with opinions divided and emotions reaching breaking point. The argument descended into which material was most likely to withstand the hostile, debris-strewn sky: the balloon's polyethylene envelope or the ripstop nylon parachutes. The envelope had endured a vast amount of stress during its ascent already. That was Ariane's argument, and she made it clear parachutes were designed for high-performance and high-wind endurance, unlike ultra-thin, high-altitude balloons that had the fragility of a paper bag.

"What's option four?" asked Lloyd.

"We stay on board, try to conserve our oxygen for as long as possible, and hope to reconnect with the ground to find out what is happening so we can make a more informed decision. We have water and the reserve oxygen tanks, and we can still choose option one, two, or three later once we have gathered more information."

"Option four for me," said Lloyd. "That's really the only option."

"Is that what you think is best?" Peta asked.

"Actually, I agree with Ariane and Donavon. I think we should either disconnect the gondola from the envelope and parachute back as a unit or jump and use our packed chutes. I'm more comfortable with the latter, to be honest, but it was only the backup contingency if we could not separate from the envelope for any reason. A full detachment was the primary plan, after all."

He let his words percolate for a moment.

"If we go now," said Lloyd, "… no, there might be fires down there. It's just not safe to return."

"I say we wait an hour. If we still get no word from the ground, we go."

Donavon shook his head. "An hour? We can't just stay up here, drifting like morons."

Not for the first time, static cut into their discussions and made everyone flinch.

"Donavon has a point," said Peta. "I know that I said we should wait, but I've just had a thought. I think the sudden turbulence we felt was from tension in the winch cable, from the explosion rippling along it. The cable might have been severed. We can't know for sure without GPS, but we could be drifting. If that's the case, we don't know where we'll end up if we wait."

Ariane put her hand up to command their attention. "Wait or descend slowly, we'll have drifted miles by the time we reach the land. That's if the balloon even survives the descent, which I believe it won't. To me, options one and four are out of the question."

Will sucked on his straw to wet his parched mouth. "So, it looks like we agree not to descend through controlled venting. And we're also not in favour of waiting here in the hope of reconnecting with the ground, especially as we could be drifting and may find ourselves over the ocean."

Peta peered over the edge of the gondola, searching for a glimpse of land between the brown blanket. "Looks like we're doing one giant leap for mankind, then. How shall we go about it? Jump individually? Or by severing the gondola from the envelope?"

"How does that even work?" asked Ariane.

Lloyd was staring at his feet but raised his head. "There are explosive bolts on the cables that connect the gondola to the envelope. All I need to do is pull the release lever next to me." He pointed at the small, yellow lever by his seat with a black handle grip.

Will checked his oxygen supply. "We each have around twenty-five per cent oxygen left, yes? That buys us about two hours, give or take, on these tanks. Plus, the secondary oxygen tanks at our disposal. That's a further eight hours, so ten in total."

"And?" asked Donavon.

"If what we witnessed was a nuclear attack, the air down there will be contaminated and unbreathable. Our spacesuits were designed to protect us from radiation, so we don't need to worry about that. Not yet anyway."

"Not possible," said Lloyd.

The comment, so out of context, threw the crew.

"Not possible?" asked Donavon. "What's not possible?"

"It's too risky. I don't feel comfortable separating us from the envelope."

"Why not?"

"What if it doesn't work? I designed the parachutes to open in an emergency, but didn't actually think we would need to use them."

Donavon held out his arms. "Ladies and Gentlemen, our chief balloon designer."

"Seriously. It's never been tested before. Something might go wrong."

Peta shrugged. "What's the alternative?"

"I don't know. You want to jump; I want to wait. Can't we make our own decisions, whichever we feel most comfortable making?"

She shook her head. "We need to stick together. We're a crew, and we must operate as one."

TWENTY-FIVE

Faced with such a frightening dilemma and the possibly fatal decision to jump individually or cut ties with the envelope, Ariane tried to shut out all the noise and spared a thought for her family. Her parents were devout Catholics who faithfully attended mass every morning without fail, their devotion to their faith a foundation of their daily lives. The church was not just a place of worship for them but where they found solace and strength. Occasionally, they would invite the priest over for dinner, transforming their modest Heyworth home into a setting for both thoughtful theological discussions and warm fellowship.

Her parents both carried old-fashioned views on love and life, profoundly rooted in traditional Catholic teachings. Their perspective on relationships was shaped by the doctrines of the church, emphasising the sanctity of marriage, the importance of family, and the virtues of chastity and fidelity. They believed in courtship over casual dating, viewing love as a sacred bond to be nurtured with patience and respect. For them, life was a gift from God, to be cherished and respected at every stage, and they held firm to the moral and ethical guidelines set forth by their faith. They had never approved of her career at NASA. They couldn't get why she would want to risk her life testing new aircraft when she should have been settling down with a family of her own.

"You know, the fear of God is the foundation of wisdom," her father said the last time she saw him.

Ariane had lost count of how many times he had said that to her over the years. "Well, every time I test out new aircraft, Pop, I'm closer to God than anyone; trust me, I always fear him."

Puerto Rican by birth, American by citizenship, fluent in Spanish and English and well-versed in Portuguese, Ariane had always dreamed of working at NASA, even as a child. She had first studied for a degree in physical science, and after that for her Masters. Neither could match the challenge of the actual job training. Each domain was integrated—cognitive strategies intellectual skills, principle theory, computer-based training, and aircraft simulation.

Nobody at NASA had taught her how to survive on board a stranded helium balloon at high altitude, faced with technical malfunctions, dwindling supplies, the fear of running out of precious oxygen, and an apocalyptic scenario awaiting her on the ground. But she had learned all about nuclear physics and radiation, understanding the science almost intuitively after her formal instruction. She trusted her knowledge would inevitably play an essential role in their survival.

Everyone was still talking, but the next step was simple and straightforward in her mind.

"We must detach and parachute as a unit, period. If it *was* a nuclear attack, the larger pieces of radioactive fallout would have dropped back to Earth in the first few minutes, while the smaller bits fall in the first few hours. The explosions began almost two hours ago."

"So, there won't be much radiation down there?" asked Lloyd.

"There'll be tons of radiation. Please, let me finish. The deadly microscopic particles can stay aloft for months or years and circle the atmosphere. That means they may fall anywhere. If radioactive clouds migrate across the European continent, the implications would be dire. The fallout could contaminate vast areas of land, making them uninhabitable and causing long-term health problems for the population: cancer, genetic mutations, and so on. Agriculture would suffer, as radioactive particles settle on crops and soil, causing food shortages and famine. The impact might not be confined only to the UK or Europe with the right atmospheric conditions; the radioactive clouds could circumnavigate the globe, leading to worldwide environmental contamination. It would affect ecosystems and health on a massive scale. The interconnected nature of Earth's weather systems means no region would be entirely safe from the fallout. I admit this is worst-case scenario; I'm probably getting way ahead of myself. I apologise if I'm adding to the fear we are all feeling right now. What is fact though is the air down there will be toxic for some time. The sooner we get back on the ground, the more oxygen we'll have in our tanks, giving us more time to assess the situation and figure out what we're going to do."

"Jefferson should have warned us about this, if you ask me," said Donavon. "He must have heard something on the news about it."

"Oh, shut up Donavon!" said Peta.

"What? He could have warned us."

"He obviously didn't know, so that's why we never heard anything."

"I think he was about to warn us before he got cut off," said Will. "Not that it would have made any difference. There's nothing we could have done to prepare for it."

"No," said Donavon, "but if we knew what was happening down there, we might know how best to respond now."

"I think it's pretty obvious what is happening," said Ariane. "It doesn't take a scientist to figure it out."

"Do you think they *were* nuclear explosions?" asked Peta.

"Yes, I do," said Ariane.

"You sound certain."

"The largest non-nuclear bomb ever made is the MOAB, a thermobaric bomb with a blast range of one mile. That's a fraction of the power a nuclear bomb has. Even from this distance, it's obvious what we witnessed were not MOABs."

"They will come find us when we land, right?" asked Lloyd, searching for reassurance no one could provide. "Right?"

A long pause ensued.

"You think we can survive it?" asked Peta. "If we avoided the early fallout?"

"Listen, I'm not going to preach false hope," said Ariane. "We know nothing about the power of these bombs or who dropped them, how much radiation they contained, or where the epicentres are. Radiation exposure will be deadly, even if you're exposed for just a few minutes."

"What makes you such an expert on radiation?" Donavon asked.

"I work for NASA."

TWENTY-SIX

Lloyd hadn't looked up from his lap for over five minutes, his ashen face concealed behind his plastic visor, curved like the horizon, tinted gold like the scorched sky below.

Peta was constantly leaning back and forth, assessing the situation below for developments. Will thought he heard a convulsive sob come from her.

Ariane was still and calm, slowly studying the crew one by one, always stoic in manner and voice. Will was relieved to have her on the crew. Her rare blend of intuition, expertise, and unwavering command of the skies brought a settling calm to him.

Donavon couldn't sit still, fidgeting in his seat, his fingers drumming against his knees. Despite his restless movements, he remained unusually quiet, his eyes darting around as he took in the expansive view.

Lloyd shot up out of his seat. Holding onto the cage, he shuffled sideways in front of Donavon and began whacking the computer equipment with the flat of his hand.

"What the fuck!" shouted Donavon.

He hit it again, this time with his fist.

"Lloyd!" Peta shouted.

Lloyd stopped and turned. "I'm trying to restore power."

"You're wasting your time," said Ariane in her calm and business-like tone. "It was an electromagnetic pulse that we experienced, caused by the bombs. The EMP would have fried anything with a circuit board or microchip. The equipment is useless now."

Following a long pause, Peta asked, "If that's true, why do our communicators still work?"

"Spacesuits are specially designed to avoid damage from EMP equivalent events, like solar radiation bursts. Same with satellites. EMPs occur in space all the time, so every spacesuit needs to have full immunity. That is why our life supports, communicators, and wrist computers continue to function."

Lloyd slowly sidestepped back to his seat and buckled up.

"You know what?" asked Donavon. "When the survivors of the Hiroshima and Nagasaki bombs told their stories, they all said the same thing; there was a profound silence during and after the explosion. No one cried or screamed. Even as people experienced horrific injuries or lay dying, they did so quietly, including the children."

"Why are you telling us this?" asked Peta. "It's hardly the time."

"I'm just saying."

"You can be so insensitive."

He shrugged. "What?"

"If you don't already know, then there's no point telling you."

"Sorry, I forgot we have to tread on eggshells around you. Everyone, be careful what you say. Peta is very sensitive and gets upset easily."

"Let's just prepare to detach," said Ariane. She turned to Lloyd. "Do you want to talk us through this? We all know the basic concept, but just explain to us what we should expect from detachment to freefall to landing."

Once again, Lloyd pointed at the yellow lever beside his seat. "When I pull this lever, a sequence of small explosions will blow the bolts that connect the cables to the gondola, separating us from the envelope."

"Yeah, then what?" asked Donavon.

"We fall."

"No shit!"

"When will the parachutes deploy?" asked Ariane.

"A series of stabilising parachutes will open at 8,000 feet to slow us down. They will automatically release to allow the second batch of parachutes to open instantly to slow our final descent." He paused and swung his head around the gondola. "I still think we should wait."

"We're not waiting!" Will said sharply.

Lloyd nodded slowly and gripped the lever, preparing to initiate separation from the envelope.

"Wait!" said Ariane. "I can't see!"

Her gold-tinted visor showed a translucent grey internally. She tapped her helmet lightly on one side, trying to clear the fog obscuring her vision, but it remained stubbornly opaque. "I think my visor heater has stopped working," she said with frustration, the situation growing increasingly uncomfortable.

She needed to address this quickly before it became a serious problem.

Donavon laughed. "You jinxed yourself with the anti-fog spray."

"Glad you find it amusing."

"What can we do?" asked Peta.

"Give me a minute."

"We don't have a minute," said Donavon.

Ariane continued tapping the side of her helmet, trying to initiate a response from the internal heater.

"Could the EMP have damaged it?" asked Peta.

"It's okay, the condensation's clearing."

"It's working?"

"Yes, I can see again."

Will took a deep breath. He looked back at Lloyd. "Okay, I think we're ready."

Lloyd grabbed the lever once more. "Everyone's strapped in properly?"

The crew checked their shoulder restraints and waist belts and confirmed their readiness.

Lloyd hesitated, his trembling fingers gripped around the lever. Shoulders raised and tensed, he looked at each member of the crew. "Shall we put this to the vote?"

"Just pull the fucking lever!" said Donavon.

"I can't stop shaking."

"We're all scared," said Will. "None of us have ever been in a situation like this before. But we have no choice. You have to do it. Now!"

"Okay." Lloyd closed his eyes, shook his hands loose, and took the lever.

Will gave him the final nod.

Lloyd pushed the button on top to engage the lever and pulled it with a determined tug. He held his breath, waiting for the inevitable plunge, but nothing happened. A frown creased his forehead as he stared at the unresponsive lever. Frustration mounting, he gripped the lever more tightly and rocked it back and forth, willing the stubborn mechanism to respond to his command, his movements growing more aggressive with each attempt.

"It's not working!" Lloyd glanced up at the envelope, then back at the lever. "The explosions are activated by a signal. The sensors must be fried. From the EMP."

Will sat in silence with more crucial seconds ticking by. He tilted his head back before making the final decision. "Looks like we're jumping!"

TWENTY-SEVEN

"I don't want to jump. I can't!" Lloyd looked from one crew member to the next, unable to see everyone's faces or gauge their reactions behind their gold-tinted visors. He could only see his own warped reflection. "I've never flown on a plane before."

The comment left everyone confused and unable to find a suitable response.

"What are you trying to say?" asked Peta.

"I'm afraid of heights."

Donavon laughed. "Oh, the irony."

"What?"

"Announcing your fear of heights at 138,000 feet above the ground. That's comic gold."

"Is that why you drove all the way to Moscow for space training when we all flew?" asked Peta.

"Aren't you the one who insisted you come along?" asked Donavon. "What was it, this personal quest to overcome your fear or a bet with a friend?"

"Shut up, Donavon!" said Peta.

"Wow, does anyone on this flight have a genuine reason for being up here, except me and Will?" He looked in Ariane's direction when he spoke but turned to Peta. "How about you, cousin? Are you really here to learn or did you come just to annoy me?"

"I came to annoy you."

He stuck his thumb up. "You're doing a fantastic job!"

Lloyd undid his belts again and slipped his shoulders out of the restraints. His breaths became gasps, his chest heaving, and beads of sweat formed on his face, blurring his vision. He stood and reached for his neck, trying to pull his helmet off.

Peta rushed to unfasten her belts and stood. "Stop that, Lloyd!"

"Latch him to the cage!" said Will. "Quick!"

Peta reached for Lloyd's bicep as he took a step back, too close to the edge for her liking. She put a firm hand on his arm and told him to calm down. "I've got you."

She steered his hands away from his helmet and clipped him to the cage ring with the umbilical-like tether.

He gasped between laboured breaths and mentioned he was seeing aurora lights.

"That's a sign of severe, atmospheric stress," Ariane said. "He needs to calm down."

Lloyd swayed like a drunk. "I can't get any air!"

"Stay calm!" said Peta. "I just want you to concentrate on your breathing, nice and slow, in and out. In and out. Nice and slow. Just breathe."

"You're doing okay," said Will. "Sit down, we can discuss this more."

Ariane shook her head. "I thought we had already decided on option three: to jump. At one stage, we all agreed. Or was I mistaken? We don't have time to go over this again!"

Donavon unstrapped himself and stood. "Fuck this! I'm jumping."

"Wait!" said Will. "We still need to talk this through."

"I'm done talking! All this fucking around is wasting time and oxygen! I'm jumping!"

Will's legs were full of cramp, and a deep ache radiated in his hip joint. He unstrapped himself. Nice and slow, he told himself, rising from his seat, working the kinks out of his back. Standing and stretching loosened him up. "We need to swap our tanks over before we jump to give us maximum oxygen on the ground."

Donavon paused, sat down, and steered his arms through the restraints, leaving them unbuckled across his waist.

The radioactive clouds were closing in. Whether Fable Sky was losing altitude or the clouds were still expanding, there was no way to tell without functioning equipment.

Will opened the cage. "First, we'll need to switch over our oxygen tanks. Then work out who jumps first, second, and so on. We also need to consider what to do when we are back on the ground in case we get separated. We must plan carefully, okay? Are we all in agreement?"

A general chorus of affirmation came from the crew, but Will still wasn't convinced. "Can I get a verbal confirmation, please?"

"Yes!" said Ariane and Peta.

Donavon nodded.

"Lloyd?"

Lloyd looked up. "Yes!"

"Thank you," said Will. "Finally, we agree on something."

In an abort, there was no need to open the vents at the pole, but they questioned whether to open them anyway to reduce the gulf between the balloon and the ground before they deserted. Priority involved replacing their oxygen tanks with the reserves strapped down inside the cage.

Will disconnected the regulator hose from one of his near-empty tanks in his life support system and secured a new tank in its clamps. He opened the valve and checked the readings on his wrist. The gauge rushed up to fifty-nine per cent. He repeated the process on the second tank, dropped the used one into the cage, and closed the lid securely.

"I'm back at one hundred per cent," he announced, a note of relief in his voice as he glanced at the gauge to confirm his oxygen levels were fully restored.

Ariane finished fastening the clamps around her own tanks until they were secure. "And me," she said, giving a firm nod of satisfaction.

"I'm ready," said Peta, having checked her wrist computer to verify her status. She took two steps to her left and assisted Lloyd with replacing his oxygen tanks while Donavon dealt with his own, their movements synchronised from countless repetitions of this routine.

Lloyd nodded in appreciation, feeling the fresh oxygen of the new tanks. "Thanks, Peta," he said, resting a grateful hand on her shoulder.

The crew was now fully prepared, each member double-checking their gear and equipment in a final pre-launch ritual that had become second nature. The gondola was charged with a mix of readiness and anticipation as they stood poised for the daunting task they now faced.

Donovon glanced up from his wrist computer. "So, who's jumping first?"

When no one volunteered, Will raised his hand. "I don't mind."

"I'll go second," said Ariane.

Peta put up her hand. "Third."

"Fourth," said Donavon.

"Can someone else go last?" asked Will. "I don't think we should leave Lloyd up here on his own. He's not in the best state of mind."

"I'm okay," said Lloyd.

Will shook his head. "You're not. I'd feel better if you went fourth."

Donavon tapped Lloyd's back. "It's fine, I'll go last."

Will leaned over the edge, then faced his crew. "We'll need to jump quickly after one another. If we are drifting, we could be moving fast; the lateral winds could separate us. I suggest we count ten seconds between jumps. What do we think?"

"Ten seconds is ample," said Ariane.

Peta and Donavon concurred.

"Lloyd, are you okay to jump after ten seconds?"

"Do I have a choice?"

"Nope!" said Donavon.

With a deep breath, Will shuffled forward until the tips of his boots hung over the edge. No longer could he afford the fanciful thoughts of space tourism, the dreamlike allure of exploring new heights. They seemed distant and irrelevant in the face of their current predicament. His duty to the flight, once his driving force, had faded like a distant star. The mission objectives and scientific goals that had once occupied his every thought now felt secondary and insignificant. Abandoning the space balloon meant consigning it to drift aimlessly until it met its inevitable downfall. All that time, money, and excitement invested in the mission would count for naught as it floated unpiloted towards a certain, catastrophic dive.

Their primal need to survive was their only priority. Their lives hung in the balance, and every decision, every action, was geared towards staying alive. He tentatively put his foot out, feeling his weight shift in unfamiliar ways.

He looked back over his shoulder. "If we get separated, we can radio through to one another. Once we have regrouped on the ground, we'll assess the situation and decide the best action to take."

"That's it?" asked Lloyd. "If?"

"It's not a great plan, I know, but the sooner we get back, the better."

"I agree," said Peta. "If we can land near each other, we stand a better chance of surviving this and can work together."

"And I agree with Lloyd," said Donavon. "These are big ifs."

Will nodded. "Yeah, I hear you. Whatever happens, I want to thank you all for your involvement with the project today. It has been a pleasure working with you."

Will still couldn't wrap his head around it. It was a day that had started with such promise. The odds against them being off the ground when a nuclear attack occurred were so high as to negate credible probability. But it had happened by luck, a fortuitous sequence of events. That was all.

Will desperately needed luck right then as he prepared for a daunting jump from twenty-six miles high onto land that was obscured from view. Skydiving from any altitude was always a high-risk activity, but this jump was compounded by a freefall that would deliver him to an apocalyptic furnace.

TWENTY-EIGHT

Standing at the edge of the gondola, Will bent his knees and prepared himself for the imminent leap. His arms hung loosely by his sides, and his torso was arched at the waist, mimicking the poised posture of a diver ready to plunge into a swimming pool. He inhaled a deep breath, feeling the rush of adrenaline coursing through his veins, but in that fleeting moment, he hesitated with an instinct to retreat. His heart beat faster than ever before. How had it come to this? The parachutes had been for contingency only. Not once had it crossed his mind they would actually have to use them. He tried to remain optimistic that their training and common sense would prevail. This was a critical moment of his so-called captaincy where he had to lead by example. He couldn't show his fear or talk his way out of it.

"What are you waiting for?" asked Donavon.

Will turned his head slightly. "I just need a moment."

Running through a mental rehearsal, recollecting all the techniques he'd learned during training, He would dive slightly headfirst, almost horizontal, with his arms pressed tightly by his sides, maximising his descent speed. This approach would allow him to reach the ground in the shortest possible time, giving him a chance to scout for a safe landing area. From there, he could guide the others to their safe return. It was why he'd volunteered to jump first.

Will's sleeve computer showed the time at 14:45.

"Okay, ten seconds everyone. Good luck. See you on the ground."

Lifting one boot off the deck, he tilted and fell square from the gondola.

A moment of utter weightlessness in the gasp that came between falling and soaring was followed by silence, floating sentient in a soundless cocoon. All he could think about in this brief interlude was returning to his son as quickly as possible, refusing to entertain the idea he might actually be dead.

Forty seconds gone, he hit supersonic speed, breaking the sound barrier. He might have broken the world record for the fastest space jump without ever knowing. Did it even matter?

One minute into the freefall, plummeting rapidly towards the nuclear fallout zone below, he had a few minutes to brace himself for the impending horrors of war. His mind raced with grim anticipation. He knew he would soon be surrounded by the alarming sight of dead bodies, victims of this unspeakable catastrophe. The frantic and impromptu evacuation attempts would have numbered in the high hundreds of thousands, a desperate exodus fuelled by absolute terror. Even as survivors might still be scrambling to escape the aftermath, he hurtled towards it at breakneck speed, totally unaware of the dangers concealed beneath the toxic shroud.

Ninety seconds.

The small drogue chute had just deployed with its primary function to stabilise his descent through the sky. The sudden pop from the chute sent a wave of tension through his body, and he began to pitch side to side, oscillating with the force of the wind. Instinctively, he made minute adjustments, subtly shifting his elbows to regain control and balance. Each slight movement was calculated according to his training. As the air thickened and rippled around him, he felt the chute working to steady his fall, transforming mild turbulence into a more controlled descent.

By his estimation, he was already a third of the way down, somewhere around 90,000 feet.

Stabilised, he focussed on keeping his limbs not too close together and his arched posture optimum to achieve effective aerodynamics.

Descending into the remnants of the dissipated mushroom clouds, his visor was suddenly showered with a flurry of black ash and grit. The fine particles clung to the transparent surface, obscuring his vision and creating an eerie veil through which his surroundings appeared only as a blur, like driving through a black snow blizzard. The earlier clear, blue skies were heavily tainted, swirling with the remnants of vaporised structures and incinerated lives.

Two minutes came and went.

Will kept his eyes on the time on the liquid crystal wrist computer, stubbornly glowing blue-green in the crushing haze as he passed three minutes of freefall. At this current altitude, the atmospheric drag had radically slowed his descent to one hundred and fifty miles per hour, creating immense pressure against his front. The force of the rushing air roared around him, drowning out the sound of his heavy breathing, and his spacesuit rippled and fluttered under intense wind resistance.

At 8,000 feet, the chute deployed explosively from its pack. It caught the air with a sudden, forceful jerk, inflating almost instantaneously into a broad, red canopy. The transformation was dramatic. Within seconds, he was decelerated from one hundred and twenty-five miles per hour to a gentle descent of ten. The abrupt change exerted a powerful upward force on his harness, momentarily squeezing the breath from his lungs and straining against his body. Profound relief came over him, the frantic freefall replaced by a serene glide, carving up the smoke and soot, but he was not safe yet. The smooth drift gave him precious time to prepare for his next challenge—executing a safe landing.

There was no drop zone or target area to aim for. No one was guiding him from the ground, warning him to steer clear of danger spots.

If he was over the ocean, he would drown.

If he came down in a fire, he would burn.

It had been a blind jump, and all his formal instruction on essential skydiving skills meant nothing.

Using the air resistance and the parachute's aerodynamic characteristics as the medium to control his final descent, he turned, trying to identify something familiar in the dark storm. Dust and ash continued to lash against his visor and suit. With still no sight of land as he knifed through ceaseless pockets of thick, black smoke, it was a frightening moment of truth as his life now lay in the hands of God, or fate, or whoever decided these matters.

All at once, the smoke cleared, parting like curtains, and he dropped out of the darkness towards a roofless building that rushed up from nowhere to greet him.

TWENTY-NINE

Ariane shuffled cautiously to the edge of the deck, her heart ablaze with anticipation. Poised and ready to make the second jump, she steadied herself at the precipice, but just when she prepared to launch herself into the abyss, a sudden disorienting, silver mist enveloped her vision, and she lost her sight again. She reached out, her hands grasping for the familiar solidity of the handrail, and her mind raced to make sense of her sudden blindness. Preparedness and training momentarily forgotten, she froze, suspended between the safety of the deck and the unknown environs below.

"Can you speed this up?" asked Donavon.

Ariane turned to face Peta, Lloyd, and Donavon lined up behind her. "My visor's steamed up again."

"You can still jump."

"Not if I can't see."

She thumped the side of her helmet, hoping to jump-start the heater motor. After repeated attempts, it came back to life of its own accord, and her visor cleared. "It's back on. I can see again."

"Jump, then!" said Donavon.

She stepped forward, glanced down, let her arms hang at her sides, and slightly spread her legs before leaping into a star position. The thin air of the upper atmosphere offered little resistance, and she experienced complete weightlessness.

Soaring towards the ground, she soon began to spin head over heel. This was where the drogue chute would play its part as soon as it met dense air. The noise of rushing wind signalled it was imminent. It would burst out of her pack and fix the spin. But it didn't, and she kept spinning. If she couldn't rectify it soon, the forces exerted could strain her muscles and joints or lead to a loss of consciousness. She thrusted out her arm against the wind, like pushing an oar out in water to stop a boat from rotating, using it as a brake. If called for, she would have to manually open her main parachute long before the auto-activation kicked in.

She had experienced a similar situation before, early in her career when flying a supersonic jet towards the stratosphere. On a standard test flight, she had revelled in the exhilaration of its agile manoeuvrability and lightning speed. As always, the twists and turns and the rapid ascent set her senses ablaze with adrenaline. The sky around her had deepened to a darker blue, the curvature of the Earth becoming just perceptible at the edge of her vision when suddenly, without warning, one of the powerful turbines stalled, and she felt the jet shudder as it lost thrust. Instantly, the wings, deprived of vital lift, began to dip, and the sleek aircraft's nose descended, turning the stable flight path into a deadly ride, where the horizon spun wildly outside her cockpit window.

Her training kicked in as she fought to control the spiralling descent. Alarms blared in the cockpit, adding to the drama, and her body tensed as she worked the controls, trying to restart the engine and regain stability. Turning the fall into a nosedive to give the wings something to bite onto, the speed increased, but the horizontal stabiliser failed and sent the aircraft into an erratic spin once more.

In such emergency situations, only a narrow window of opportunity existed to correct a problem. She couldn't afford to black out, even though she was on the verge.

"Ground Control, initiating abort."

She was hurtling towards the ground, only 4,000 feet from disaster when she pulled the ejection lever. It engaged, flinging her out of the cockpit and into the air. The parachute instantly blossomed above, and she landed in a field of maize a hundred metres from the plane.

Walking away from the flaming wreckage with her helmet in her hand and every bone somehow intact, she pulled out her St. Christopher necklace and pressed it to her lips.

Propelled back to the present, Ariane watched a silver wall of condensation crawl across her visor until she could see nothing again. What lay beneath the clouds deeply concerned her. If she landed in the ocean, she could stay afloat until she used up all her oxygen. Lifting her visor, she would breathe radioactive air, and water would seep into her heavy suit, making her a deadweight. It would drag her beneath the surface to a cold womb and a return to the lightless source of all life. Drowning in a scary, black silence, her last thought would be whether they should've heeded Lloyd's advice and not jumped; should they have waited instead? These thoughts would be quickly flooded by the encroaching seawater and her deep regret.

When the parachute straps yanked Ariane's shoulders back, everything settled, including her senses. Then, right on cue, as if it had been waiting for the perfect moment, the heater sprang to life. Slowly, the condensation lifted, and she could see black soot driving against her visor, obscuring her vision almost as effectively as the condensation before it.

When the toxic clouds rolled back, she viewed the gnarled landscape, engulfed by fire. A giant flare spiked up into the sky, and she used the burst to digest the scene. Banking sharply, she passed over a small town of broken roofs and structures reduced to rubble and ash, their skeletal remains charred by the relentless fires feeding on whatever was left.

A second pass, lower, slower, drifting in a tactical wide arc, bought her some time to seek somewhere safe to put herself down. Through the haze, she spotted a patch of grass between the scattered fires and dove towards it in a swift descent.

The landing almost knocked her legs out from beneath her, but somehow she stayed on two feet as the canopy bunched up around her.

THIRTY

At the ten-second mark, Peta breathed deeply, preparing to abandon ship. She looked over her shoulder at Lloyd and her cousin. "Okay, I'm going. Be safe and good luck."

Then she was gone.

Donavon and Lloyd leaned over, watching as she vanished from sight like a dropped toy.

Donavon shoved Lloyd to the gondola's edge. "You're up next."

Lloyd cleared his throat. "I don't think I can jump."

"You can, and you will!"

"What if my parachute doesn't open?"

"When we land, come and see me and I'll pack you a new one."

"Seriously?"

"Seriously? I'll come and mop up your bloody entrails.

Then I'll use a shovel to gather your shattered bones, which I'll give to your mum."

"My mum's dead!"

Donavon shrugged.

Holding onto the cage, Lloyd slowly leaned out, then took a half-step back. He checked his parachute harness and saw two cords hanging. "There are handles on my left and right."

"They're called ripcords."

"Can you remind me which one is for the main chute and which is the reserve?"

"The one on your right is main. If that doesn't work, use the left one. The chute will open automatically at 8,000 feet, so this is a pointless conversation and you're wasting my time."

"Where are the steering lines?"

"You should've paid more attention during the training."

"Please!"

"The toggles will appear after your chute opens."

From the moment he stepped onto the balloon, his fear, a relentless companion, had clouded his judgment and dulled his reflexes, leaving him perpetually a few steps behind where he needed to be. His lax approach to his training was also being exposed. As he reflected on his performance, he acknowledged he had coasted through exercises and drills, reluctant to push himself beyond his comfort zone. Now, faced with the harsh reality of his shortcomings, he realised his complacency had left him ill-prepared for the numerous challenges that lay ahead, filling him with regret.

He peered over the edge again. He looked at the time on his computer, still on solar charge. "We really should wait, you know."

"You're starting to piss me off now!"

"They could be preparing a rescue."

"Who's they?"

Lloyd drew a long breath. "I don't know. Jefferson? The Army Reserve maybe? NASA? They know we're here. They're not going to forget about us."

"Why *are* you here, Lloyd?"

Lloyd frowned. "To join the flight."

"But for no reason."

"That's not true."

"Then show me. Do something worthy. Prove me wrong. Make a contribution."

"What?"

"At this moment, you're delaying me from jumping, which means you're risking my life, and I'm losing patience. So, take your fat arse to the edge of the gondola, jump, and prove me wrong."

"I can't."

"I knew you weren't cut out for this."

"Why?"

"I was outvoted by Will and Jefferson. I had my doubts about you from the start, but they wouldn't listen. I was right, as usual. You shouldn't be on this flight. You know it, I know it."

"I designed the balloon."

"Not very well."

"What?"

"How many fucking times did we have to postpone the flight? How many problems have we had to deal with in the last few years? And how many times have we lost contact with the ground today? You couldn't even disconnect the gondola from the envelope."

"That was hardly my fault. It was caused by the EMP, not through flaws in my design. And the communication issue was because of the duplexer in the lighthouse, not because of the balloon."

"You should've thought about EMPs when you designed the balloon. The best engineers always consider every possible outcome. You obviously didn't do enough research. Just like your skydiving, you seem to approach tasks half-heartedly, and that's why we're in this situation right now, adrift and without communication."

"But that's because of the EMP."

"Hey, Lloyd, shut the fuck up!"

Lloyd turned away and mumbled, "We should wait."

"You've got five seconds."

He shot round. "What?"

"You've got five seconds to jump."

"I still think we're making a serious mistake. They must be trying to find a way to communicate with us. It makes more sense to wai–"

Donavon grabbed Lloyd's shoulders, spun him round with force, and shoved him one-handed in the chest.

Lloyd instinctively flung out his arms in a desperate bid to steady himself. The sudden movement caused him to lose his balance completely, and he crashed down into his seat with a jarring thud. His head slammed into the headrest with a sharp impact, sending shockwaves through his skull. Disoriented, he blinked rapidly, hoping to clear the stars dancing in his vision. Everything spun momentarily as he clutched the armrests and attempted to calm himself. Donavon came into view, standing before him. He caught a glimpse of himself sprawled in his seat reflected in his crewmate's visor.

Donavon turned his hand into an imaginary gun, pointing it at Lloyd's chest, and pulled the trigger. "I'll be waiting with my shovel."

He turned and jumped off the balloon.

THIRTY-ONE

Lloyd climbed out of his seat, steadied himself on the compact deck, and stepped slowly to the edge of the gondola. Leaning over, he watched Donavon disappear into the dark clouds with contempt.

What was it like down there? Were there any survivors? Had Will, Peta, and Ariane survived the freefall?

Only because the altercation had occurred so quickly and unexpectedly, leaving him in a state of shock, had Donavon not been treated to every obscenity he could muster.

Shaking uncontrollably, he collapsed back into his seat like a puppet whose strings had been cut. Panic and his anxiety had him firmly in its grip.

He couldn't jump.

He couldn't jump.

He couldn't jump.

During the pre-flight checks and the nerve-wracking three-hour journey towards the stratosphere, he had been incredibly tense. At launch, the anxiety had peaked, leaving him on the verge of throwing up. Now, that feeling was back.

He stared at the empty seats on the gondola, spooked by the silence and darkness. His body froze, every muscle. He wasn't getting enough oxygen, even though ninety-eight per cent remained in his tanks. What he *did* consume scorched his throat.

"Can any of you hear me? Is it safe to jump? Will, do you copy? Did you make it back? Is it safe to jump? Can you hear me?"

The chances of a rescue were slim. Deep down, he knew he had to abandon the balloon, but his feet were anchored to the deck. He needed confirmation that he wouldn't jump into water or fire.

As a kid, he used to have a habit of singing to himself, usually without words, a deep and joyful sound that rose from his soul. He had been a skinny, anxious boy given to stuttering when he got scared. Singing had been a therapy: emotional and mental. He had not carried it with him into adolescence and adulthood and was always self-conscious if ever he *did* try to sing. At ten, he had fallen out of an oak tree, breaking several bones. It had been his scariest experience, the catalyst for his vertigo. It marked the end of his singing. This, however, was way beyond that.

If ever there was a good time for his training to kick in, it was right then, but it had been some time ago, and he'd missed key elements. The crew, Ariane excluded, had completed ten high-altitude jumps, including two solo, with six hours of pre-requisite training. He had attended the classroom instruction, had practiced on the parachute jump tower and trapeze swing, and had spent time in a wind tunnel with gusts of up to one hundred and eighty miles per hour. Of the ten skydives, he had completed seven, all tandem. He had gone to great lengths to avoid the remaining three, especially the solo jumps. Attending the wrong airfield, engine problems with his van, and a severe migraine were the excuses he gave. In that order. What chance would he have if the worst happened?

"To hell with this!" he muttered.

Locating the cord that vented helium at the balloon's pole, he gripped it tightly with his gloved hand and pulled with a firm, focussed motion, as if sounding a train horn. With the valves releasing a large amount of helium, he sat in his seat and fastened the straps. He braced himself for the long journey back with a mixture of anticipation and readiness for whatever might happen.

The majestic ascent was now a gradual descent with the balloon slowly but surely falling from the sky, providing Lloyd with too much time to ponder the perils awaiting him below. For one, a vast body or water loomed as a high possibility; if the balloon had indeed drifted out to sea, drowning seemed almost inevitable unless a ship happened to be passing nearby. Conversely, the thought of landing in the sea brought slight relief compared to the alternative. On land, a nuclear aftermath presented a harrowing array of dangers that included raging fires, ruins, and radiation.

He assessed the gondola and considered its fate should it impact with water. Made of aluminium, it would certainly sink, offering little chance of survival. Regret filled him as he realised he should have designed the gondola with flotation in mind. Donavon's words echoed in his head. He had dismissed the need for a design that accounted for all possibilities, such as the electromagnetic pulses that had disabled their on board equipment. Now, in the quiet descent, Lloyd acknowledged his design shortcomings and the gravity of these oversights, laid bare for all to see.

Before long, the expansive and menacing mass of the toxic mushroom cloud loomed directly beneath the balloon. The sight was both terrifying and surreal. Disturbed by the volume and proximity of the fallout, his body reacted instinctively. His bladder relaxed, and a warm sensation at his crotch appeared as his diaper was further saturated. He had consumed a lot of water. His drink pouch still held some. Less than a litre. But something.

Even so, Lloyd had faith in his balloon. He'd designed the envelope with a translucent polyethylene material using special additives to strengthen performance against strong crosswinds and high-altitude temperatures. He still believed it would hold steady and braced for impact as the balloon dipped into the disturbed airspace. The churning ash cloud sent the gondola in a cycle of erratic movement, pitching when the envelope fabric came under pressure. Lloyd felt the deck vibrating through the soles of his boots. With a series of sickening lurches, the Fable Sky balloon plummeted, jarring movements that sent shudders through Lloyd and the gondola. Black ash coated his spacesuit in a thick, grimy layer. The fine particles clung stubbornly to every inch of exposed equipment and obscured the deck with a dense, soot-like film. The descent had turned into a struggle against the forces of nature.

"It's not going to hold."

After a minute of indecision, he undid his restraints and rushed around the deck, unfastening the metal clamps securing large ballast bags to the side of the gondola. Ten in total, the ballast comprised ten per cent of the balloon's total weight. Cutting and releasing them would cause the balloon to rise out of the vortex, buying him time to reassess.

Having jettisoned the first two ballast bags, he reached for the third, stepped on the discarded solar wing controller, and lost his footing. As his reflexes snapped to stabilise his centre of gravity, his feet left the deck and he plunged backwards, his breath gone with the shock of suddenly falling. His eyes bulged and strained in their sockets as he tumbled, turning the world upside down. Fable Sky, now a suspended ball in the sky, was fleetingly framed in his visor upon each revolution. The red transponder beacon light, triggered by Donavon for ground control to triangulate their position, flashed on the underside of the gondola like a beating heart, but he lost sight of it when the mushroom clouds folded around him.

With only minutes to live, he felt unprepared for death. He didn't experience flashes of his life; there wasn't a great deal of content.

Deployment of the drogue parachute arrested the spin, gradually stabilising him in the fall. He fixed his arms and legs in the optimal positions to facilitate a steady descent, recalling important elements of his training.

At 8,000 feet, the parachute deployed with a crisp pop, bringing a sudden and welcome stability to his rapid descent. Everything settled, including his frantic heart. As the rush of adrenaline ebbed away, an overwhelming wave of exhaustion swept over him. His eyelids grew heavy, and before he could muster any resistance, his eyes rolled. Consciousness slipped away like a receding tide, leaving him adrift in the darkness as though cast out into space. The last thing he registered was the sound of his breathing before descending into an inescapable grave spinning up to swallow him.

THIRTY-TWO

Ariane had known it would be bad, but nothing could have prepared her for the sheer magnitude of the destruction. It was worse, much worse, than she had imagined. It looked like the town had been struck by hurricane, earthquake, and firestorm simultaneously. The explosions had ignited vast, uncontrolled fires, obliterating the sun with black smoke, and plunging the town into an unnatural darkness. Over in the east, a line of fire raged relentlessly along the horizon, compounding the deadly debris that rained down from above, blanketing the landscape in suffocating layers of filth.

Nearby, a church, unremarkable by design, burned fiercely, and she watched, sparing a thought for her religious parents as the upper half imploded. The weakened structure leaned to the side with protection of neither the roof nor walls, succumbing to the fire as easily as a house of matchsticks.

Ariane craned her neck to the west, where the fires burned with less intensity. Between the two contrasting horizons sat the small town she had passed over. The temperature inside her spacesuit had risen, as though the heat from the fires had penetrated its protective material. Though the liquid-cooling tubes in her spandex garment staved off some of the excess body heat, she deduced the air-cooling ventilators might have ceased working.

She drank some water and set off for the town. A gust of wind blew against her parachute and dragged her back several steps until she calmly pressed the quick-release buckles and shrugged the pack off her shoulders. The canopy blew several feet into the air before deflating into a flat, red sheet.

Every few seconds, she glanced up, searching for Lloyd and Donavon, due any moment. "Will, Peta, do you copy? I've landed safely. Where are you?"

She searched for signs of life, the crew, and anyone who might have taken refuge underground to escape the explosions. It wouldn't be long before they crept back to the surface where everything was demolished with efficiency as true as an atomic clock.

"Ariane here. I'm in a small town. I don't know where this is, but everything is on fire. I don't see any survivors here. Can anyone hear me?"

Her visor heater packed in again, causing her to halt in her tracks. This new unreliability in her vision was unnerving. She waited for it to regain power as the town gradually vanished from sight, obscured once more by a wall of mist. The seconds ticked by painfully slowly, turning into agonising minutes, but the heater stubbornly refused to cooperate and continued to engulf her in an impenetrable fog. She drew a small mouthful of water from her drink pouch, pursed her lips, and sprayed her visor, clearing a hole in the condensation. With restricted vision, she proceeded cautiously, every step ultra-slow as the ground began to alter, the soft turf giving way to asphalt. "Will? Peta? Do you copy?"

The provisional window in her visor had begun to close, but the fog-over suddenly receded and dissolved owing to the reactivated heater. Relieved and full-sighted, she crossed the road, filled with smashed-up and burning cars where the EMP had damaged all modern vehicles as they were equipped with and reliant upon computer technology, sending them coasting out of control into one another. The subsequent heatwave had provided the erasure, obliterating human existence within the vehicles. The power lines had come crashing down. Fires raged. The townspeople were dead with not much remaining except blood and shadows.

She was spared further horror when the heater shut off and her visor slowly misted over again. Their flight to the edge of space had involved calculating the risks and accepting them if things went wrong. The same logic applied now. She had to accept nothing about the next eight hours would be easy; the standard survival mechanism was just to try and maintain one's composure at all times.

Using her hands to sweep the air to compensate for her blindness, she found a wall and felt her way along it. This must have been how a partially sighted person felt. She groped her way through the darkness, arms extended like the undead in an apocalyptic setting. She had seen all the zombie movies. Now she *was* one.

She spat more water onto her visor, buying her a few extra minutes of sight to avoid running into unexpected changes in the landscape or unknown dangers, eventually giving up. She leaned heavily against the wall, her breath ragged. "If anyone can hear this, I'm in a town. That's all I know. My visor heater's failed again. I can't continue like this. I'm going to wait here; hopefully you can find me. I'm at the edge of the town, near a forest."

Lacking any options, she dropped in a kind of fugue state of sadness and fear. She rested her head back against the wall and clasped her gloved hands around her knees, drawing them to her chest. There was little point in walking around if she was sightless, and she didn't want to waste any more water on her visor. Radiation was the most significant threat now. Invisible, tasteless, odourless, insidious. The moment the suit became a redundant life support, there would be no escaping it as it was absorbed into the body like some possessive spirit, triggering cancers, carcinomas, blood disorders, cataracts, and eventually whole-body shutdown. In a matter of days, she could expect internal bleeding, DNA damage, and collapsed immune system followed by multiple organ failure. A brutal, painful way to die.

To increase her survival odds, she now had to conserve her energy, water, and oxygen. She had to wait for the others to find her. Her life depended on it.

THIRTY-THREE

"Aerodynamic law is, in my opinion, fascinating physics," said Donavon, spinning his black board marker into the air and catching it between two fingers at the front of the classroom, his eyes focussing on the twenty students facing his whiteboard and lectern. "It's an engineering science with four forces to consider."

He pulled a ten-pound note out of his trouser pocket and held it above his head, waving it like a mini flag. "If one of you can tell me what they are in the next five seconds, I'll give you a tenner."

"What do you mean, exactly?" asked a young student at the front, her hair beaded into two plaits.

Donavon ignored her question and stared at his watch. "Time's up. Propulsion, weight, lift, and drag." He wrote them on the whiteboard and repocketed the note. "These were the discoveries of Sir George Cayley at the end of the 18th century. He was the very best of British minds."

He drank some water and screwed the cap back on the bottle. "There's a diverse range of aerodynamic inventions. For example, decelerators such as parachutes and thrust reversal devices. And a vast range of spacecraft. Micro air vehicles to hypersonic wave riders."

A man in the front row with his leg in plaster cast raised his hand.

Donavon acknowledged him with a nod. "Yes."

Wearing a grey suit jacket and a mauve shirt opened two buttons down, the man, late twenties, younger than Donavon but the oldest student in the room, asked, "In terms of lighter than air vehicles, as in balloons, is there a height and capacity limit?"

"Sorry, what's your name?"

"Will."

"It's a fair question. While there are no set universal limits, hot-air balloons for recreational use generally don't fly much higher than 14,000 feet without supplemental oxygen. Most air balloons are around 100,000 cubic feet, but they have been known to go six times that. That said, if the material is strong enough, you can build bigger. Ripstop nylon and polyethylene terephthalate are the most robust materials and are commonly used in modern-day air ballooning. Capacity can range from a single passenger to twenty or more, depending on the balloon's design and size. A cubic foot of air weighs roughly an ounce. Heat it to around thirty-seven degrees centigrade, and it weighs about seven grams less. A single cubic foot of air contained in a balloon can lift seven grams. Not a great deal. So that's why hot-air balloons, airships, aerostats, blimps, are so large. The more heated air they contain, the more weight they can lift. My advice is to always adhere to manufacturer specifications and aviation regulations."

Most students took notes. A few looked at their mobiles, not even pretending to be interested.

After class, Donavon spotted Will hopping on crutches across the college car park. "Into balloons, yeah?"

Will threw the crutches into the back of his Jeep. "The only way to fly."

An apple bitten down to its core was pinched between Donavon's thumb and forefinger, which he dropped onto his boot and kicked high into the air, watching it land in a bush. "I'd argue that helicopters are more exciting, but that's just me being biased. Anyway, I have a cousin who loves ballooning. I can put you in touch with her if you want?"

"I have a hot-air balloon, actually; I run my own company. Business is slow, especially as I'm unable to fly at the moment." He pointed at his crutches and closed the boot down.

"What happened? The wife kneecap you?"

"Let's just say a lethal concoction of red wine and false bravery."

Donavon gave him a lazy grin. "Been there. What brings you to my class if you already fly balloons?"

"I'm looking into a new kind of ballooning business."

"You came to the right place."

Will half-smiled but said nothing.

Black eyebrows locked in a frown, Donavon folded his arms. "What's this business, then?"

"Space flights."

The gears in Donavon's mind churned, his thoughts racing as he mulled over Will's words, sensing an opportunity, so he invited Will to the pub, persuading him with the offer to buy the first two rounds.

Drinking eight pints to Will's four, Donavon listened to his audacious plan to take a helium balloon into the stratosphere with paying tourists on board. A high-end client experience. A niche market with limited competition in the burgeoning space tourism industry. High revenue potential, with ticket prices set at a premium. Zero emissions; no impact on the environment. An out-of-this-world perspective of the Earth. Educational value, teaching passengers about the atmospheric layers, space, and the science behind high-altitude flight. A tourism boost for St. Ives and its neighbouring towns. The only obstacle holding the project back was his lack of finance and a small team.

Donavon was an opportunist, someone who thought in terms of achievement and self-interest, and by the end of the night, he had made his intentions clear. He wanted a slice. It took a gallon of beer to convince Will, who struck Donavon as a prudent, smart individual, even after a skinful. Will said he needed to talk to his business partner, Jefferson, and financial terms had to be considered, but Will had seemed optimistic, if not excited.

Royalties from interviews, documentaries, and chat shows could make the endeavour a lucrative investment opportunity. Not to mention the income from running flights to and from the edge of space. Donavon had logged several balloon flights in his life. They were interesting enough but could grow boring at times with the lack of motion and adventure compared to the dynamic capabilities of flying helicopters. However, Will's enterprise was something else entirely.

Nine days after adjourning their discussion to the pub, Will contacted Donavon with great news. Jefferson was keen for him to join the team and wanted to meet for dinner at some point in the next week to discuss his involvement and how his investment could catapult the project forward.

Donavon zipped past two minutes of freefall, covering more than half the total distance, but his mind was entrenched in thoughts about his pivotal role in the Fable Sky project. The crew remained oblivious to the extent of his contributions and the lengths he had gone to ensure the project received enough funding. They had no comprehension of the myriad risks he had undertaken, the personal sacrifices he had endured, and the colossal financial burden he had shouldered. Nor did they grasp the inherent dangers he had faced head-on. Some details, Donavon knew, were better left unspoken so as to maintain the crew's morale and focus. The true value of his investment needed to be acknowledged openly, though, because the initial success of the mission and, more importantly, surviving the nuclear attack, were the outcomes of his efforts. Without him, none of the crew would have ever experienced this incredible journey—or lived to tell the tale.

The charges cut the line holding the parachute in place, and it bloomed at 8,000 feet like a red flower. Donavon took hold of the toggles on either side and turned himself towards a long, straight road that cut a black line through a fiery orange vista. He bent his knees and braced himself as the ground rushed up at him, and he heard a dull thud where his space boots touched down on the asphalt.

Gathering his bearings as the chute floated gently to the ground, he swung his head left and right, surveying the trees on the sides of the road, either burning or blown to stumps. The dark orange sky was a scene straight out of Mars.

The dual lane road ran to the horizon in both directions. He had to strain to see through the smoke encompassing him. In the east, fires burned harsh and bright. The orange glow was less intense in the west, so he set off in that direction.

And then, out of nowhere, a cloud of dust on the side of the road announced the arrival of one of the crew. Judging by the clumsy way he landed and lost his footing, then became entangled by the parachute, it was obvious Lloyd had plucked up the courage to jump.

Donavon walked over and peeled back the parachute as he fought his way out. "I guess I don't need a shovel, then."

An arm reached out from beneath the canopy, and when Donavon grabbed it, he saw the nametag on the suit's upper sleeve read Peta.

"Where are we?" she asked, looking up and down the long road.

Donavon stepped back with stunned surprise. "You took your time getting here. You jumped before me."

"I'm much lighter than you. And I decided to pull my chute early and circle for a while so I could search for a safe place to land. Then I saw you." She turned her eyes around the scenery. "I can't comprehend what I'm seeing. This is unbelievable."

Donavon nodded. "Whoever caused this, I guarantee our military response will be twice as severe."

"Where's Ariane? Have you seen her?"

"I just landed myself."

"Have you heard from her or Lloyd?"

"No."

"We need to look for them."

"Is that a wise idea?"

"Is that a serious question?"

Donavon checked his sleeve computer. "We don't have a lot of time."

"We're searching for them. They should be nearby."

"They could be anywhere."

"Lloyd and Ariane jumped ten seconds either side of me. They must be close by. Will may be further away, but I'm sure he'll contact us when he can. Let's go."

They followed the road, their senses on high alert in such unsafe territory.

"This is Peta. Does anyone copy? Are you okay? Where are you?"

Nothing came through their receivers.

"Lloyd, do you copy? Where are you?"

"Forget him," said Donavon. "We've got..." He paused and looked at his oxygen gauge, "We've got about seven and a half hours to figure out where we are and where we should go. That's not long at all."

Peta scanned the road to the horizon. Then glanced up at the radioactive particles swirling in the sky like the inside of a vacuum cleaner. "I guess they'll reach out to us as soon as they can."

Further along the road, they came across a vehicle with its bonnet up and smoke belching from its torched engine. It was so charred, she could not determine the make, model, colour, or registration. The interior was also gutted black.

She carefully rubbed the scorched number plate, her gloves turning black from soot. The lettering underneath was barely legible, but she could make out just enough. "This is a foreign car," she said, her voice tinged with curiosity. "It looks like it has the Euro logo on it, and the letters are smaller than UK plates."

Donavon peered over her shoulder, squinting at the plate. "Which nationality?"

Peta traced the faint outlines of the characters with her finger. "I think French," she said, a note of uncertainty in her voice.

"You think it's possible we could have drifted that far?" he asked, looking all around him as though the landscape might suddenly reveal the answer.

Peta put her hands on her hips and looked up and down the deserted road. "I honestly don't know."

Could they really have drifted so far without realising? If they'd crossed into foreign territory, it would mean rethinking their entire strategy.

"We need to figure out where we are and what to do," she said. "Let's keep moving, see if we can find any more clues."

With a final glance at the burned-out vehicle, they started down the road.

THIRTY-FOUR

Located in the county of Cornwall, St. Ives was celebrated for its charming narrow streets and quaint, traditional cottages. This idyllic seaside town drew tourists worldwide, enchanted by its promise of clean air and vast unspoilt beaches. Visitors eagerly explored its scenic coastal walks, offering breathtaking views of the rugged coastline and azure waters. The town also boasted a thriving arts and crafts scene, with local galleries and studios showcasing some of the finest creations in the region. With a population of just 6,000, St. Ives provided the perfect retreat for those seeking an escape from the hustle and bustle of everyday life, its intimate size instilling a warm, welcoming atmosphere. Whether wandering through the cobbled streets lined with artisan shops and cafes or relaxing along the sandy shores, its tranquillity and charm made the tiny beach town a beloved destination for rejuvenation and inspiration.

It was Ariane's first time in St. Ives, but she hadn't come for the tourism. She had been sent by NASA on business.

From sleeping under the euphoria of prescription pills to awaking suddenly, disturbed at dawn by some jackass revving his motorcycle inside a garage on the opposite side of the road, Ariane threw back the duvet and opened the curtains to the spectacular sea view, but her eyes were drawn to the biker. The heavyset man switched off his engine and rolled the motorcycle into a lock-up storage container, closed his garage door, and vanished inside his house.

As neither a fan of loud bikes nor early mornings, Ariane stumbled peevishly to the bathroom to freshen up.

Will had recommended the charming boutique guesthouse, situated on the hill overlooking the St. Ives Bay, famous for its splendid, cooked breakfasts using all local produce and fresh fish. She was the only guest, not counting Heidi, the sweet owner.

Breakfast lived up to expectations, and with a full stomach of poached eggs and an exquisite pork bagel, she walked along the streets footed in ancient cobblestones, passing the various galleries and craft shops riding out the quiet end of winter before the tourists flooded back in droves for mid spring.

It took twenty minutes to arrive at the garage just outside St. Ives.

A man dressed in a waterproof jacket, a black beanie, and a trendy beard strolled towards her. "You must be Ariane." He held out his hand. "I'm Will."

She shook it. "Hi."

"Sleep well?"

"Until some douche on a motorcycle revved his engine loudly at some ungodly hour. Apart from that, no complaints.

The guesthouse is lovely, and the breakfast was divine. Thanks for the recommendation."

"I've stayed there many times. Heidi treats her guests like family."

"Does she take care of thoughtless bikers? With some kind of medieval weapon?"

Will shrugged. "She's open to requests." He pointed at the garage door, wide enough to accommodate two cars side by side. "It's in here." He unlocked the door and raised it above his head, inviting Ariane inside. Taking up most of the interior was a large trailer draped with a black tarpaulin. He untied the tarpaulin and slid it off, unveiling a circular, six-seater gondola.

"It will be towed out to the cliff on launch day. We have two helium trucks arriving at around four in the morning to inflate the envelope."

Ariane studied the white writing below the insignia on the discarded tarpaulin. "What does Fable Sky mean?"

"Fable is an acronym for First Aeronautic Balloon Launch Expedition."

"First? Haven't there been a few over the years?"

"Yes, true, but this is the first space balloon operating as a passenger-carrying vessel with a crew."

She examined the red gondola in detail, running her hand along the external rail and across the back of the seat headrests. "You've had issues, I hear."

"We've had to postpone the flight for the past few years because of ruptures in the envelope. Some deficiencies were found in the balloon when we did tests in January, but they've been mended. We're still waiting for the new ballast we ordered weeks ago from an independent supplier. It's possible a sudden change in weather on the day could delay the launch again, but

I'm confident we'll fly on schedule this time. Let's go and see the lighthouse. If the white room doesn't impress you...."

In the ten minutes it took to drive from the garage to the lighthouse, Ariane learned things about Will. Following a bad marriage and an even worse divorce, he had lost his appetite for relationships, immersing himself in the balloon project as it kept him constantly busy. It was clear his obsession with the flight was like a drug addiction. Every dime he had went into it, he neglected friends and family, slept little, and looked tired and drawn, judging by the black circles beneath his eyes. The broad strokes of his past were obvious enough to a woman like Ariane, though the depth of his pain was something he chose to carefully hide.

Stopping in front of the lighthouse, Will killed the engine and climbed out of the Jeep, walking round to the passenger side to open Ariane's door.

"Thanks," she said.

"Where in the States are you from?" he asked, closing the passenger door.

"I was born in Puerto Rico but grew up in Illinois with my parents. These days, I spend most of my time at the research centre in California."

"High-speed jets to slow-rising balloon. Quite a change."

"Not really. My role is to carry out specific research in the upper stratosphere. Something I can't do from a scramjet."

Entering the faintly lit lobby of the lighthouse, Will pushed the lift button, biting his nails as he waited. The faint hum of machinery and the distant sound of waves crashing against the rocks outside created a ghost-like atmosphere. The creaks and groans the old lift made deepened Ariane's frown. During the lengthy wait, her eyes adjusted to the darkness, revealing the worn, weathered walls and the faint outlines of nautical maps and ancient photographs hanging in their dusty frames. She sensed Will had picked up on her impatience when she crossed her arms, making him hit the button three more times. Finally, the lift doors opened.

"Not the fastest lift," said Will.

Ariane remained mute as they stepped inside.

Will pushed B for basement and they waited for the lift's mechanics to kick in and take them down.

"Got stuck in here recently."

She viewed the interior, her frown even more pronounced. "Figures."

"I was out in time for Christmas, though."

She shot him a look. When she cottoned onto the joke, her serious face showed a faint smile.

The lift finally came to a bouncy stop, its worn springs groaning under the strain. For several seconds, an unsettling silence filled the compact space. Then, with a grating rumble, the lift doors shuddered open, revealing a low-lit foyer.

Red-faced, Will led Ariane into the foyer and opened a large, steel door. He located a panel for the lights and switched them all on. "We call this the white room."

She roamed her eyes around the facilities, checking out the benches and vast floor space. The white walls were immaculate with powerful spotlights brightening the room. In lieu of the overhead lights, the ceiling glowed with milky iridescence.

"Because it's white by any chance?"

"When the lighthouse was first opened in the 19th century, the basement was a storage room for mined chalk." He pointed at a sealed hatch in the ceiling, used for transferring the chalk directly from a delivery cart decades ago.

She could just make out the hatch between the lead pipes, crusted with white sediment.

He smiled. "And yes, because it's white."

Her attention was drawn to the spacesuits encased inside a glass locker. She strolled over to inspect them. The mission to the stratosphere would expose the crew to multiple dangers. The vacuum of space was an extremely hostile environment. Breathable air and the atmospheric pressures that prevented haemorrhaging were absent at high altitudes, so the spacesuits had to be top-notch, with every component in perfect working order.

Will rested his forearm against the cabinet. "Your spacesuit should arrive next month. I've sent them your measurements already. Thanks for those."

Ariane levelled her sparkling eyes on him, their radiant green reminiscent of a newly unfurled leaf glistening with dew. "Are you confident about this flight?"

"I guess so."

"Either you are or you're not."

"I'm apprehensive, but I think I'm entitled to feel that way, all things considered."

Ariane snapped out of her trance to a headache and dry mouth. She sipped some water, just a smidgen, and let it moisten her lips before swallowing. She wasn't sure how long she had been curled up against the wall without a visual on a clock. Tiredness dragged her eyelids down, but she wouldn't sleep. How could she? She had pictured the day going a whole lot differently. No one could have imagined this afternoon playing out the way it had. With time on her hands, she tried to make sense of the sociological mechanisms that had led to this catastrophic turn of events. What was this, Doomsday? A declaration of war? An invasion attempt? An accident? An act of God? The act of a dictator who thought they were God? Which guilty party had their fingerprints on the button?

The ground shook; the wall behind her shook against her back. Was a second attack taking place? Her heart raced, but the shaking stopped as quickly as it had started.

A hazy shape loomed in front of her, haloed in the silvery mist clinging to her visor. Years of training kicked in. She had taught herself never to panic when confronted with danger, to keep a clear mind and approach situations logically, calmly, and sensibly. She rose and took a cautious step forward. The shape took a human form, and she realised someone was standing in front of her. One of the crew?

"Will?"

Bright light knifed through her visor, flooding her face. It compelled her to squint. When no response came, her initial relief gave way to a rising fear.

THIRTY-FIVE

The office block was a skeleton of its former self, its grandeur lost to the blast that swept through the town. Rows of glassless windows stared out like hollow eyes, exposing the building's ravaged interior and oozing smoke like ghosts escaping from their graves. It seemed on the verge of collapsing at any given moment like a Jenga tower ten moves in, leaning unsteadily yet with defiance to succumb.

Will emerged from the ruins onto a wide road that used to be the main square. Making several trips back and forth along the road, trampling papers and documents strewn across the asphalt, some burned, others completely untouched, Will swung his head left and right, trying to absorb and process the scene. Walking sideways, forward, circling twice, heading backwards, throwing out his hands, he turned, walked forward some more, stopped, then resumed, figuring out the best route to take. He stepped off the footpath onto another road, checking out of habit for oncoming cars. There *were* cars, thick with debris and pulverised glass and concrete that had settled on them. Bodies lay smothered in black dust and soot, scattered all across the road. Some were in full form like burned mannequins. Some were so charred and shrunken it was hard to tell if they were male or female. One, its cadaverous face gripped in agony, lay in a twisted heap of broken bones. The sight of so much death highlighted the fragile nature of human existence and personal vulnerability. Still, he found strength and transformed his fear into a fierce, unyielding drive to find his son, believing he was still alive.

"Will again. Not sure if you heard my earlier transmissions, but I'm in a town that is completely in ruins. I have no idea what town it is. I can't make out any familiar landmarks. Where are you?"

He continued into the maze of ruins, lost in the town like a hopeless tourist. "We agreed on ten seconds between jumps. That means we should be relatively close. If you can hear me, I'm following a road at the moment, heading out of a small town. I'm trying to figure out exactly where we are. I'll reach out again when I see something familiar, and hopefully we can reconvene there. Stay safe."

He raised the gold shield on his visor. Ultraviolet radiation was not a concern anymore. There was different radiation to fear.

Rounding a large pile of rubble, he found a young woman covered in sticky wounds beside her handbag. A melted purse was gripped in her right hand. Will prized it from her slackened grip and poked through the compartments. No money was inside, not even a coin. He hunted for ID, bank information, store cards, anything that might contain her address or give an indication of the geographical whereabouts. The atomic heat had transformed the cards into molten plastic.

Across the road was a sign hanging perpendicular to the path, suspended by a brass bracket on a crooked wall. When he twisted it round, he saw it read *Le Bistro*. Turning slowly, he noticed another sign wedged among a pile of bricks. Curiosity and a faint trace of hope propelled him towards it. His gloved fingers, dirty and shaking, flipped it over to reveal two words: *St. Day*.

The sudden clarity struck him with the sharpness of an icicle, piercing through the fog of confusion and despair. St. Day. The name sparked a flood of memories. The image of his son, possibly lost, injured, or alone, became sharper and more insistent. With newfound determination, he tightened his grip on the sign, as if it were a lifeline. Checking the time and his oxygen, he ran through the sums.

Will spent the next ten minutes constructing a message in the road, using the bricks to form letters. He climbed upon a car roof and checked the legibility of his writing from up high.

Satisfied and mind made up, priding himself on his usual instinct to make the right call, eyes sharp and alert, he hurriedly crossed the road. "I know where we are and what–"

A wall collapsed in front of him, hurling bricks across the ground like a packet of spilled sugar. He stepped around the fallen wall and, when he glanced to see what it had concealed, locked onto a figure slumped against a wall twenty metres away in a cul-de-sac.

He hurried through the building's remains and emerged on a road on the opposite side. As he got closer, he saw the faint rise and fall of their chest—alive, perhaps barely. Their steamy visor obscured their features, but the nametag on the upper arm of their spacesuit told him everything he needed to know.

"Ariane, it's Will! Are you hurt?" He waved his arm to flag her attention. "It's me, Will!"

She hardly moved, and he feared she had passed out. It was dark in the lane, so he switched on his headlamps and shone them on her visor, hoping the bright light would cut through the condensation.

Her head moved; she looked up, then stood. She stepped towards him. "Ariane, it's me, Will! I can't tell you how happy I am to see you."

She didn't respond; she wasn't receiving him in her headset, suggesting she had lost audio. Or perhaps he could no longer relay outgoing messages. It might explain why he hadn't heard from the crew since he jumped off the balloon. Either that or they were already dead.

To make himself heard through two insulated helmets, he had to yell, "IT'S WILL!"

A small splash materialised on the inside of her helmet, and water cascaded down the visor. Ariane's flushed face appeared behind the plastic.

"ARE YOU HURT?"

She shook her head.

He held out his palm for her to see. "TAKE MY HAND!"

Mouthing the word *okay*, she cast a glance at her oxygen readout on her sleeve.

They lumbered out of the cul-de-sac, leaning on each other and linking arms. The road ahead was long and fraught with danger, but the sign had restored his orientation and resolve and he would follow it, no matter what obstacles stood in their path.

THIRTY-SIX

Rocking back and forth at the bottom of his parachute, Lloyd resurfaced from the depths of unconsciousness. His awareness slowly trickled back into his senses, and his first realisation was the absence of solid ground underneath his feet: a disorienting discovery. He was suspended, buoyed by an unseen force, and any movements he made were met with the surreal sensation of weightlessness.

As consciousness tentatively reasserted its dominion and his mind groped for information, he remembered the balloon. A vivid recollection emerged of his descent, the frantic struggle against gravity as he tumbled from the safety of the deck. What confused him was the strange scene stretched out before him: countless rectangular grids illuminated by flickering black and orange shards of light; barbecued debris lay among numerous scattered vehicles, as if dropped from above, with many lying on their backs like dead animals. It was a car park, two hundred metres in length, perhaps ninety wide at its greatest extent.

He looked up at the sky. His parachute canopy hung above him. He looked down at his suspended boots, swaying gently in the air. Was he still falling? If so, he must have imagined the car park. When he saw the smouldering coach, close enough for him to make out the scorched metal replacing the paint, its tyres melted into black puddles, and its charred driver fused to the seat, he knew it was real.

More painstaking seconds passed before Lloyd's cognitive faculties could piece the fragmented clues of his surroundings together and he deduced that he was stuck in a tree, oscillating in its branches.

He took a tally of his injuries. He hurt all over, but a few areas stood out, principally his injured shoulder. No internal alarms had been triggered on his spacesuit, meaning it hadn't become damaged in the fall. He could not assess the readings on his wrist computer; the parachute lines had pinioned his left arm behind him. Scratches in the polycarbonate plastic of his visor meant he couldn't see well. He was confident that his life support kept his oxygen and blood flowing, keeping his organs performing, keeping the radiation out, keeping him alive.

More attuned to his surroundings now, he determined the car park belonged to a medium-sized stadium, belching smoke from its ruins.

"This is Lloyd. I made it back, but I'm stuck in a tree. I'm tangled up and can't move my left arm. I've hurt my shoulder. I don't think it's broken, but it could be dislocated. I'm not sure. Do you copy?"

He waited for someone to acknowledge his mayday but got nothing. He was out of the stratosphere, but the drop he faced was no less dizzying. An awkward landing could still leave him injured. He had been terrified before, but sheer panic was in his eyes now. It was ridiculous, a man of his age letting his fear overcome him. He started hyperventilating, aware he was using up precious oxygen. But this just made him panic more.

He turned his head, a slow and painful process. "Help! I'm stuck in a tree from the jump. I can't get down. Will, are you hearing me? Ariane? I'm in a stadium car park. Does anyone copy me?"

Below him was a smashed-up SUV, one of a few cars still upright. He hung directly above the windscreen, where glass shards resembling prehistoric teeth stuck out from the seals, waiting should he fall. Other than falling, he could think of no other way out of this predicament. The margins were narrow if he wanted to avoid falling through the windscreen.

He suddenly missed his mother. They had lived together in a cluttered house. He'd been single his entire life. His needy mother and his demanding career had taken precedence over romantic relationships. He had dated a few ladies but had never been in love or even remotely infatuated. Women had never found him attractive, anyway. He had buckteeth that his upper lip couldn't conceal and a large forehead. He found looking in the mirror an ordeal. He never allowed himself to get close to anyone, partly because of his unusual living arrangements.

Confined to her double bed, his mother had suffered from numerous illnesses: pneumonia, bowel complications, strokes, to name a few. He had always been there to see her through the turmoil, giving her bed baths, feeding her medication, and ensuring she ate and stayed hydrated. Because all his attention was divided between his mother and work, he often neglected household chores. As a result, the rooms were dirty, cluttered, and smelled of rotting food in the overflowing bins. He and his mother were used to the foul odours that they had stopped noticing years ago.

On a regular Wednesday morning, he received tragic news from the hospital. "We've had the results of the latest tests," said the doctor, who put his hand on Lloyd's shoulder. "I'm sorry to say your mother has stage four breast cancer."

"Can you do anything? Is it terminal?"

"I'm afraid so. Sorry to be the bearer of such bad news."

"How long has she got?"

"Not very long. Months, weeks perhaps."

Lloyd tried to continue normally after the prognosis. His smoking increased from a single pack of cigarettes a day to two. The melancholia that had hung over him like a dark cloud in the beginning became more of an encompassing fog.

The breast cancer soon metastasised to her bones, brain, lungs, and liver. He watched her body shrink gradually in her hospital bed until one day, he arrived at the ward to find her room empty and sanitised, knowing she had passed. She *was* eighty-two and had lived a long life.

Lloyd was sentenced for tax evasion the day before her funeral and was forced to mourn her death from his new cell. His six-month sentence served as both a prison and a crucible for self-reflection, convinced the world had passed him by and that his best years were behind him. His mother was gone, his career in tatters. Life had nothing left to offer, leaving him stranded in the stagnant backwaters of his own disillusionment. As the days stretched into weeks and weeks into months, a spark of defiance ignited within him. He seized control of his destiny, prepared to rise from the ashes of his self-imposed exile and reclaim his rightful place in the world because he had nothing left to lose. It was time to start taking risks and strive for something that could pass for a life. Fresh starts and new beginnings, as soon as he made it out of prison.

And just like that, shortly before his release, Will turned up at the prison with a proposition, as if Lloyd's wish had been heard. In the space of a week, he had been accepted to join a flight on a balloon of his design to the edge of space, earning him a healthy pay packet. The inaugural flight was always the most dangerous because it was a trial by fire, flirting on the razor's edge of catastrophe, and things could easily go wrong.

But what had just transpired surpassed any definition of the term *wrong*. *Wrong* was an understatement. In the annals of aviation history, *wrong* did not encapsulate the magnitude of what had occurred.

Now he was stuck in a tree in a burning wasteland, quickly running out of oxygen. Then he remembered the quick-release buckles. Pressing them would detach him from the parachute, releasing him from this nightmare. In his haste to escape, he pinched the buckles without much thought, further twisting his shoulder as he slipped out of the harness, tilting his fall. He slammed into the roof of the SUV, landing on his front, and his visor gave an ominous crack. The impact was so forceful, it left a serious dent in the metal. As much as he tried to avoid the windscreen, his right leg swung through the gap, catching on the glass.

Rolling off the roof to the ground, he used his elbows to inch forward, clawing across the asphalt. He stuck his head up when he reached the tail end of the SUV and tried to stand up. He only managed to raise himself as high as the brake light. Pain like a hot nail had pierced his leg made it difficult to stand. He raised his knee and looked beyond the crack in his visor to find a thick shard of glass protruding above his ankle, slicing open the protective foam wall of his boot. No internal alarms had pinged yet. His suit still functioned, even with the breach and damaged visor. It would doubtfully hold and circulate the oxygen if he removed the glass, and he'd be left watching the readout count inexorably down from ninety-one per cent to zero. It would have to stay embedded in his foot for now.

Nearing the coach, still burning brightly, his shadow grew long and shaky as he dragged himself along. Breathing heavily through his nose, blood streaming into his boot, he fought to stay upright and focussed.

The next step was to try and find Will or hope for Will to find *him*. He trusted Will. Failing that, he would have to count on humanitarian aid. In a perfect world, rescue helicopters, military ambulances, and paramedics would all converge upon the scene, treating the injured and transporting them to safety. But this was far from a perfect world. In a perfect world, this would not have happened in the first place.

THIRTY-SEVEN

A blizzard of white-hot embers fluttering like fireflies filled the air as Peta and Donavon followed the perforated white line in the middle of the road, frequently brushing cinders off their suits.

They passed a male corpse on the side of the road, dressed in a tracksuit melded to his blackened skin. What looked like a dog leash was stuck to his burned hand. His broad shoulders were hunched in anguish. His eyes had boiled in their sockets, and the lips and gums had melted, exposing a set of teeth that seemed to accentuate a sneer of contempt.

Peta turned away. She had seen dead bodies while working in the hospital, but not like this, in such desecration.

"I blame Ariane," said Donavon.

"For the attack? I'm not sure she has the power or ability to nuke a country."

"I don't like her."

"You don't like anyone. But how is this her fault?"

"All that bullshit with the visor. Because of her, we've all been separated."

"It was hardly deliberate."

"She should have jumped after ten seconds."

Peta shrugged. "She couldn't see."

"No one invited her on the balloon. I objected to it. Will and Jefferson said nothing, even though they felt the same way. I knew it would end in trouble."

"Let it go!"

"Say that to me when our oxygen runs out and we take our last breaths."

Upon approach to a petrol station, the air ignited with two explosions. The first when the petrol pumps burst into flames; the second was an enormous eruption, causing burning fuel to stream from the broken pipes. Oily smoke curled into the sky, adding to the polluted ceiling.

They gave the station a wide berth to avoid the flames, but a third explosion shook the ground with concussive force, blowing Donavon off his feet. Giant jets of flame propelled wreckage high into the air like an active volcano.

"Are you okay?" asked Peta.

Donavon lay still, fearing he'd sustained an injury, or worse, a ruptured suit. According to Ariane, breathing in radioactive dust this soon after the bombs could prove fatal. Standing and inspecting his condition and that of his suit, he saw he'd been wrong on both counts. "I'm fine. We need to get away from here."

"How on Earth are we going to find a safe shelter?" Peta asked.

"I don't know. There's nothing here."

"What now, then?"

"Try and get our bearings. Do you know France at all?"

"I never said we were in France. That car we saw may have been French, but that doesn't confirm anything."

"That should be priority, then. Finding out where we are."

She suddenly turned and raced back to the petrol station.

Donavon held out his hands. "Where are you going?"

Peta ran across the forecourt, shielding her eyes against the brilliance of the fire as the heat threatened to blister her suit. She approached a blazing inferno of cars, the flames roaring with such intensity that she couldn't venture any closer. Forced to maintain a safe distance, she examined the cars, scrutinising their interiors and taking note of the licence plates. The heat radiated in waves, distorting the air with a hellish glow, but she remained focussed, determined to gather any clues that might hint at their whereabouts.

Donavon stood on the road in front of the petrol station. "What are you doing?"

Another explosion disturbed the darkness, a large flash of daylight for the barest moment as gushing petrol erupted from the pumps, dispatching fireballs, and causing tremors like the end of the world all over again.

Peta recoiled with a shuddering growl of terror and joined her cousin in the road.

"What the fuck was all that about?"

Peta glanced back at the petrol shop as a plume of black smoke burst through the windows, the roof caved in, and the walls folded neatly down on top of it.

"I think we're still in England," said Peta. "That's the good news."

Donavon grabbed Peta's arm and marched her along the road, away from the fire, stopping a safe distance. "How do you know we're still in England?"

"Those cars were all right-hand drive. All European cars are left-hand drive."

"Okay, detective. What's the bad news?"

"We could be anywhere."

"We're still fucked, then."

"Let's try and find the others."

She started walking. "This is Peta. I'm with Donavon, on a long road. This area, wherever it is, appears to be nothing but woodland. Anyone getting this? Do you copy?"

"Look who we have here!" said Donavon.

Peta spun round. A tired-looking black dog with massive legs and a jowly face trotted out of the woods and stopped in front of them, watching with sorrowful eyes, as if it had done something wrong and knew it. It pricked up its ears before sitting on its haunches. Donavon stroked its head. "Probably belonged to that dead dude in the tracksuit."

"Where did it come from?" asked Peta.

Donavon pointed at a gap between the woods where the surrounding fires had not yet converged. "Let's go see what's through there."

The path through the woods led to a human-made clearing by the felling of trees. It turned into a field, and a small town in the distance revealed itself through the smoke.

Donavon turned his head slowly from side to side. He had been prepared for destruction, but this was something else.

Peta swept her eyes across the harrowing sight, assessing the scene. "It's all gone. How many people have lost their lives here?"

Donavon's voice was stripped of emotion. "Everyone."

"I can't believe this is happening. Who caused this?"

"My money's on the Russians," said Donavon.

"That was my first thought, too."

"They fired a missile at the UK six months ago and then attempted to cover it up."

"Wasn't it a failed test missile that veered into the North Sea?"

"The perfect excuse for an intended but failed attack. I guarantee they're behind this."

"Why attack us, though? What did *we* do?"

"They're a law unto themselves. They think they can do what they want without consequences."

"I know someone just like that," said Peta, looking at her cousin.

"Funny."

"Perhaps it was a mistake," she said.

Donavon exhaled loudly. "Yeah, someone in the Kremlin accidentally pushed a button and set off a load of missiles. Get real!"

"There's been rising tension with Iran. They might have been behind this?"

Donavon started walking across the field. "The Iranians have several miles of North-Korean built tunnels where they stash ballistic missiles, chemical warheads, and nuclear bombs. But I doubt it was Iran."

When they came across a red parachute tangled up in its lines, they were relieved at least one of their crew members had landed safely. "I wonder whose it is," said Peta.

Donavon looked up at the crimson sky. "They probably went into the town. That's where we should go."

Peta spotted a survivor wrapped in a black shawl, sinking to her knees, softly and silently, the eyes of someone who had just seen people die. Without urgent treatment, she wouldn't live long. Hospitalised or not, no treatment in the world could undo the effects of severe radiation sickness.

Peta pointed at the woman. "Look!"

Donavon followed her finger. "I see her."

"Should we help her?"

"How?"

Peta shrugged. "She could be badly wounded."

"There's nothing we can do for her."

The woman struggled to her feet, turned, and went on her way, holding her hand against her head.

"I don't think she's seen us yet. Let's follow her."

"Why?"

"We're going that way, anyway."

The woman moved cautiously, her head bowed as if trying to avoid attention. Every so often, she glanced up to verify her surroundings.

Peta and Donavon followed her into the town, leaving a cautious gap between them. Instinct told Peta the woman was no threat, though the situation was as unpredictable as bizarre and understood Donavon's reservations.

The mere fact there were any survivors at all was nothing short of miraculous. Among the destruction, this was the silver lining: not everyone had perished. But those lucky enough to have survived had received high-dose, whole-body radiation and would go downhill fast.

The woman dragged herself along a narrow path between destroyed buildings, turning left at the end of the alley, which fanned into a broad esplanade, and lumbered out of sight.

Donavon stopped. "That's enough. We're wasting time."

Peta entered the alley, her eyes raised above her to avoid the dangling steel and concrete that could fall at any time.

"Why are you still following her?"

"I want to see where she's going."

"This is ridiculous. We don't have time for this."

She blanked him and kept going.

On the other side of the alley, something stopped her in her tracks.

THIRTY-EIGHT

St. Day was once a thriving copper mining town, experiencing significant wealth and growth during the peak of the industry. This period of prosperity led to the development of terraces of granite cottages and numerous shops, reflecting the affluence and activity of the time, and built to accommodate and serve the growing community of miners and their families flocking to St. Day in search of work and opportunity.

Like any good thing, the copper industry began to decline and eventually collapsed, ending St. Day's economic fortunes. As a result, the town, filled with the sounds of commerce and daily life, gradually fell silent. Now the cottages and shops that sprang up during the boom years lie in ruins, their once-sturdy walls reduced to rubble.

Peta checked the time and her oxygen supply, making her calculations as Donavon came up behind her.

"Stop running off! You're like a hyperactive child."

"Look!" she pointed at the ground.

Here St. Day. Lighthouse 18 miles west. Go quickly. Will.

The message, crafted out of bricks spanning the length of a city bus, was to the point and very clear.

"Will left it for us," said Peta. "It was his parachute we saw. I told you we were still in England. He wants us to go to the lighthouse."

"The white room," said Donavon. "It's deep underground, away from radiation. Do we have enough oxygen to get there?"

"We'll have to move fast."

Donavon ran through some calculations, using his fingers to help him count. "We'll have to maintain an average speed of about three miles per hour. That will take about six hours, as long as we don't get lost or injured. Possible under normal circumstances, difficult in a spacesuit."

"We can make it."

"How can we be sure the lighthouse is still standing? If the winch cable attached to our balloon was severed by the bombs, it means the lighthouse was probably hit, too."

"Possibly. All we can do is pray."

"Pray? That's your plan?"

As plans went, Peta knew getting to the lighthouse was their only option. "Do you have any better ideas?"

Donavon turned his eyes around the scene and threw out his arms. "No."

"Then shut up; let's go!"

"Wait!" Donavon started kicking the bricks, breaking up the message.

Peta pushed him back. "Ariane and Lloyd might not have seen this yet."

"Nor any survivors. May as well be handing out maps and invitations."

He finished destroying the message, earning him a look of contempt from Peta. Nearby, the black dog reappeared with its melancholy eyes fixed on them. Its sorrowful expression bore a silent disapproval, as if tacitly siding with Peta.

Leaving the town, they took off up a hill and headed west, moving slowly in their heavy spacesuits. Unlike the hundred and twenty-seven-kilo spacesuits worn by astronauts on the international space station, theirs weighed forty-five, though still substantial.

Donavon rechecked his computer without breaking stride. "My oxygen's at eighty-nine per cent. Yours?"

"Ninety."

Peta radioed Will repeatedly. He might not communicate back, but he might hear her status reports. She informed him she and Donavon had seen his message and were on their way to the lighthouse.

"Will must have written that message because he can't get through on the radio. It must have been damaged during the skydive."

Donavon nodded. "Ariane's, too."

"Yes, and Lloyd's. I'll keep trying them."

Peta took the lead, and Donavon slotted in close behind, slipstreaming like a cyclist, not that any physical benefit was gained.

Passing through the ruins of a small village, they stopped at a body pinned beneath a fallen post, barely recognisable as human. Peta saw something shiny poking out of their trouser pocket and removed it. Attached to a set of keys was a Swiss Army knife with a three-inch blade. The other sharp tools were tucked into the handle. She couldn't pull them open with her gloved hands but thought it could prove useful. She slipped it inside the utility pocket on her thigh.

The sight of the body made her suddenly anxious, and she twisted round in a panic, as if unseen eyes were studying her and Donavon from every angle. Every corner seemed to hide a lurking presence, and she couldn't shake the feeling of being constantly watched.

Donavon had walked ahead already but paused mid-step and turned back to face her.

"What is it?" asked Peta with alarm.

"Nothing."

She walked quickly and caught up with him, glad she was not alone. "You okay?"

He nodded. "Absolutely fine."

She shook her head. "How can you say that?"

"What?"

"That you're fine."

"I suppose it's a long story and not that interesting."

"We have plenty of time."

"Do we?" He glanced at his wrist computer. "In less than seven hours, we could be dead."

"And still, you're fine? Absolutely fine?"

"I'm alive, aren't I?"

Whether he was really fine or not, she stopped talking. As much as she didn't want to be alone right now, if she had to be stuck with him, it was best they didn't speak. They had to conserve every bit of oxygen they had, anyway, and talking was taxing. Still, she continued with the radio announcements, just in case the others hadn't seen Will's message. "Ariane, Lloyd, if you can hear me, we are heading to the lighthouse in St. Ives.

The white room is our best chance at riding this out. We landed near a town called St. Day, eighteen miles from the lighthouse. Head west if you get this message. Will is already on his way there now. Out."

"You're wasting your breath. If they can't transmit, they probably can't receive."

"You just worry about yourself. You usually do."

"That's how you stay alive."

"Well, let's hope—"

Out of nowhere, a badly injured man lurched at Peta. His face was a bloody rictus, blistered and cut. His clothes were soaked in blood, and the buttons on his shirt were ripped open, revealing a bloodstained bandage haphazardly wrapped around his chest. His lips moved, but she heard no sound; it seemed like he was saying *help me* over and over. Without warning, he grabbed her savagely by the arm, his grip tight and desperate.

Peta shrieked, her voice piercing the inside of her helmet, and frantically shook him loose, stumbling backwards in terror.

Donavon lunged and punched the back of the man's skull, sending him tumbling headfirst into the ground. He remained still for a moment, then gradually pulled himself to his hands and knees. He tried to stand, but Donavon stomped on his back as if squashing a can with the sole of his boot, flattening him out on the grass. He turned the man over and threw slow punches, crushing his face with left and right blows. Blood skooshed from his mouth and nose, yet Donavon continued to beat the remains of his face to a mash of skin, blood, and bone.

Peta planted her hands on her helmet, sickened by such an awful sight. "You killed him!"

"He was almost dead, anyway."

"You didn't have to kill him!"

"The right choice keeps us both alive. It's not hard."

She shook her head. "You psycho!"

Donavon wiped his bloody fists on the grass to clean his gloves. He raised himself off the corpse, acting like nothing had happened. "There'll be desperate survivors everywhere. We need to keep out of sight. Can't risk an ambush."

THIRTY-NINE

Will and Ariane marched across a large field, the scalded grass brushing against their boots. Her right hand was tightly clasped in his, a constant anchor in their journey. She maintained her position a half-step behind him like she had for the last four, perhaps five miles.

They hadn't exchanged one single word during that time. With communication only possible by shouting, they had to opt for silence. The difficulty of walking in a spacesuit was already considerable, but navigating the treacherous, nuclear-blasted landscape made the long journey exponentially more challenging. Every step demanded concentration and drained their stamina. The ground was uneven and littered with debris, forcing Will to carefully manoeuvre himself and Ariane. It left them battling not just the terrain but their own physical and mental limits, making progress sometimes slow but constantly exhausting. In preparation for their flight, they had followed a strict exercise regime devised by professional trainer and had attained the highest fitness levels, but in their heavy spacesuits, it was akin to carrying a ten-year-old child across a long, sandy beach.

With the attack now four hours old, they slogged on, every minute precious, maintaining a steady pace to make it back to the lighthouse before their oxygen ran out.

"Will again. I'm with Ariane. We are close now to a town called Portreath. We must have detoured. I can see the coast already. If you can get yourselves to Hayle, you can follow the Great Western Railway into St. Ives. That's your best bet. We will follow the coastline all the way down to Hayle. Hope you hear this. See you soon. Out."

Will had set himself milestones. Not so much in terms of miles, but minutes. He wanted to make it to Portreath in the next quarter of an hour, and for the fourth time in a hundred paces, he checked the time on his computer.

Will stopped Ariane suddenly. "You hear that?" He heard no reply from her; she couldn't hear him either, but he kept speaking. "Sounds like a helicopter."

The visor deadened most noise. Still, Will was convinced he heard the whir of helicopter blades.

Striding up a small hill and crossing a flattened fence, he discovered it was not a helicopter but a large turbine engine, its propeller in motion. A chunk of warped metal was catching on the spinning blades. Will could feel the staccato sound deep in his chest.

Moving beyond the engine with a safe enough distance, he stepped on a fallen sign that read: *Remote Radar Head Portreath operated by the RAF.*

Judging by the destroyed planes scattered on the asphalt, he deduced they were on a runway. No standing watchtowers were at the base and, from what he could see, no guards either. A dome-shaped structure resembling a golf ball half-trodden into the turf might have offered a refuge had it not been for the gaping hole in the roof, from which smoke billowed.

"RAF Base at Portreath, Cornwall. We require a rescue. If anyone can hear this transmission, please send a rescue."

Will repeated the message, hoping the airwaves were being monitored by military personnel somewhere in the country.

The engine exploded in a sudden powerful blast, causing shockwaves.

Will and Ariane dropped to the ground as mini asteroids rose and fell, lighting up the sky.

"ARE YOU OKAY?" he shouted to Ariane.

He heard a stifled, "YES!"

Giant, orange tongues spewed out from the windows of a crashed plane. It had left a trail of luggage and warped metal across the airfield. Will visualised its instruments going haywire from the EMP, crashing as it attempted to land, both wings snapping as they dug into the ground, fuselage cartwheeling, crew and passengers dying instantly.

Walking the length of the runway, they arrived at a fence crowned with barbed wire. Further along, the fence had fallen, leaving a large gap to pass through safely so as to avoid tearing their spacesuits.

Staggering, sometimes tripping, their space boots growing heavier on their feet, they crossed fields and meadows, passing dead livestock and charred bodies. A burning barn overlooked a large pond, the flickering flames reflecting against the water's surface.

St. Day to Portreath was manageable, but the long journey to Gwithian and then Loggans drained their energy, leaving them in desperate need of a rest. Will's hunger and thirst were affecting his ability to think clearly, and the darkened sky threw off his navigational sense, sowing doubts in his mind about the quickest route back. Nevertheless, he was satisfied with their progress. Ten to eleven miles had been covered already, and after a short trek beyond Loggans, a sign announced Hayle.

Will and Ariane found the path up the hillside hard going. The terrain was rocky and became steeper. Will decided to wait to take a break until they reached the top. Just the anticipation of resting spurred him on. Upon arrival, weak and breathless, Will sat Ariane down in front of a boulder at the summit and slid languidly to the ground beside her, leaning his head against the rock. Every time they reached the top of a hill or broke through the trees, he imagined, with a fragile thread of hope, that the land was unharmed, and the air was untainted, colour flourishing back, spreading shades of green like floodwater across dry land. As before, he was left bitterly disappointed as he stared out at the desolation.

Following the five-minute break, Will's brain told him to get up, but he couldn't, much too tired to move. Ariane must have been exhausted, too. He was impressed at the grace with which she had carried herself this far without her sight. What must be running through her mind? Was she distressed? Her experience and training had taught her to react and behave in adverse situations with calm and composure. Apart from the fleeting glimpse when he found her in St. Day, he hadn't seen her face since 50,000 feet when they had all pulled down their gold shields to avoid the ultraviolet and infrared rays, and her beautiful face had vanished behind her visor.

The steep uphill climb had been a slog. The downhill was their reward. The slope levelled off and led to the outskirts of Hayle, another town razed by fire. It was a disheartening sight, making the final leg of their journey an eternity of daunting reckoning as Will waited to find out if St. Ives had survived the worst of the onslaught. He knew it had been hit. Not only had they seen the bombs strike from the balloon, but they had also been on the receiving end of the shockwave, which violently rippled along the cable and rocked the gondola. The explosion may have been powerful enough to topple the lighthouse, but Will remained optimistic that it had stood firm, shielding the white room beneath it like a bird protecting its eggs.

He checked his oxygen supply, depleted to thirty-nine per cent. Ariane's read a concerning thirty-two per cent. Another rest stop was in order, but it would tighten the noose around an already constricted timeframe. He had to consider Ariane's oxygen, too, as she was burning through her tanks much faster than him. Time was now their enemy. They couldn't build any slack into their journey, so instead of taking another break, Will took their pace up a notch.

They reached a river as a body drifted past, twisting and turning in the current. They followed its banks for a time until it veered off into a patchwork of pools and streams, mashed into a muddy porridge. The remains of a wooden trestle bridge seemed like the only way across the river, even though it could collapse under the slightest pressure. They advanced slowly across the bridge, holding tightly to the rail and each other. It held, and on the other side, Will saw orange flames spiking through the trees. Impatient to find the Great Western Railway, he glanced at the time. That he hadn't come across the railway line yet threw his navigational sense into further doubt. Had they detoured again? One wrong turn, one more delay, and they wouldn't make it back before their oxygen ran out. The same questions crowded his mind. Was the lighthouse intact? Were Jefferson and Todd still alive? Would he find his son? Was the white room even accessible? Would they be safe down there? Were rescue parties scouting St. Ives?

Stopping to catch their breaths, Will ran a bearing check. Reassessing their surroundings and above to determine where the sun was setting behind the black smoke choking the sky, recalibrating his inner compass, running brief checks on their oxygen supplies, he set off again, towing Ariane as he would a reluctant child.

Thrown by the darkened sky and change in landscape, he had to overcome his disorientation, trust his instincts, and try to identify landmarks which, however altered, he'd committed to memory over the years.

His doggedness paid off when, just ten minutes later, he stumbled upon the railway line.

FORTY

Five hours since the bombs...

Avoiding main roads and steering clear of towns and villages to prevent any unwanted confrontations, Peta and Donovan travelled cautiously across the landscape. Their path eventually led them to a river running beside a cluster of trees standing proudly in full leaf, miraculously untouched by the blast. The lush greenery provided a hopeful contrast to the surrounding destruction, offering a moment of respite and a rare glimpse of nature's resistance.

Donavon glanced at the data on his wrist computer. "What, fourteen more miles?"

Peta had been quiet for some time, still reeling from the shock encounter with the injured man. She had learned a hard lesson. It was each to their own; this was no environment in which to play the good Samaritan unless you wanted to wind up dead. In a sick sort of way, Donavon was pleased it had happened.

"Fourteen would you say?" he asked again.

Receiving no response, he turned to find Peta was nowhere to be seen. "Where have you pissed off to now?"

He turned full circle and spotted her lumbering to the top of a nearby hill, crowned with an obelisk that looked damaged even from this distance. He chased after her up the steep hill, battling against the cumbersome weight of his space gear, ill-suited for such activity. He could feel the sweat trickling down his back and his breath growing heavier. He put his hands on his hips at the top, walking in a wide arc, and doubled over to replenish his lungs.

Peta roamed the summit, her eyes fixated on the ground as if looking for something.

"What the fuck, Peta? Will you... stop running off?" He paused to catch his breath. "What are you looking... for?"

Her behaviour became even stranger when she dropped to her hands and knees.

Receiving no answers, he threw his arms up and headed to the obelisk, reduced to wreckage on its cracked concrete base. With his headlamps switched on, he angled the light to flood the obelisk, inscribed: *The County of Cornwall to the memory of Francis Lord de Dunstanville and Basset A.D 1836.*

He knew where this was. The historic landmark, the oldest obelisk in southwest England, confirmed they were in the right region. He verified his oxygen, estimating the miles standing between the site and the lighthouse and if enough remained in the tanks to get them back in time, but was still none the wiser as to Peta's odd behaviour.

"Are you done?" he asked, returning to her at the summit.

She was still on her hands and knees, crawling in endless circles. "No!"

She stopped. With the Swiss Army knife in her right hand, she stabbed at the soil, chopping it loose.

"What *are* you doing?"

Her teary eyes widened behind her visor.

One look at Peta's face and he knew. This was where it had happened.

"He's here!" she said. "My father's here!"

Peta was transported back two decades to when she was eight, remembering the day of his passing like it just happened. She had been turning cartwheels and doing handstands on the hill when her palm hit a sharp stone. "Ouch!"

"Show me!" said her father.

A spot of blood pooled on her skin. He wiped it clean with a handkerchief. "You'll live."

He found the smooth, pointed flint that had caused her the injury. "You know what this is, don't you?"

"What?"

"It's probably part of an ancient arrowhead. It's believed that several tribes fought over this site during the Neolithic settlement."

Peta looked at her hand and sucked off the fresh blood oozing from the nick.

"Am I boring you?" he asked, suppressing a smile.

"You said we were going to get a hot chocolate."

His smile grew. "Well, seeing as it's Christmas, I think we should take this present out of your ear in case it gets lodged there forever."

He drew his fist back from her neck. A locket on a bronze chain fell out of his hand, swinging on his finger.

Peta's eyes widened and sparkled. "A necklace?"

He opened the heart-shaped locket, revealing a picture of them together. "If ever you feel scared or lonely, open up this locket and you will see everything is fine because Daddy loves you."

"I love it!" She hung it around her neck and tucked it inside her coat.

He smiled. "Now, about that hot chocolate. I'll race you to the bus stop."

Peta sprinted down the hill with the smooth, powerful motion of a young greyhound, every muscle propelling her forward, her breath pumping steam.

At the bottom, she paused to rest and, as she turned, saw her father had collapsed at the summit.

Peta charged back up the hill, reaching the top to find him prostrate and blue in the face. She stared, waiting for him to get up, smile again, and start talking.

"Daddy, wake up!"

When paramedics arrived a half-hour later, they declared him dead at the scene. He had suffered a heart attack.

His funeral had been a small, solemn affair, unfitting for a man with such a large appetite for life and adventure. Standing at the spot of his passing with a handful of his close friends and family, including a nineteen-year-old Donavon, Peta had never heard a silence so eloquent. His ashes were placed in a hand-carved, wooden box together with the arrow-shaped flint he'd been holding at the time of his death. Peta had added her bronze locket. A shallow hole was dug, and the box was buried in the ground. Peta, her heart sad and empty but helped by prayers, bade farewell. It was a day of tremendous significance. Not only had she lost her father, a loving, stable influence in her life, but she was also now in her mother's primary care and knew and feared her true nature. It marked the beginning of seven long years of physical and psychological abuse.

"I want my locket!" said Peta.

"It's buried here?"

"In a wooden box with my father's ashes."

Open the locket in times of fear and loneliness. That had been her father's only wish. She could lay claim to both and wanted to see his face, that moment frozen in time.

Donavon bent down until his face was level with hers. "It will take ages to find it. We don't have time for this. We will die if we stay here."

"It's right here, I know it."

Donavon stood. "You really want to vandalise his grave?"

She stopped digging, the grief curled up and smouldering inside her like contained smoke.

She examined the grey land stretching in every direction beyond the hilltop, rolling dunes of scorched grass like she was adrift in the ocean during a severe storm with enormous waves surrounding her. In between the hills, toppled pylons, nothing more than twisted and warped steel frames, dotted the land, with fires burning in every direction.

She turned to the obelisk, feeling the hurt child in her all over again. "You're right. I don't know what I was thinking."

Donavon put his arm around her and hoisted her up. "We don't have much time. We must go!"

FORTY-ONE

Donavon and Peta arrived at a gate that opened onto a wide belt of land with a scrawl of drystone walls dividing the fields into multiple rectangles. For some reason, it evoked memories of Donavon's time in the RAF as a helicopter pilot. Training had been mentally and physically stressful, involving military field skills that included handling weapons and first-aid. He'd been forced to leave the RAF after nine years of service. For failing to abide by rules. For violent misconduct. For suspected substance abuse and excessive drinking. Take your pick. He'd been in training one week when he experienced his first brush with authority. Punching a colleague for dissing his untidiness was one of his more regrettable mistakes, tainting his reputation.

Even at an early age, he had demonstrated both a reflex and a skill for engaging in violence. School in London had been a grim place, where Donavon had gained a reputation for his constant playground fights. Whenever angered in adulthood, he couldn't deal with his rage without a trail of blood or beer bottles. He had always resolved disputes with his fists, but this was not considered an attribute in the RAF, despite a strong patriarchy and military-style loyalty to his country.

Donavon's trained eyes scanned the scene for any potential threats but failed to spot the one beneath him, tripped over a rock, and stumbled. Luckily, it was of no consequence as his reinforced boots protected him from injury. He drank some water through the straw connected to his in-suit drink pouch. Water wasn't doing it for him right then; he could've murdered something a little stronger.

"Why were you dismissed from the RAF?" asked Peta, the Swiss Army knife still gripped in her hand. She hadn't spoken in almost an hour since the bizarre hill incident.

Donavon looked back over his shoulder. "Huh, I was just thinking about that."

"I have a sixth sense."

"And a big nose."

She shook her head. "Tell me, then!"

"None of your business!"

The gap between them widened until Peta hurried to catch him up.

"Why were you late this morning?" she asked.

"What's this now?"

"You were late this morning. We were all told to be at the lighthouse by five o'clock. You didn't arrive until seven. Why were you late?"

"What is this, the Spanish Inquisition?"

"Just a question."

"I had a late night."

He had forgotten to set his alarm the night before. He had also forgotten to close the curtains, so the sunlight streaming through the window replaced his alarm with true efficiency. He had left Simone… Sierra – whoever his latest one-nighter was – in his hotel bed. It had been a wild night of blissful sex under the spell of ecstasy—the *love drug*. This reminded him of the pills stored inside his backpack. Added motivation to reach the white room. If this *was* the end of humanity, he would go out in a transient state.

Sometime later, Peta stopped at a glade, crouched, and studied the merging and crisscrossing footprints on the ground. "More survivors?"

Donavon barely acknowledged and pushed on. About ten of the eighteen miles covered, Peta found the journey easier, her body now marching on autopilot as she thought about her father. Standing at the site of his passing had reignited her pain, inducing memories of their brief time as father and daughter. Sadly, she could barely remember his face and regretted not recovering that locket.

She had streaked ahead of Donavon but, as much as he antagonised her, didn't want to increase the gap. He wasn't thinking about the bloodied attacker he had dispatched. She was. It had freaked her out. Donavon had also spooked her with talk of an ambush, elevating her insecurity. Coupled with the footprints, fires, and the time restraints, her anxiety had gone into overdrive. She found it morally difficult turning her back on these poor injured strangers whose bodies were visibly breaking down. On the other hand, she knew Donavon was right to be cautious; she could do nothing to help them, and in times of desperation, people were capable of anything.

She stopped and enjoyed a long sip of water, relieving her dry throat, resisting the urge to have a second in case this was the last for a while.

Donavon caught up, and she carried on walking.

They completed the next hour without any interruptions, covering three more miles.

Peta thought it might be a good idea to stop and rest for a minute or two, so they sat against a tree.

"We made some good progress," said Donavon.

Peta concurred with a nod. "I wonder how far we are now behind Will."

"A mile or two."

"I hope Ariane and Lloyd are with him. If not...."

Donavon shrugged. "That's life!"

Peta shot him a cold look. "Do you even care if they're okay?"

"They're not my friends."

Peta stood, shaking her head, and walked away to show her disgust, muttering, "Do you even have friends?"

The next stint passed by in silence, with Peta avoiding any conversation with Donavon, now way ahead of her again. She could not keep up, the rest-stop having broken her momentum. Her life depended on being able to push herself when her lungs were begging for mercy and her stomach sat empty. It had been twelve hours since they had eaten a meagre breakfast, and her hunger made her weak and irritable. It was the ultimate test of endurance, especially with the bulky spacesuit hindering her agility, making the journey an even more arduous endeavour. Despite the challenges, she pushed her limits, determined to catch up to her cousin, driven by urgency and the family bond that tied their fates together.

She was still pondering his caginess. He was often innately secretive about his life, always keeping his cards to his chest because it allowed him to keep his options open and his dirty deeds confined. Which was why she hadn't yet challenged him about the money he had invested in Fable Sky. Money was supposed to be worked for, earned with toil and perseverance. Stable jobs had been scarce since Donavon had left the RAF. Despite occasionally teaching aerodynamic law at a few colleges and sometimes piloting for a helicopter charter service, the fact he had come into so much money so fast suggested it had been dirty.

He was a complex man, and she had always suspected he might be on the autism spectrum, though this was unproven. He tended to judge other people and looked down on anyone he considered stupid or ignorant, and as far as Donavon was concerned, it included almost everyone. He had a reputation for taking what he wanted and asking questions later... if he asked them at all. A trait that ran in the family. His aggressive nature came from having a tyrannical mother. She'd demanded best behaviour, utter obedience at all times. No whining. No showboating. The punishments had been hefty and harsh. On one occasion, seven-year-old Donavon had been strung upside down by both his ankles, leaving him vulnerable to a brain haemorrhage and causing him temporary loss of vision and crushed lungs from the weight of his organs. He had always been a troubled, hyperactive child, given to sudden tempers and difficult to calm and restrain once provoked. By twelve, he was already self-sufficient, and his mother became powerless to control him. The similarities in their backgrounds were not lost on Peta. Their mothers, who were sisters of similar age, had identical approaches to corrective behaviour. As a result, there was an understanding between them, a kinship spawned from being only children to abusive parents. But they were not similar, and they often ran out of things to say to each other, with different perspectives on life. They had known each other forever, but in the last decade, since Peta had turned twenty-one, they rarely saw each other. He had been a prominent part of her life during childhood, the best and the worst. Though she hesitated to admit it, for all his flaws, he was a good enough man, albeit constantly annoying, constantly getting into trouble. He would always be a social outcast of his own doing.

When they reached the next town, Peta had no idea how much time had passed. Within the silence of her helmet, at the mercy of the scorched environment, she completely lost track.

"Keep up!" said Donavon.

"I'm trying." She couldn't afford to dawdle but needed to rest. "Can we stop for a minute?"

"Again? I thought you were the fit one."

She bent over, hands on her knees, catching her breath to relieve a stitch.

From their elevated position, Donavon and Peta looked out over the alien Cornish landscape.

"I'm worried about Lloyd," she said.

"Why?"

"Ariane can take care of herself, but Lloyd's too…"

"He shouldn't have been on the balloon, anyway."

"Why?"

"He had no reason to be there. He did nothing during the flight, just sat there trembling like a frightened cat."

"Okay, so Lloyd and Ariane weren't supposed to be there. Anyone else? How about our captain? Should Will have sat this flight out as well?"

"He's not the captain."

Peta sighed. "Maybe go on your own next time."

"Maybe."

She shook her head. "Come on, I'm ready to continue."

By dusk, they reached St. Erth, as the many signs hanging above the damaged shops informed them. It was bordered by Hayle and on the periphery of Carbis Bay, home to the River Hayle.

The plan, Peta decreed, was to locate St. Erth station where the railway line split in three directions.

One line ran east.

One went southwest to Long Rock and Penzance.

The final route, the Great Western Railway, terminated at the end of the line in St. Ives.

FORTY-TWO

Eight hours since the bombs…

The sky was growing darker when Ariane and Will arrived at Lelant Saltings station. The single platform was marked with black stains, and Will was horrified by the thought they might be the remains of people caught in the blast wave. His head dropped, sickened right through again. What stories lingered in their immortalised shadows?

"Will, here. Ariane and I have just arrived at Lelant Saltings station on the Great Western Railway line. We're about to set off along the train tracks. I estimate that it will take us ninety minutes to reach St. Ives. Another twenty to thirty minutes to reach the lighthouse. We have about two and a half hours of oxygen left. You'll have about the same. You must hurry. See you soon. Out."

He held onto Ariane's hands and helped her down from the platform. He guided her onto the train tracks and steered her feet onto the sleepers between the ballast. "WE FOLLOW RAILWAY!"

Ariane spat water on the inside of her visor to create a clear spot. She looked around her and down at the tracks, and faced Will, mouthing *okay* to indicate her readiness. Will was happy to see her face again. Her fringe was soaked, her cheeks circles of rouge. They spared a smile for each other.

The tracks ran in a north-westerly direction. Following the light from the headlamps, they stepped from one sleeper to the next with their arms linked and strides perfectly synchronised. Will couldn't avoid imagining himself leading Ariane down the aisle. The thought brought a brief smile to his lips, knowing it would have looked comical under normal circumstances. Two aeronauts processing arm in arm along a railway line. This was anything but normal, and the contrast between the solemnity of a wedding procession and their current situation – following a deserted railway track under the encroaching darkness – was no laughing matter. Will remained vigilant. With some distance still to cover, it was beset with potential hazards. He couldn't afford to let his guard down.

After the first mile, Ariane was slowing them down. Her visor had fully steamed up again, and her steps had fallen out of sync, often tripping between the sleepers until Will caught her and corrected her stance. With such slow progress, meeting the deadline was a tall order, and their exhaustion threatened to halt their pursuit. The muscles in Will's legs had begun to cramp up as lactic acid seeped into them past the pain barrier and beyond. Would his body finally fail him, his muscles no longer responding to his brain?

Reaching Carbis Bay, Will recognised a petrol station on the road that ran parallel to the railway line. Still marked with lanes for cars to form orderly queues at the pumps, it reminded him he'd refuelled his Jeep there the day before. The attendant had started his dayshift sporting a piece of bloody tissue stuck to a shaving cut, he recalled.

The body sprawled across the tracks inside a tunnel that yawned like a hungry mouth caught him by surprise. The lips were drawn back in a silent scream; the bones were barely held together by sinew and cartilage. They stepped over it as though it were driftwood.

Seconds after emerging from the tunnel, he saw the body of a teenage boy lying next to a man. His father? The boy's head was intact. If you only looked at his top half, you would think nothing was wrong. His eyes were closed, and the skin on his face was untouched. But from the chest down...

Anthony flashed into his mind. Was he safe? The thought his son might be a victim of this atrocity was unbearable, and he swiftly rejected it, clinging instead to the desperate belief that he'd somehow escaped the danger. He clung to this hope with a father's steadfast commitment to protect his child at all costs.

He looked at Ariane. Perhaps her faulty visor was nothing short of a blessing. She had been shielded from the grisly sights and widespread destruction surrounding them. The protective bubble that kept her from witnessing the carnage also trapped her inside a prison of terrifying possibilities, where the unseen world bred fears more intense than any she could see. Sounds, from distant explosions to the faintest rustle, would only feed her imagination, making her conjure up vivid and terrifying scenarios.

At nine-thirtyish, they finally drifted wearily into St. Ives station. The old transport hub stood broken and deserted. Will carefully helped Ariane step up from the tracks, his grip firm and reassuring, and joined a road that led into the heart of the town. The bombs had knocked out the electricity, but the faint glow from the multiple fires, lighting up piles of rubble two and three storeys high, guided them.

On the other side of the town, they followed a path that ran uphill. By the time they reached the top, Will was out of breath, and his calf muscles had cramped. Tired right through, he paused at the top of the path, facing the empty clifftop that stretched out before him. From his high-up position, he had a panoramic view of the town's shattered peace below, and the scale of this catastrophe became even more apparent. The bay area was lit by the glow of hundreds of fires, their reflections shimmering across the otherwise dark waters. An unimaginable toll of human remains buried in the wreckage had Will shaking his head in despair. He turned his back, facing the black void of the clifftop once more.

A quarter of a mile and they would finally be back at the lighthouse. He could see it, showing like a white pinprick on a sheet of black paper. It was a critical moment, the unknown element. To think he had been there only that morning when life was still normal, and ignorance was bliss.

"NOT FAR NOW!"

Unsure if Ariane heard his voice, he glanced at his wrist computer. Approximately forty-five minutes of oxygen was left in his tank. He grabbed Ariane's left hand and checked her oxygen. She had much less than him. It jolted him forward. He had to press his other hand against his ribs to soothe a stitch he had acquired climbing the hill, now threatening to debilitate him. Despite the pain, he increased his pace, virtually dragging Ariane along as he hustled her towards the lighthouse. She did not resist, silently willing to endure the necessary measures to reach safety. Dehydrated and desperately hungry, their oxygen supplies dwindling to critical levels, they pushed themselves the remaining distance and, finally, against all odds, they were back.

Will had spent the last seven hours reassuring himself the lighthouse stood unscathed and in its full form. It had endured almost two centuries of intense weather, a towering presence of stability and strength, its unwavering light slicing through stormy skies and suffocating fog, offering a semblance of hope and order to the sailors who had always relied on its guidance. That even after the shocking events of that morning, it stood in defiance of a world turned upside down.

Reality shattered his conviction.

In that dark moment, as hope evaporated and his heart sank, the remains of the old lighthouse mirrored his own sense of disillusionment. It left him grappling with the harsh truth of the situation. He immediately experienced that sinking feeling you got when you knew you had made a wrong decision, only this time it would cost them their lives.

"IT'S GONE!"

FORTY-THREE

The lighthouse was a ghostly silhouette against the night, both tragically beautiful and profoundly haunting. A quarter of its normal height, the tower was mostly missing, ripped away by a powerful force, and all that remained of the hollowed-out base was its crumbling walls, somehow still circular and full of holes and marks as if it had taken a pounding from a division of army tanks.

Will just stared at its shell with tears, utterly defeated at this point.

"DESTROYED?" shouted Ariane.

That word pierced him like a knife.

The shock on Ariane's face was concealed behind her visor, but he saw her shoulders sag.

Stepping gingerly over a broad circle of scattered bricks, twisted metal, and shattered glass, he made his way through a gaping hole in the wall, wide like the mouth of a cavern. His headlamp beams brightened the darkness. Somewhere beneath the rubble was the white room, entombed by the tower that had stood sentry above it.

Sickened and sad, he left the ruins and headed out into the darkness to the launch site. The explosions had scorched the landscape for miles and miles, burning foliage brittle and black. Taking in the stark scenery, reliving that morning's anticipation and excitement, he looked up at the sky and traced the vertical path their balloon had flown. Taking small steps forward, he trod on something solid. When he looked down, he saw it was the metal frame that had tethered Fable Sky to the ground. The winch drum, crushed like an empty beer can, lay on its side in the distance, and the procession of parked cars that owners had brought to the launch site had been picked up and hurled across the clifftop like toys, some hanging precariously over the edge.

Where were the spectators? Their bodies? Will stared at the burned grass, stained with the blood and shadows of a thousand onlookers. There one minute and gone the next. Instantaneous non-existence. Slaughtered together, smashed by the powerful shockwaves and flames, and flashed to vapour and carbon dust. Had they known it was coming? Had they tried to run, or had they understood running was futile and dropped to their knees, hundreds gathered like Muslims turning towards Mecca? He thought about those young boys holding onto their balloons in support of the crew before launch. And all those women, all those men, all those children. Incinerated together as they tried to escape, caught up in a stampede as the blast engulfed them. Had his son been among the victims? He could only hope his ex-wife had picked Anthony up after the launch and taken him back to their house in Salisbury, out of the blast range. Unless a massive swath of the country had also been hit? Something in his gut told him this wasn't an isolated incident, with more to the story. This led him to bitter recriminations about the government and its role in this. What had it done to protect its citizens from its enemies: domestic and foreign? How had it allowed this to happen? If this *was* widespread, the politicians, true to form, would have considered themselves before the greater population.

Quickly coming to terms with what could only be perceived as the end, he found himself strangely calm. It was as if he had stepped outside his own body, becoming a detached observer of his own fate. The situation should have filled him with panic and despair, but instead it left him oddly at peace. This out-of-body experience allowed him to see everything with an almost clinical detachment, as though he were a spectator in some play whose conclusion was inevitable and beyond his control. In this such state, he could reflect on the unfolding events with unusual clarity, accepting the finality of his circumstances with an inner peace that defied the world around him.

He glanced up at the ill-fated lighthouse where the flight control room had been. Jefferson and Todd were both dead.

Something's happening.

He thought about Anthony and Jaqueline one more time with sadness ripping through him. He had fallen out of love with her years before, their connection long since faded into distant memories. In these final moments, warm thoughts of her surfaced in his mind. These reflections were not born from rekindled affection but rather a symptom of his acceptance and reconciliation with the world. As he faced the imminent end, he found himself making peace with his past, understanding that soon he would be gone and none of this would matter. The love that had once been and the subsequent indifference were insignificant in the grand scheme of these last moments.

His head dipped, aware his life would end tragically. His final days would be spent waiting to learn which would kill him first: dehydration, starvation, or radiation.

If their lives *were* about to end, they could choose how to end them. How. When. Where.

There were several options. They could suffocate in their spacesuits. They could stride out to sea and drown. They could cremate themselves in the many fires still raging in St. Ives. They could throw themselves over the cliff. Or they could let the radiation take them under its deadly spell. He had thirty minutes of oxygen to decide how he wanted to die.

He closed his eyes, taking a deep breath as he struggled to hold it together, a string of curses escaping under his breath. In this pivotal moment, and not for the first time in his life, he faced a grave choice: he could surrender to his fate, letting it consume him, or he could muster the strength to confront this final challenge. It was a familiar crossroads, reminiscent of the countless battles he'd faced before, each demanding resilience and courage. With a determined exhalation, he decided this too would be a test of his fortitude, another obstacle to overcome in the story of his endurance.

Think. With a final anxious scan of the clifftop, he hurried back to Ariane, his pace quickening with every step.

She stood patiently, arms by her side, her headlamp beams bathing the lighthouse walls. What went through her head? She would know by now that all was lost, her mind reeling with frightening possibilities. Time was running out for Ariane, too, and soon she would be forced to suck down toxic air.

As he neared the lighthouse, something caught his eye and got him thinking, but his focus was drawn to the two people in the distance, both wearing spacesuits and closing in on the lighthouse.

FORTY-FOUR

Sunset had come and gone. There may have been a moon, but there was no trace. The power in St. Ives was out, and the mountains of rubble created gloomy canyons. A few buildings remained standing but looked as if the slightest cough might bring them tumbling down.

Leading Donavon through the town, Peta relied on the scattered fires to find her way along the cobblestoned streets, shimmering with a kaleidoscope of grey and orange light. She struggled to believe these human constructions had been so easily erased until all that marked one location from another was a pile of bricks.

At the intersection of two roads, she came to an abrupt halt, her posture tense and wary as if anticipating oncoming traffic. The strong wind whipped around her, creating a vortex of dust and glowing embers. A ribbon of smoke curled lazily from a nearby phone box, adding to the unsettling ambiance of the scene. She noticed a child's bicycle chained to a post, its tyres misshapen and oblong, its frame warped and buckled by intense heat.

"I have an awful feeling about this," she said, sensing they were headed to a promised destination that no longer existed.

Behind Peta, Donavon stepped over a dog, charred and disintegrating like his hopes. "I have from the start."

Further along the street, Peta threaded through scattered bodies. Some were like mannequins pre-arranged for a drama, others a more realistic sculpture of death.

"Sayonara, suckers!" said Donavon.

Peta twisted round. "What is wrong with you?"

"What?"

"Arsehole!"

To which he responded it was hardly the time for insults.

"You're so insensitive sometimes. What the hell is wrong with you? Seriously."

She shook her head, stunned that what was unfolding did not arouse in him the same shock or fear it did in her. She couldn't resist repeating herself. "Arsehole!"

The town gradually slipped behind them and the disturbing ruins gave way to a slope that ascended to the clifftop. It was steep; easy enough were it not for the speed limitations of the spacesuit and the fact they had already travelled eighteen miles on empty stomachs.

It was so dark on the clifftop they could scarcely find their way, despite their headlamps. For a moment, Peta imagined it was what deep space looked like as she maintained her pace, turning her head frequently to ensure Donavon was still close by. At one point, she waited to let him fall into step with her.

It had taken seven hours, but at last they arrived. Two sets of headlamps lit up the pale lighthouse, its details shrouded in uncertainty. From this distance, it was hard to discern whether it was intact or in ruin. The shimmering headlamps created an illusion of solidity, yet hints of external damage showed at the edge of perception.

Normally, the lighthouse could be viewed from miles away with its iconic lantern crowning the tall tower, dominating the skyline on a clear day.

As they grew nearer, it was clear all that remained now was a mound of rubble encircled by its jagged and shattered walls.

"I knew it!" said Donavon. "I fucking knew it!"

Peta was momentarily rendered speechless until she said, "At least we're all together."

"Great!" said Donavon, throwing his hands up into the air. "We don't have to die alone."

"Let's see what Will and whoever's with him have to say. They might know something we don't."

They stopped in front of their crewmates, four once again. They hugged each other awkwardly in their bulky spacesuits.

When Donavon drew back, the twin headlamps from his helmet illuminated Will's sullen face.

A foggy visor covered the face of the crew member by his side, casting little doubt as to who was behind the veil.

Donavon declared his frustration with a loud sigh. "What now, mastermind?"

Will pointed to his ear, his expression tense. Donavon and Peta saw his lips moving, but no sound reached their helmets, indicating his extravehicular communicator had malfunctioned. Frustration etched on his face, Will conducted a series of hand gestures, emphasising his plight. He then pointed at Ariane's helmet, signalling she too was without verbal communication. The urgency of the situation was clear; they had to rely entirely on visual signals and hand gestures to coordinate.

Will carefully lowered Ariane into a seated position on the ground, ensuring she was comfortable and could get some rest. Turning to the others, he beckoned them forward with a wave of his hand, miming a message that unmistakably conveyed, "This way!"

The urgency in Will's movements left little room for doubt, prompting them to follow.

FORTY-FIVE

Followed by Peta and Donavon, Will hurried through the cave-like opening in the wall, trampling glass and sharp, metal debris, his feet protected by the silicone soles and stainless-steel layers of his boots. He led them to the mound of rubble extending from wall to wall, spanning twelve metres. What remained of the lighthouse encircled the rubble like the fractured edges of a shattered bowl. He gestured towards the severed steel cables scattered limply across the rubble, their twisted forms akin to lifeless black snakes. The sight had caught his eye earlier as he made his way back from the launch site. The cables, once vital and taut, now lay discarded and inert.

Peta and Donavon exchanged puzzled looks, attempting to understand what Will wanted to say.

Determined to make himself clear, Will clambered over the bricks and seized hold of one of the cables, pulling it taut. He pointed at the sky, sketching box shapes with his hands in a game of charades, followed by a cross using his forearms to indicate there was *no lift*. Pointing at the ground, he popped up his thumbs, intuiting the lift could be intact below ground. To his way of thinking, if the lift had been stationed at the top of the tower when the bombs had knocked the lighthouse down, it would have been destroyed, and the empty lift shaft below ground would have filled with rubble. That would make getting inside the white room impossible. Conversely, if the lift had been underground, the rubble filling the shaft would be much shallower, extending only from ground level to the lift's roof, which he estimated to be twenty feet thick. This rationale led Will back to the cables. Since they appeared to be lift cables, there could be an intact lift. In fact, he was confident the cables were still connected. It was a small but telling detail.

Any hope of survival now hinged on the crew uncovering the lift so they could climb down inside and gain access to the white room. If it was there. If it was still in one piece. They had survived the flight. They'd survived the explosions. Now they had to survive the next half-hour. To do this, the recovery of the white room was their only chance. Whatever anguish or pain they felt, whatever tiny shred of hope remained, they had to take their bruises, pick themselves up, and work together to get the job done. He couldn't be certain the white room was undamaged or even radiation-free, or that trying to unearth the lift was a rational idea, but he had gone about as far as possible with caution. Will couldn't articulate this. He could try, but Peta and Donavon would hear only muffled, fractured sentences, and with time rapidly running out, they could not afford any more delays. Knowing they each had thirty minutes of oxygen or less, he positioned himself between the severed lift cables to do what needed to be done. Brick by brick, he set to work digging out the lift.

Donavon and Peta joined him in a triangular formation on top of the rubble between the cables.

Peta took a deep breath and burst into action.

Lean and quick with powerful arm and shoulder muscles gained during a lifetime of gym work, Donavon also burrowed through the wreckage.

Ten minutes into it, Will's strength waned as the adrenaline fuelling him dissipated. His lungs and eyes throbbed with pain. Aware of the limited time, he pushed through his aches and pains and crushing fatigue. His face had turned purple with the strain, his neck a web of sinew and muscle. He was down to reserves, running on autopilot with his last scraps of energy and determination feeding his tired muscles. It had been the most physically gruelling day of his life.

Part of the wall on the west side cracked and tore away, collapsing inwards and hurling more bricks onto the remains. It neither harmed anyone nor added to their workload. After a momentary pause, they got back to work, launching the bricks from the centre of the pile. Slowly, surely, they burrowed down, exposing more of the lift cables, which stretched through the debris like a lifeline, guiding their desperate efforts.

Overcome with a sudden spell of dizziness, Will put his hands on his knees to steady himself, waiting for the episode to pass through his deep breathing. He straightened his aching back and stretched his arms.

"No time to rest," said Donavon, launching a large slab of wall out of the forming crater. "You can rest when you're dead, which will be soon if you don't get a move on."

"He can't hear you," said Peta.

Something, Will didn't know what, urged him to see about Ariane before continuing. Peering over the rim of the crater, he saw her through the gap in the wall. She was on her feet, waving her arms frantically as if under attack by a swarm of bees. Alarmed, he climbed up the side of the crater and darted through the gap in the wall. He gently touched her shoulder to announce his presence.

She tapped her wrist, signalling with urgency. The images and text on her computer were flashing red. She had run out of oxygen.

FORTY-SIX

Ariane's in-suit drink pouch was completely empty, leaving her without water to either drink or clear her visor of condensation build-up. She had drained it over an hour ago and had become desperately dehydrated.

All she knew was that the other crew members had arrived fifteen minutes ago, yet they could not relay updates. Her mind raced with impatience and anxiety, frantically seeking details but feeling utterly helpless. The uncertainty amplified her thirst and the suffocating tension of the situation.

Things went from bad to worse when an alarm from her computer rang through her like a surge of electricity. She knew immediately what it was. She couldn't see. She couldn't move safely. She couldn't communicate. In a few minutes, she would no longer be able to breathe because the alarm warned her she was on the brink of running out of oxygen. All she could do now was stand and wave her hands to attract attention, hoping someone might rescue her before it was too late.

Showing the first signs of breathlessness, her shoulders and chest heaved with each laboured effort to stay alive. She tried to yell but couldn't find her voice; the air had been squeezed from her lungs, like her chest was trapped in an unrelenting vice. Sweat streamed down her brow, along her cheeks and jaw, and continued down her neck.

Her last full breath had already expired, and she was forced to starve herself of oxygen to protect herself from radiation. As the need for air grew unbearable, she knew she might have to remove her helmet. That moment of decision was just a few seconds away.

Supernovas of pain lit up her vision as the pressure in her chest intensified. She was on the verge now of passing out.

Then someone tapped her arm. *Will*.

She raised her hand and pointed at her wrist. What could he do, though? The spare oxygen tanks were inside the white room, and everyone would be showing similar oxygen readings to hers. Every second became indescribable torment. Forced to exhale her final breath, she gasped for air that was no longer available. Her quickened heartbeat throbbed in her head like a drum roll to certain death. Her chest and lungs were in agony. She started to convulse, head and shoulders gripped by seizure. Her legs gave way when she passed out, slipping into a deep, dark hole of painlessness. But gravity did not take her. Will, ever her reliable saviour, had anticipated her falling before her knees buckled completely and caught her.

Fresh oxygen unexpectedly flowed into her suit. Her breath caught with a loud gasp, bringing her back from the dead.

"TEN MINUTES!" Will shouted.

Will helped her to her feet and held onto her until she got her balance back. But she remained lightheaded, and her chest was still tight, making her nauseous.

Ten minutes Will had said. Until what? Her oxygen ran out again? Before something happened? What? WHAT?

Will grasped her hand firmly and guided her forward as he had done for the past seven hours. The flat ground beneath her feet gradually gave way to a rocky, uneven surface. Was the lighthouse completely in ruins? Her heart sank at the thought, but she had to see it to believe it. She hated this, not knowing anything. All she knew was Will had saved her life twice that day, and she had used more oxygen than him because she had perspired; it was the body compensating for the loss of fluids owing to the faulty heater inside her helmet and likely issues she suspected with the air-cooling ventilators.

She heard the muffled sound of bricks crashing against one another. She had to presume the crew was now digging out the white room, buried beneath the collapsed lighthouse ruins. She wanted to help them, but what use was a blind woman?

Weakened and weary beyond anything she had ever before experienced, she sat down on the rubble, unable to remain on her feet. If she passed out again, it'd be safer to eliminate the potential of a hard fall.

Her worst fears were then realised when the low oxygen warning alarm sounded again, the sinister shrill putting her on edge. Was that ten minutes already?

How many times had the spectre of death loomed over her that day? The alarm would be the last sound she heard, like a heart monitor flatlining. When her final few minutes of oxygen were depleted, she would have to resist the overwhelming urge to remove her helmet again, no matter how intense the agony became as radiation poisoning inflicted a slow, merciless death. Suffocation, by contrast, was a much quicker way to die, akin to drowning. First, she would pass out, then pass away.

FORTY-SEVEN

Donavon's oxygen tanks had plunged, like his optimism, to a critical three per cent. His breaths felt more precious and came with the anticipation the air would soon be thinner and more inadequate. "How much oxygen do you have?"

Peta glanced at her gauge; the daunting percentage glared right back at her. "I reckon seven or eight minutes."

Will had rushed back to Ariane at the summit of the crater. He had already given her one of his oxygen tanks as she'd run out. Now they were both on the verge of suffocation and held onto each other like a married couple sticking together to the end. All it needed was some melancholic violin tune to set the scene.

"Same. But these lovebirds are almost out of air."

Peta looked down at the foot of the crater, still a bed of rock and debris. "I'm not sure we'll make it. What do we do?"

"Just keep digging, Peta, or we'll never get invited to their wedding."

Peta bent over and continued digging. "Have you *ever* been invited to a wedding?"

"Shut up and dig!"

The crater formed organically, becoming a perfectly circular hole with gently sloping sides. Through relentless digging, the base of the crater had transformed into a cube with its sides squared off as they excavated deeper inside the lift shaft. The rubble was mounded in the corners, creating sloped banks. Every layer removed brought them closer to the lift, but there was still no sign. They'd dug about sixteen feet so far. If the lift was down there, they should reach it soon. If not, they would never get the white room back.

Peta's strategy involved carrying bricks and large chunks of timber out of the hole, using the slopes to climb from the shaft to the crater.

By contrast, Donavon hurled them, launching the bricks and concrete and lumps of metal like a shotput thrower. He was working twice as fast as his cousin, three times faster than Will had managed before relinquishing his post and tending to Ariane, who proved about as useful as Lloyd on board the balloon. Peta kept pausing, so technically, he was putting in the work of four in his determination to get the job done and save his and everyone else's lives. He wondered if Will had been over-optimistic and puzzled over alternative ways to get inside. Without access to the white room, their options declined to a dire choice: either remove their helmets and inhale poisonous air or face the consequences of asphyxiation within their sealed spacesuits. The latter was obviously not an option. They'd have to take their chances in the open and hope the radiation was weak or non-existent. Whatever the next few minutes revealed, they crept closer to the precipice of disaster.

The burning question was whether the lift was even down there, but he received the answer when he unveiled a sliver of metal. He pushed aside the bricks, revealing a smooth metal surface that could only be the lift they desperately sought. His adrenaline propelled him to clear away the remaining debris, uncovering the access hatch—a small portal, no larger than a car window, holding the key to their salvation.

"We're in!" he said, kneeling over the hatch.

Peta arched over his shoulder. "Is the lift damaged?"

Donavon leaned his head inside the opening and swept his headlamps around the interior, searching for signs of damage or obstruction that could hinder their descent.

Will peered down from the top of the crater and saw the light from Peta's helmet reflecting on the shiny metal surface, raising his hopes.

Donavon pulled his head out and looked over his shoulder, first at Peta, then up at Will. "Looks like it's still intact."

Climbing to the top of the crater, he approached Will to share the good news, but Will pointed at Ariane's life support system, then drew a line across his throat to indicate she had run out of oxygen again. Donavon saw the flashing lights on her wrist computer. He also noted Will's oxygen had dwindled to one per cent, giving him a few more minutes. He gave Will a thumbs-up signal and pointed to the bottom of the crater, confirming the lift had been uncovered and was safe to climb inside.

Will unclamped his last oxygen tank and disconnected the regulator hose, swapping out Ariane's redundant tank with his, buying her a few extra minutes.

She almost collapsed again, but Will held onto her, gently easing her down so she could sit. She nodded to confirm fresh oxygen flowed into her suit and she could breathe.

Will still had the excess oxygen circulating inside his suit. That bought him an extra minute, two at most.

FORTY-EIGHT

The total depth from the edge of the crater to the bottom of the lift shaft measured a daunting twenty-something foot. A small clearing emerged in the centre, revealing a flat sheet of metal that belonged to the roof of the lift.

Spooked by his internal alarm and the oxygen going stale in his suit, already feeling the stress on his lungs, throat, and eyes, he stood at the edge of the shaft at the bottom of the crater. The rubble inside the shaft had formed dunes at each corner, making it possible to climb in and out, but Will didn't have time to make his way carefully down the unstable slope. He jumped into the shaft, dropping almost ten feet and landing heavily on a pile of bricks, jarring his weak knee. He raised the hatch and fed his legs through the rectangular opening as if it led to another dimension. He slipped inside, flailing his arms as he dropped into darkness, once again jarring his dodgy knee upon landing. He already ached. Every limb and muscle. How much more could his body take?

Relying on his headlamps to illuminate the lift's interior, he swung his head from left to right. His mirror reflection looked superimposed like a hologram within the glass. He gasped for air, his chest tightening as he drew in his final breaths. The cacophony of his alarm persisted, a relentless warning that his tank was now dry, and he struggled against the suffocating grip of his suit.

As much an optimist as a realist, he knew the worst-case scenario might still come to pass. The white room might have imploded under the collapsed lighthouse. Radiation may have seeped inside. Holding his last breath, reliant upon everything going in his favour, he stepped up to the lift doors, his heart thumping with anticipation and the lack of oxygen reaching it. He placed his hands between the vertical line where the doors met. But without the power-assisted hydraulics and with his thick gloves making it impossible to establish a firm grip, he struggled to pry them apart. He grunted with the effort, his fingers slipping on the metal surface as he frantically wrestled against the stubborn doors. Desperate and on death's door, only seconds away from suffocation, he uncoupled his gloves, flexed his fingers like a pianist to improve his agility, and stuck his sweaty hands on the cold metal surface, sticking like the feet of a gecko. Summoning all his strength, he pried the doors open, managing to create a two-inch gap. He jammed his boot between the doors and squeezed himself into the narrow space, using his body to force them wider still until he pushed himself through to the foyer.

His eyes widened in his effort to stay awake, fighting for a few more seconds of life. His chest bore the brunt, as though an adult was sitting on his chest. He launched himself through the door, stumbling inside the white room, where he pulled off his helmet and gasped loudly for air. His communication cap slipped off his head onto the tiled floor when he arched over, violent coughs tearing from his mouth, leaving his throat raw. His breath clouded as he exhaled into the frigid air and had to compensate with another deep, desperate gasp.

Helmet tucked underarm, he used the headlamps to carve through the gloom. The white walls bounced into life and the concrete pillars threw dramatic shadows across the tiled floor. With a cursory glance around the room, he saw no immediate signs of damage. In fact, the room seemed untouched, pristine in its silence, leaving him astonished by the improbable sight before him. He swung the headlamps on the mop and bucket in the corner, briefly fooled into thinking someone stood there. He lit upon his backpack hanging on a hook beside his blazer with a peculiar sense of familiarity and homecoming. Whatever he stumbled on rolled away, crashing into the wall and startling him in the cavernous space.

He lowered his head, closing his eyes, scarcely believing the ordeal was over, that he could breathe again; an extraordinary feeling of release like a fish cut free from a fishing line. He turned the headlamps around the room once more, picking out the stepladder. He dragged it inside the lift and positioned it beneath the hatch, inviting the others to join him.

With gentle care, Donavon lowered Ariane's lifeless body through the hatch. Her computer screen blinked red, a clear indication of the life-threatening state she was in. Realisation struck Will like a blow: Ariane had lost consciousness again from oxygen deprivation, her very life hanging in the balance, even contemplating the possibility she might be dead.

She hung for a moment, her feet brushing the top of the stepladder. Will climbed the first three steps to grab hold of her waist.

Donavon released her, and she fell deadweight into Will's arms. Somehow, propping her up under her arms, he found the strength to drag her backwards into the white room, where he laid her down and twisted off her helmet.

Her face and hair were soaked with sweat and her lips had turned blue. He tapped her cheek a few times, trying to revive her from her unconscious state. She didn't wake up. When he checked, he discovered she was not breathing. He pulled her gloves off, sat her upright, and then detached her upper torso assembly from the waist. He lifted it over her head and lowered her back onto the floor. He began chest compressions, fighting through the fog in his mind and fatigue in his bones. With calm, he recalled his first-aid training, and after thirty compressions, he pinched her nose, tilted back her head slightly, sealed his mouth over hers, and gave her two long breaths.

Will's hands moved with urgency, transitioning seamlessly into the next cycle of chest compressions, willing life back into her still form. The next two breaths he administered seemed to yield no change, her body remaining stubbornly motionless beneath his touch.

"Come on, Ariane!" His voice strained with emotion as he pleaded for her to awaken from death.

He continued, refusing to give in to the creeping despair threatening to engulf him. He heard someone climb down the stepladder into the lift and the sound of a spacesuit venting its remaining oxygen.

"My God!" said Peta, standing in the doorway, holding her helmet. "Don't let her die, Will!"

Will continued with another thirty chest compressions in a desperate plea for life, a race against time to revive her before it was too late. Gently pinching her nose once more, he leaned in to deliver another two breaths, willing his own breath to be the spark that reignited her dormant lungs.

Will paused, hesitant to continue, reluctant to give up. He performed another round of chest compressions and blew two more breaths into her mouth. "Wake up!"

"Do you want me to take over?" asked Peta. "I'm a trained nurse, remember."

"Yes."

"Keep trying while I take my gloves off."

Will continued, another round of compressions, another two breaths, another agonising wait for a response that did not come. He stared at her serene visage, thinking she had found peace in her final moments, a calmness that eluded him even now.

He struggled to see Peta through the tears streaming from his eyes, shaking his head in defeat.

Peta also gushed tears as she uncoupled and pulled off her second glove. "No!"

Outside, Donavon gritted his teeth as he struggled his way through the narrow hatch. He finally emerged on the other side, planting his feet firmly on the stepladder. With a swift motion, he reached up and pulled the hatch down behind him, sealing them in. He found himself instantly engulfed in darkness, the only illumination from the reliable beam of his headlamps. His breath came in ragged gasps, his oxygen levels dangerously low.

Passing through the open doors of the lift, he wasted no time closing the gap, moving quickly and decisively despite his exhaustion. With one final push, he applied more force until the doors met in the middle with a resounding thud, sealing off the only potential entry point for the deadly radiation that lurked outside.

He twisted off his helmet, releasing the last of his oxygen, and removed his communication cap. The first thing he saw when he entered the white room was Ariane lying next to Will, dead. It was obvious she was dead by the way Peta looked at him with teary eyes.

Will resumed with the resuscitation techniques, his hands pressing down on Ariane's sternum with increased pressure.

As he leaned in to administer the two breaths, a sparkle of hope ignited in him. And then, finally, it happened. Ariane's chest rose with a slight gasp, her body responding to the influx of air.

"Ariane, can you hear me?" asked Will, drying his eyes.

Receiving no response, he thought she had passed. He let out a long, tense breath when he saw her eyes flutter open, the sight of her blinking bringing such relief. He waited patiently for her to revive and return.

Peta had one hand on top of her head. "Thank God!"

Will hoisted Ariane into a sitting position and Peta held onto her while she recovered.

Will left her to fetch a bottle of water from his backpack and returned hurriedly. Removing the lid, he helped her drink some, and when he saw how thirsty she was, insisted she finish it. He wiped her wet chin with his hand, and she looked at him, breathing in the air gratefully.

His relief sounded in his voice. "Welcome back!"

FORTY-NINE

The next ten minutes were spent in feverish activity as the crew assembled in the foyer and rushed to shed their contaminated spacesuits, discarding them on the floor.

Will assisted Ariane, still weak from her ordeal, removing her suit until she wore only her spandex garment.

Peta, having swiftly removed her spacesuit, now stood in her streamlined spandex suit, a contrast to the bulky gear she had carried on her body all day.

Donavon doffed his spacesuit one component at a time, peeled the biomed sensors off his chest from underneath his spandex suit, and double-checked the lift doors were sealed properly. Finally, he closed the main door, listening until the latch clicked into position. He leaned against the nearest pillar, waiting for his eyes to adjust to the gloom, the headlamps from Will's helmet providing barely adequate light to see the entire room. He went to his backpack hanging above the bench and changed into jeans and white shirt with the sleeves still rolled up from early that morning. After, he approached Will, who had just sat down. "Good call, getting us to come here. Have to admit, I had my doubts, but here we are, safe and sound. Nice one."

Will stood and nodded once.

They shared an awkward man-hug, separated uneasily, and Donavon got in a final slap to Will's back.

Will looked away, uncomfortable with compliments. "Glad you both made it back safely."

Donavon shook Ariane warmly by the hand as though they were old friends. "Glad you didn't die. Well, glad you didn't stay dead."

He veered towards Peta, ready to unleash another round of awkward remarks that were intended to flatter but inevitably fell short. His hand sincerely gripped her shoulder. "Hey, we made it. We're alive. You're welcome."

She said nothing and didn't smile.

The room wasn't exactly bio-sealed from the outside, but its thick sandstone walls provided a formidable barrier, turning it into a temporary fortress of protection and security. Also, its geographical location had played a crucial role in its survival. Nestled in the clifftop shielded by rock and earth, the room was strategically positioned to minimise exposure to external threats. The combination of the thick, ancient sandstone and its sheltered position had helped it endure, offering a sanctuary against the turmoil raging outside.

Some damage had occurred, though. Will had already given the place a more thorough inspection and had discovered a number of issues. The air conditioning unit sat lopsided on the wall and looked like it might topple under the slightest tremor. Multiple cracks had formed in the ceiling, spiking off in jagged forks like bolts of lightning—runoff from the ground quake and heavy downward pressure from above. Concrete chunks had broken away, leaving piles of grey dust laden with small rock fragments on the tiled floor. All said and done, these were minor inflictions compared to the rest of the lighthouse.

Donavon reached inside his backpack and took out a half-eaten ham salad roll from that morning. He wolfed it down in three bites in front of his hungry crewmates. He then collapsed to the bench, picking his teeth clean, and exuded a loud sigh of weary despondency.

It raised eyebrows among the crew.

"Better now?" asked Peta.

"No, I'm fucked!"

"Yeah, we know how you feel," she said with a second hint of sarcasm that seemingly went over his head.

To keep himself warm, Will wore his blazer on top of his spandex suit and fastened the buttons, dusting his shoulders out of habit as if about to attend an interview. When he turned, Ariane stood in front of him. She pulled him towards her. He fell into her embrace and wrapped his arms around her, resting his chin against her scalp. It was unexpected, but the sentiment also came as no surprise.

She detached herself from him and wiped her eyes with her fingertip. "I'm good." She held his arm. "Thank you."

He frowned.

"You saved my life." Her voice trembled with gratitude and relief.

He raised his brows slightly. "We're not out of the woods yet."

"No, but thank you, really, for getting me here safely, for saving my life. I'll always be grateful." She reached out and held both his hands, her grip warm and reassuring.

He tried to muster a smile, but the effort felt hollow. His heart wasn't in it; the uncertainty of their long-term survival and the knowledge of Anthony still at risk or even dead left no room for relief or joy. Instead, he nodded, acknowledging her gratitude while his mind remained focussed on the challenges ahead.

He turned to face Donavon and Peta. "Did either of you see or hear from Lloyd?"

There was a collective shake of heads.

FIFTY

The alarm penetrated the silence inside the cocoon of Lloyd's space helmet, its high-pitched, continuous wail a dire warning about his dangerously low oxygen. The sound was relentless, cutting through his thoughts and igniting panic. He stared at the readouts on his wrist computer and the numbers flashing ominously, confirming his worst fears. He had precious little time to find a solution before he was exposed to radiation and it was too late.

Hours of relentless walking in a heavy spacesuit in pitch darkness with a visor marred by cracks and scratches had taken a severe toll. The world around him had shrunk to the narrow beam of his headlamps, one of which had shattered when he fell out of the tree. This combination of factors had left him hopelessly lost, traversing blindly through the countryside in complete disorientation.

Now the alarm signalled his journey was nearing its critical end. The sharp pain from the glass embedded in his foot had become a dull ache, something he had forced himself to ignore as he pressed forward. His muscles felt as if they had torn apart, sending waves of agony through his splintered limbs. Footsore and severely dehydrated, throat parched and lips dry, having drained the last of his water long ago, it left Lloyd with nothing but his determination to keep him going, knowing he couldn't afford to stop with his life at stake.

He had to be close to the lighthouse. Just two hours earlier, he had passed a sign indicating eight miles to St. Ives and had picked his pace up a notch to ensure he made it back in time, following the hazy orb of the sun behind the smoky veil until it dipped below the horizon. In truth, he was convinced he had been walking in circles, passing the same landmarks, taking the same paths.

With the last of his oxygen running thin, he followed a road that plateaued in a small valley. The blast wave had continued its path of devastation here, sweeping through village and town, taking everything with it. He stopped in the middle of a brick bridge whose sides had collapsed into the river below, needing a moment to reorientate himself. Struggling to breathe on the fumes circulating inside his suit, he wasn't sure he could handle what was to come. With nothing left but fear and anticipation of a horrible death, he didn't think he could handle the pain and suffering induced by acute radiation sickness.

Then he took his final breath with a gasp, raised his visor, and exhaled into the frigid darkness. At first, falling prey to his imagination, he sensed radiation all around him, contaminating his spacesuit, seeping into every nook and cranny: ears, nose, every pore. The air didn't seem poisonous, however. It smelled and tasted like normal air. Was it possible the bombs hadn't been packed with nuclear fission materials? Had their fears been unwarranted? After all, no one had told them anything about what happened, apart from Ariane, whose assessment had been guesswork.

He tore his gloves off and launched them off the bridge, watching them sail into the river, carried downstream. Sitting on the asphalt, he bent his knee and pulled his boot within proximity of his face. He finally removed the two-inch shard of glass, covered in blood, and tossed it away.

He resumed his solitary journey at the typically brisk pace of a desperate survivor, enjoying the newfound mobility in his hands and right foot, and the improved visibility.

The road split in three directions: left, right, and straight. He headed straight and had to tackle a punishing uphill slog. He wanted to take off his suit and helmet, removing forty-five kilos of deadweight, allowing him to tread lighter and faster. But he needed his suit. Without it, he would have no footwear or the means to converse with the crew if they tried to get in touch.

The road led him to a pitch-black town. Was this St. Ives? A wave of noxious vapours engulfed him, a poisonous mixture of chemicals, burned textiles, melted plastics, and ignited fuel. The smell seeped through his open visor, stinging his eyes and assaulting his senses with its acrid scent. It reinforced his fear that the air could be contaminated with radiation. As he passed through its toxic wave, the fallout zone's obliteration became ever more tangible.

Against the brick wall of a dilapidated bus station stood a vending machine brimming with an assortment of snacks and drinks. Its glass front remained securely intact until Lloyd put a brick through it. He removed two chocolate bars, devouring them in seconds. He guzzled two bottles of water and slipped another two in each utility pocket on his thigh, saving them for later.

He walked gravely on, heading deeper into the burned-out town, searching for the lighthouse and crew. Ahead, a small group of men and women carrying bags and dragging suitcases trudged in a solemn procession along the same road, heading in the same direction. There was no way of telling if they were friend or foe, but they bore no resemblance to rescue workers, that was certain.

Lloyd switched off his headlamp just as one looked over their shoulder in his general direction, their face just a black smudge in the darkness. He hid behind a vehicle, sinking into the pause that followed, letting out a relieved breath when they vanished.

Continuing his journey in the opposite direction, he glanced over his shoulder every few seconds. He sensed no immediate threat lurking in the darkness. Assured whoever he'd seen was gone, he pressed on. He needed to find out if this was St. Ives. If not, how far away was he?

A sign at the top of an embankment leaning drunkenly where the heat had buckled its legs raised his hopes. But with a clumsy misstep, he attempted to climb onto a low wall only to stumble and fall hard on his injured shoulder. A sharp cry of pain escaped his lips. Gritting his teeth in agony, he hauled himself to the top of the embankment where he stood before a green sign, illuminated by the faint glow of his headlamp. His heart sank; St. Ives was *still* eight miles away.

FIFTY-ONE

Ariane untied her ponytail, letting her hair drop in a cascading wave. The strands tumbled down her back in a mass of twists and turns like tangled seaweed. Tucking her hair at her temples behind her ears, she turned to face the crew, standing under the light shining from Will's helmet suspended from a hook above the bench. "Listen everyone, our spacesuits are heavily contaminated. We might still receive a lethal dose of radiation from them."

"What do you suggest we do?" asked Peta.

"Around eighty per cent of residual radiation a person will receive is on their clothes. The other twenty per cent is in their hair. By disposing of any contaminated clothes, most of the radiation is removed. Then, all you need to do is have a shower and wash your hair. With us, because we had helmets, we just need to deal with the suits."

Peta stood, stretching her arms behind her back. "Okay, so dispose of the spacesuits? How? Burn them?"

"We don't need to dispose of them," she stated. "In fact, we're going to need them at some point, so we won't be getting rid of them. They just need to be decontaminated, and we need to do it now."

"How?"

"We have a mop and bucket and access to plenty of water from the containment block. There's also a bottle of bleach at the back of the white room somewhere and liquid soap in the restroom. I saw them in here this morning."

"What about the radiation that's drifting in the air? How do we get rid of that?"

"That's not how radiation works. It's not floating in the air; it's the tiny particles within the air. Down here, no particles were exposed to radiation. Only those that fell from the sky will be heavily radioactive. That is what our suits were exposed to."

"Okay, so who's on laundry duty?"

"I'm going," said Ariane. "I'm feeling better. But I need help out there."

Will put up his hand. "I can help."

Ariane turned to Peta and Donavon. "We're going to need several buckets of water. Each time I knock on the door, can one of you fill the bucket from the containment block and add some bleach and liquid soap?"

"We can do that," said Peta, with Donavon right behind her nodding in agreement.

While Peta and Donavon set up the water and bleach, Will and Ariane grabbed a reserve oxygen tank each from the walk-in vault and relocated to the foyer. Closing the door and suiting up, they clamped down their new oxygen tanks, opened the valves, and watched as their oxygen levels rose to fifty per cent, giving them four hours. Only one reserve tank remained inside the vault. After that, no more oxygen was available because the compressor used to refill the tanks ran on electricity.

To begin the decon cycle, Will stood holding the top half of Donavon's suit as if Ariane was about to judge whether he looked good in it.

Taking the mop out of the bleach-infused water that Peta delivered to the doorstep, Ariane ran the wiry head over the suit: shoulders first, arms second, across the midriff, washing away the grime and radioactive dust. She scrubbed the legs and boots, creating a foam from the liquid soap component. Then she washed the helmet. Finally, the gloves, heavily stained with blood. She used the remaining water to rinse the suit before Donavon came and took the bucket away for a top-up.

A small drain sat in the centre of the floor, its metal grate rusted and worn from years of use. The contaminated water, a murky grey, trickled slowly through the narrow holes, swirling around the drain's edges before it was swallowed and carried away through a network of pipes to the ocean below.

The next bucket came, the water tinged blue by the bleach and liquid soap. Ariane held up Peta's suit, and Will repeated the steps, scrubbing away the nasties into the drain. He had to work extra hard to remove the bloodstains on the sleeve and shoulder, further evidence that she and Donavon had endured a bloody encounter with someone or something.

Two suits clean, two to go. Ariane scrubbed Will down while he stood in his suit with his legs splayed and his arms outstretched as if about to perform star jumps. Knee hurting, body stiff and sore, he struggled to remain upright amid the sloshing noises and rubbing sensation on his body, yearning for some physical therapy and a professional massage. What he wouldn't give for a hot shower, the powerful jets pounding the trauma and angst from his body, caressing away the aches and pains.

Ariane wiped the mop strands across Will's helmet just as Peta appeared at the door with another full bucket, her outline blurred by the water streaming down his visor as if he were passing through a car wash.

When it was her turn, Ariane stood in the same star-shaped position while Will dipped the mop in the bucket and applied it to Ariane's spacesuit and all its components, scrubbing off the radiation particles, dust, and filth.

With the fifth and final bucket, he tipped the water across the floor, spreading it all around, and used the mop to steer the puddles into the drain.

Ariane wearily entered the white room in her spandex suit while Will finished up.

"All done?" asked Peta.

"Not quite. I think we should move the locker outside into the foyer. It's airtight, and we can hang our suits inside. Best to be precautious."

"Agreed," said Peta.

As soon as Will returned, they took a corner of the locker and carried it across the room, out through the door, tucking it snugly against the right-hand side wall in the foyer, which reeked of bleach. The pungent fumes rushed up Will's nostrils, causing an immediate reaction. His throat constricted, and a burning sensation spread, making him cough involuntarily. His eyes stung and watered, blurring his vision and forcing him to blink rapidly to clear the tears. The others coughed, their eyes streaming, too, the chemical scent so strong that breathing felt like inhaling a sterilised fire, leaving an unpleasant taste at the back of their throats.

Peta raised her hand over her nose and mouth. "Are you sure the radiation won't get stuck in the drain and contaminate the foyer?"

"Jefferson had all the drains and sewage pipes cleaned and surveyed two years ago," said Will. "The radioactive water will flow out to sea."

Identifying their spacesuits by name badge, they took turns hanging them inside the locker before returning to the white room.

FIFTY-TWO

The clock struck midnight, marking nearly twelve hours since flocks of missiles had flown across the ocean and rained down on the country with devastating force.

Lloyd had been missing now for nine of those hours. His oxygen had expired. Peta prayed he had found somewhere safe to spend the night, someplace as secure as the white room. The alternative was unthinkable.

Visions of the attack as she sat helpless on board Fable Sky would not leave her. She wanted someone to shake her awake and assure her it hadn't happened. How much had the helmet cameras captured? Had the EMP destroyed the circuits? In any case, the cameras had been connected to a central system, and the footage fed back to monitors inside the flight control room. Because Jefferson hadn't upgraded from analogue technology to the cloud, there was no way to salvage the data remotely.

The hard drive, along with everything else in the tower, had surely perished. What would it look like to watch? A significant moment in history captured from above. Scary trails of smoke and vapour tracing the missiles' paths until they lit the country in a blaze of fire. Their supersonic freefall through radioactive mushroom clouds. The long march across apocalyptic land to reach the lighthouse. The race against time to unbury the white room before their oxygen expired and they suffocated in their suits. The compilation would make hard viewing.

Using her bag as a pillow, Peta, dressed in black leggings and a purple hoodie, flattened her spandex suit, turning it into a makeshift futon, providing a thin cushion against the cold tiles of the floor. She curled up in the foetal position, hugged her knees, and raised her hood, clenching with deep and dark grief. She struggled to find comfort on the unforgiving floor, but she knew it was a fair trade compared to any alternative, aside from her own bed in a safe environment. The white room was not about aesthetics or comfort. It was simply a base in post-flight quarantine to ride out the tragedy until tomorrow or the next day when a rescue came.

"I hope Lloyd's safe," she said softly.

It did not arouse a response from the crew, sitting on the bench and floor in contemplative silence, their eyes glazed, their minds shocked into numbness.

It took another hour before she could start to relax. After the longest day, the night offered her a chance to recuperate. Being out of the spacesuit and around other humans was vital for her psyche.

The worst was over. Or perhaps worse was still to come. She had an awful feeling manifesting in her gut, rising to her chest.

Fear of the future. Of the unknown.

Finally, she fell asleep.

Will heard Peta snoring and turned to Ariane and Donavon. "We should try and get some sleep, too."

Sitting on the bench next to Ariane, Will leaned against the wall. He let out a disconsolate sigh, relieved to be safely back in the white room, the centre of his obsession to conquer space tourism. He strapped on his diving watch, feeling reconnected to his father, hoping he was safe.

He rubbed Ariane's shoulder and drew her in, feeling her body relax against his. She had experienced the most gruelling journey after the malfunction inside her spacesuit, a harrowing ordeal that had pushed her to the limits of human endurance. Despite her valiant efforts, she had ultimately succumbed to a lack of oxygen, willing to take her chances to avoid exposing herself to the outside elements. It had paid off.

"How are you holding up?" he whispered.

"Okay. You?"

Will said he was *fine*, but the day's horror would not leave him for one second. To think they had witnessed the unfolding scene from above. It should have been a day for rejoicing a milestone in his career, having reached the stratosphere. There would be no celebrating, however. The grim reality of their situation left no room for joy or victory. No accolades awaited them, not even praise or recognition for their efforts. The dire circumstances had stripped away any semblance of festivity, leaving only a sombre atmosphere. Feelings of triumph and achievement were merely residual. Instead of receiving a hero's welcome, they confronted the aftermath of heavy losses. The accomplishments, though significant, felt hollow in the face of the overwhelming tragedy, overshadowing their personal and collective success, reminding them all survival, not celebration, was priority now.

Will imagined Anthony in his mother's arms in the back of a rescue helicopter, travelling safely away from the radiation zones. Happy memories flooded back to him when Anthony was an infant and his marriage was amicable enough, though at times cold and loveless when all their attention was on their son. Like a baby monkey, he always wrapped his legs tightly around Will's waist, clinging onto his neck as if his life was dependent on not falling.

Will jolted awake, forgetting where he was until the room pulled into focus as the realistic dream receded. Despite his exhaustion, sleep remained elusive, slipping away each time he thought he had found it.

He heard Peta sobbing on the floor and calling out for her mother in her sleep.

Donavon was slumped on the bench, his head tilted back against the wall, mouth flopped open. He wasn't quite snoring but breathing loud enough that he could be heard from the other side of the room.

Ariane was asleep on his shoulder, warming his jaw with her gentle breath, stirring the fine hairs at the base of his neck. Her hair was stuck to his beard like velcro until he detached himself from her and stood up from the bench. She raised her head with her eyes still closed and leaned gently back against the wall.

Will laid out her spandex suit and used her duffle bag to fashion a pillow. He guided her to the floor and onto the suit, propped the bag beneath her head, and removed his jacket, covering her upper body and shoulders. He reached for the helmet hanging on the hook and switched off the headlamps, encompassing them in impenetrable darkness. Their exertions demanded their due. The day had been filled with relentless demands and nonstop horror; it was time to rest their weary muscles and heavy hearts, shutting their eyes to escape the haunting visions of the tragic day. It was then he realised he was shaking, subtle but noticeable, a lingering response to the intense stress he had endured. He thought sleep might take a while to come with the terrifying images seared into his mind, a rerun of the attack and the exposure to such widespread death. But he did slip off, quickly and deeply.

A mobile phone trilled sometime later that morning, its ringtone an electronic rendition of *Penny Lane* that pierced the silence and darkness. The familiar melody, transformed into digital notes, echoed throughout the white room.

Will, still sitting on the bench, was in a surface-level state of sleep and incorporated the sound into his dream, where a spirit version of himself reached for the mobile.

The tune had been playing for almost a minute before the crew stirred, slowly at first, then in a sudden rush of panic.

A small window of bright, bluish light emanated from the bench, creating a dim glow. It flickered gently, drawing their attention to its source. An incoming call on a forgotten device.

No one dared move.

Realising it was his mobile, Will stiffened and reached over to answer the call. Was this Jefferson ringing to see if they were alive? His son, reaching out to report he was safe and not to worry? His heart raced, desperate to see a familiar name on the call screen. When he raised the phone to within inches of his eyes, his expression transformed from surprise to sadness, and he switched the mobile off.

"Who is it?" asked Peta.

"My alarm."

He had set yesterday's four o'clock wake-up call to repeat by mistake.

They closed their eyes, seeking solace in the darkness as they settled back into their most comfortable positions. Sleep came swiftly, enveloping them in its secure embrace. But for Will, he was unable to quiet the tumult of thoughts circulating in his mind. This day, etched into his memory like a permanent scar, marked a pivotal moment when the world's history was forever altered.

FIFTY-THREE

Ariane surfaced gradually from her blissful sleep, her dreams dissolving gently. She lingered in the delicate state between rest and wakefulness, in no rush to rejoin the waking world just yet. The relentless pounding in her head, reminiscent of a migraine, was exacerbated by hunger and a dry throat, likely from relying on bottled oxygen for sixteen gruelling hours. She wasn't alone in her suffering; the others had voiced complaints of painful headaches before they went to sleep last night.

With a groan, she sat up, ready to confront the challenges of the new day, the first of this national apocalypse, having died yesterday. Her stomach rumbled. The meagre breakfast from the extreme dietary regimen, imposed by the medic three days earlier, suddenly seemed appetising.

Blinking open her eyes, she saw a silhouetted figure lurking in her periphery by the door, startling her. He had a light in his hands, causing pain to her vision, forcing her to squint. But it was the gun gripped in his other hand that seized her attention and gripped her heart.

First, it was the cold blast of light that penetrated Will's eyelids, stirring him from sleep, followed by the cold rising from the tiled floor that infiltrated his flesh. The third and most intense discomfort originated in his right knee and hip, customarily aggravated whenever cold. Sleeping had done little to reduce the swelling around his kneecap, and his muscles were resigned never to move again.

Something pricked at his brain to awaken. He attempted to push himself up, but his body refused to comply. Struggling open one eye, a bright light forced him to close it just as quickly, but he had seen a man near the door, his form obscured by the dimness of the room. He reared up, sensing imminent danger, trying to identify the shadowy interloper. A quick glance at his watch in the dim light told him it was 06:30, customarily when Will concluded his sunrise flights with his customers. Around this time, they would disembark the balloon as the hot air was expelled and the envelope deflated. He would then serve them a chilled flute of champagne and go through his usual custom of speech, toast, and handing out souvenir flight certificates, a ritual much loved by his patrons.

Donavon was by the door holding the helmet under his arm with the headlamps switched on. And when he turned the headlamps on Ariane, Will saw him more clearly. You didn't need a keen eye to spot the heavy-looking gun held in his other hand. It had a large trigger and a narrow barrel.

Will smoothed his beard, rumpled by sleep. "What's going on?"

Donavon just stared at them, his black eyes soulless and animal-like.

Peta sat up and rubbed her eyes. "Donavon?"

He pressed his index finger against his lips, a gesture both commanding and perplexing, urging them to say nothing. An unspoken implication came with his action, as if it conveyed the chilling message: "You're mine now!"

What was Donavon planning? Had he completely lost his mind?

Ariane and Peta slowly rose to their feet, standing close to each other. They looked small and fragile, the same way elderly people looked when life had startled them into submission.

Will stood up, his legs shaky and his movements unsteady. "What are you–"

"Shush!" Donavon silenced him with a sharp hiss and a scowl to match.

The anticipation felt interminable until, finally, Donavon lowered the gun, his eyes narrowing as he focussed on the door. "Someone's outside!" he murmured.

Peta broke from Ariane and stepped forward a few paces. "Who?"

He turned and shrugged. "I heard banging out there, above the lift."

"A rescue!" said Peta. "At last!"

"Unlikely," said Donavon. "They would have called out to us."

Peta lowered her head but raised her eyes to the firearm in his hand. "Why do you have a gun?"

Donavon stooped slightly to bring his ear against the steel door. He set the helmet down, its headlamps angled in a way that made seeing everything in the room easier except his face, like he was relying on the darkness to avert the attention from him. "Someone was definitely out there."

Ariane brushed her long, black hair off her face. "Aren't guns illegal in this country?"

Donavon turned from the door and picked up the helmet. "Not since those bombs went off."

"Why do you have a gun?" Peta asked again.

His face tightened as if put out by the question. "Does it matter?"

"Yes! You've got us all worried."

Stalled in his reply, he finally said, "Self-defence."

"Against what?"

He looked away, seemingly deciding how to say what he wanted or even if he wanted to say it at all. "In the last five years, I've run up a lot of debt with a loan shark company. I've fallen behind with the repayments and my life's been... how can I put this? Compromised."

"What do you mean?" asked Peta.

"Use your brain!"

"In danger?"

He opened his fist and held up his four fingers, stressing his missing digit.

"You said it was a work accident," said Peta.

"I lied. They killed my dogs, too. So I got a gun."

"How much debt are we talking here? Thousands?"

He shook his head. "Half a million."

Peta cupped her hand over her mouth. "How did you get into so much debt?"

"How do you think we pulled off the flight yesterday?"

Will was unable to keep the shock from his eyes. "Your investment?"

"We should have launched years ago. I was supposed to pay them back in lump sums. All these postponements have caused me so many problems!"

"Why didn't you say anything?" asked Will. "We could have helped out."

He shrugged. "The people chasing me are dead now, so it doesn't matter. They were based here in St. Ives."

Peta put her hands on her hips. "So *that's* why you said 'sayonara suckers' yesterday. I thought you meant everyone."

He shrugged again. "Erased debt collectors. Erased debt."

She didn't prod him about money, but she was appalled by the harm the thugs had caused him. "I can't believe they cut off your finger and killed your dogs."

Will rubbed his eyes. "Put the gun away. If anyone's out there, it'll be rescuers. No one else could have survived."

Donavon frowned. "We saw a few, hey Peta."

Peta looked at Will. "It's true."

"Is that why there was blood on your suits and gloves?" asked Ariane.

Peta nodded. "Someone attacked me."

Donavon held up the firearm. "Lucky we've got a gun."

Ariane crossed her arms. "They might have survived the bombs, but they won't survive the radiation. Not for long."

Will limped to the door, unable to shake off his stiffness. "We should go looking for Lloyd. It might be him you heard out there."

"Be serious!" said Donavon.

"We can't just leave him out there."

"This is prime real estate right now. You going out there puts this place *and* us at risk."

"He's one of our crew."

"It's his fault he never jumped." Donavon paused with a hint of realisation crossing his face, as if he had misspoken. He cleared his throat and added, with a measured tone, "After the count of ten, I mean."

"Did he take a while to jump?" asked Peta.

"He was shitting bricks. He shouldn't have been on the flight in the first place. I *did* say."

Everyone had thought the same, that Lloyd wasn't up to the task. His big, brown eyes were always wide and averted from the crew like he was formulating hypotheses about the world around him.

"How long after me did he take to jump?" asked Peta.

"Sixty seconds, maybe longer."

"We have to go and look for him," said Will.

"Nah," said Donavon. "You reap what you sow. He's on his own now."

Will turned his back on Donavon in annoyance, gauging Peta and Ariane's willingness to go and find Lloyd. The girls were hardly receptive to do anything but stay put.

"Donavon has a point," said Peta. "It's dangerous outside. We need to rest. And we're out of oxygen."

"We still have some in our reserve tanks. And a spare tank in the vault."

"I agree with Peta and Donavon," said Ariane. "If it *was* Lloyd, don't you think he would have knocked or tried to come in? I want to find Lloyd as much as you do, but the chances of finding him are slim."

Donavon, gripping the gun loosely in his fingers and with a cold shrug, said, "Lloyd's dead! If not, he soon will be."

FIFTY-FOUR

The dark, compact room evoked a sense of profound solitude and introspection. Sparse furnishings were barely discernible in the dim light, which lit up Peta sitting quietly on the floor with her back against a pillar, turning her diamond ring around her finger.

Ariane finished changing out of her spandex suit and into jeans and a loose silk T-shirt narrowed at the waist by a fancy belt before walking over to Peta. "Nice ring."

Peta kept her focus on the ring. "My ex gave it to me."

"What's his name?"

"*Her* name."

"Sorry, I didn't…"

"Dani."

"What?"

"Her name's Dani."

Ariane sat beside her on the floor, shuffling up close. "Why did you break up?"

"I had an affair about a month ago."

"With who?"

"Sam, an old friend."

"Was it a one-off? Or did you want more with her?"

"*Him.* Sam's a bloke."

Ariane palmed her forehead. "I'll just shut up now."

"It was a drunken one-night stand. Dani found out, went berserk." She looked down at her lap. "I got what I deserved. Lost the only person I ever loved."

"Sorry to hear that."

"I can't stop thinking about how pleased my mother would have been that we broke up. She never approved of me having a girlfriend. Then again, she never approved of anything I did, so I guess it doesn't matter."

"You were calling out for her last night."

"Dani?"

"Your mother."

"Really?"

Memories of her mother's death regularly crept into her nightmares. Whenever anxious or frightened, they had a habit of resurfacing. It was a secret she had carried with her since, one she had longed to unburden herself of.

"It's instinctive," said Ariane.

"What do you mean?"

"It's a sign of the stress you're under at the moment and the maternal comfort you're seeking."

"She wasn't capable of maternal comfort. She bullied me for years, even stabbed me with a pencil. I almost died from internal bleeding and can never have children."

"Seriously?"

"Yeah, I know. I struggle to believe it, even after all these years. She got what she deserved, though."

Donavon, sitting close by on the bench and eavesdropping on their conversation, laughed. "Bitch fell down the stairs and broke her neck."

Peta glanced at her crewmates, hesitant to say any more. A major regret. Forgotten sorrows and hidden secrets. So many terrible memories. Such guilt about things that were absolutely not her fault. But everyone had their secrets, and she realised the truth couldn't harm her down here.

"She didn't fall. I pushed her!"

Donavon snapped his head in Peta's direction, his face lighting up. "Priceless."

It was the first time she had volunteered any backstory to her life. It seemed right, that it would be overshadowed by the attack, and her confession would be met with sympathy and understanding. Maybe that was why Donavon had shared his debt crisis with them. If this was the end of humanity, what harm could come of sharing your darkest secrets? Still, half a million was a lot of money for a man in his circumstances to scratch up.

"Not intentionally. I mean, I pushed her, not to kill her; she was strangling me, shouting in my face. I was worried she was going to stab me again."

Ariane couldn't hide her concern or confusion. "What did the police say?"

"I told them she fell. When they did the post-mortem, they discovered high blood-alcohol levels and amphetamine in her system and put the fall down to an accident caused by serious intoxication."

Ariane put her hand on Peta's shoulder. "It must have been an awful time for you."

Peta lowered her head, on the verge of tears. One spilled down her cheek; she quickly batted it away. Crying provoked nothing but the sound of its own sadness, counterproductive under these extraordinary circumstances. Which was why she normally cried in silence, something she had done throughout her adolescence in such a way nobody ever saw the tears.

"Not having my dad around made it hard."

"Where was he?"

"He died of a heart attack when I was eight. That's what changed my mother. It was like a switch. She had always been aggressive and emotionally distant, like disconnected, and my father protected me from her when he was alive. Thankfully, I grew up to be nothing like her and took after my father."

Donavon laughed out loud. "You killed your mum. That's brilliant."

"I'm glad you find it funny," said Peta.

"I knew her. Trust me, it's funny. I should have done the same to my mum. Looks like the Russians have taken care of that for me."

"What makes you think it was the Russians?" asked Ariane.

"Most nuclear-equipped nation in the world. Near the UK. Hates the West. And our government has the competency of a chimpanzee. It was inevitable."

"We know nothing yet," she said.

"Come on, open your eyes. Today's world faces numerous challenges: climate change, social inequality, overpopulation. Capitalism and socialism can't address these issues. Capitalism has led to environmental degradation and economic disparities. Socialism, while it does push for equality, relies on centralised control that stifles innovation and individual freedom. No, this attack is a wake-up call for change; our government needs to take a long, hard look at itself. Now is the opportunity to prove themselves with a strong response to this attack."

"Why would Russia care about any of that?"

Donavon frowned. "I thought you were educated! Since the collapse of the Soviet Union, Western ideologies have been forced down Russia's throat. The entire political system was reformed based on Western democratic principles, including a multiparty system and competitive elections. The West is seen as a model of *normal* life, always has been, and many believed Russia should follow its example, but these ideologies often clashed with Russia's historical, cultural, and political realities. It only created resentment and resistance among the Russians. National identity and pride became rallying points against what was seen as external interference. In the last decade, Russia's perception of the West has become increasingly negative. We are a rash, and how do you remove a rash?"

Tired of listening to Donavon's political rhetoric, having been subjected to it many times over the years, Peta raised the hoodie she had been cradling in her lap to her nose, breathing in the freshening scent of the fabric softener. A sudden chill ran through her, so she slipped the garment on and pulled the hood up.

"Where's Will?" asked Ariane.

Peta stood and peered between the pillars to the other side of the room, neither seeing nor hearing any movement. "I've not seen him for a while."

"He left the room about ten minutes ago," said Donavon. "I thought he had come back already. Maybe he's in the toilet. I'll check."

By the time Peta had tied her shoelace, Donavon was back. "He's not in the toilet," he said. "I think I know where he is, though."

FIFTY-FIVE

Suited up with his helmet between his feet, Will was about to seal the lift doors when Donavon, followed by Peta and Ariane, emerged from the white room into the foyer. Their confused faces appeared in the narrowing gap.

Will paused, his hands pressed against the cold steel of the doors. He watched Donavon charge towards him, wagging his finger. "No, you don't!"

"Where are you going?" asked Ariane.

"To look for Lloyd."

Peta shook her head quickly. "It's not safe out there. Don't go!"

"There's a risk, I accept that. I could use some help."

Will could tell Peta and Ariane were wrestling with their guilt.

"Absolute waste of time and oxygen," said Donavon.

"If it was one of *us* out there, you'd want *someone* to come and find *you*." A note of pleading had entered his voice.

Peta slowly unfolded her arms. "Lloyd doesn't know the area at all. He's from the north. To be honest, I don't think he knows how to get here."

"Where do you plan to search?" asked Ariane. "Not where we landed?"

"If what Donavon heard this morning *was* Lloyd, I doubt he would have gone far. I'll be an hour, two tops."

Donavon gave Will a snarky grin. "You're too nice, that's your problem."

"Wait!" said Peta. She ran back inside the white room and returned holding her camera, fitted with the lens extension. "It has a thirty-times zoom range so you can use it like a pair of binoculars."

Will connected his helmet without the communication cap while Peta lengthened the strap to fit the camera over his head. She gave him a hurried hug.

Ariane stepped closer, whispering, "Be careful out there."

"Find food and drink," said Donavon. "And look out for rescue parties. They are priorities right now."

"I will look for them all," he said.

He wanted their help, and thought about how to bring it up again, if at all. They had been through so much already, he didn't want to say anything that could be wrongly interpreted as criticism. They clearly struggled with the dilemma, vacillating between obligation and reluctance. It was not his intention to force them to act against their instincts. The choice to go and look for Lloyd was his and his alone. Pulling his visor down, returning to a world of silence, Donavon's disapproving glare was the last thing he saw before he closed the lift doors.

Will's helmet collided with the ceiling when he reached the top of the stepladder. He straightened, raising the access hatch with his head, and pushed his hands down on either side of the opening, levering himself out.

Turning his headlamps around the deep hole, he assessed the daunting twenty-foot climb. Realising the challenge, staring at the broken blocks and bricks in the corner that Peta had methodically stacked to create a makeshift staircase, he made careful steps to the top. Coming out of the shaft, he ascended the rubble belonging to the crater, careful to avoid causing a brick slide. The last thing he needed was for the rubble to turn into an avalanche of bricks and seal his crew in, forcing him to go through the painstaking task of digging the lift out again.

Will started his search for Lloyd at the launch site, evoking memories of the flight. Having rectified the vulnerabilities each failed launch had revealed, they'd finally got Fable Sky off the ground when it mattered most, avoiding a violent death. The ocean was dimmed by the bruised orange sky looming above, flaming like a stunning sunset and veiled by a hazy blanket of smoke. The absence of seabirds, often seen circling the top of the lighthouse, defecating all over the lantern room windows, reminded him this tragedy was not confined to humans. The clifftop would normally be heaving now with coastal walkers, dog owners, and fitness fanatics. His mind was a whirlpool of emotion, still trying to come to terms with this shocking turn of events, aware venturing back into a blasted wasteland was not the best decision of his life. He had certainly made worse decisions, though nothing capped flying a hot-air balloon while intoxicated.

Relying solely on his instincts might lead to a hasty and incomplete search for Lloyd. With limited oxygen and time, creating an invisible but pressing countdown in his mind, he decided against venturing too far into the unknown. Instead, he resolved to stay within the immediate vicinity. By remaining local, he increased his chances of encountering a search and rescue team. Their expertise and equipment would be crucial in conducting a thorough and effective search for Lloyd and other survivors.

He surveyed the scattered vehicles, combing through the unintentional scrapyard and peering into the empty, glassless windows. Finding no trace of Lloyd, he headed inland until it made no sense to go any further because nothing could be seen for miles. Trekking back to the broken lighthouse, he studied the grey sea for rescue boats. A capsized fishing trawler was bobbing along the surface, and a rowing boat with high prows fore and aft was beached on the sand near an upside-down car, its red paint scorched, its roof crushed. He was suddenly drawn to a washed-up corpse clad in a white outfit. Could it be Lloyd? Using the camera's wide-angle lens and twisting the zoom ring, he studied the display screen. The man, professionally attired in a white coat typically worn by doctors and scientists, had blonde, wavy hair and a surgical mask on his face. Ineffective against radiation, which a man of either medicine or science would have known. Radiation warranted specialised equipment, such as lead-lined suits or respirators with specific filters, to shield the body effectively. His reliance upon a surgical mask underscored either his ignorance of the true dangers he faced or lack of access to more suitable protective gear. The man was sprawled face-up across the beach, hands stretched out limply above his head as if exhibiting a futile attempt at surrender before the bombs struck. The sea bucked and broke, whipping into white foam over his legs.

Panning the camera to the right, he witnessed a grim and disturbing scene unfold before his eyes. More bodies, lifeless and adrift, bobbed in the surf, rolling back and forth with the rhythm of the breaking waves, which gently lifted them, only to let them fall back onto the wet sand. Will pushed a button on the camera and took a picture by mistake. The body-strewn shoreline filled the display screen. The general lack of dexterity with the gloves meant he couldn't push the tiny delete button. For the benefit of the crew, he would erase the picture upon his return. They didn't need any more visual reminders of the horrors lurking outside their haven.

Will made another wide circuit of the clifftop. Nearing the lighthouse, he saw footprints in the fine mantle of soot and ash on the ground. He may have missed the tell-tale markings had it not been for the sharp lump of metal he stepped on. He knelt beside one print. Space boots didn't fit the profile; they were too narrow with a sports tread. If the footprints didn't belong to Lloyd, whose *were* they?

When he looked up, he saw a bloody handprint smeared across the ruined wall of the lighthouse. The sight sent a chill down his spine, a visceral confirmation of Donavon's earlier suspicions. Someone had prowled around the lighthouse after all, and judging by the ominous stain, they were in a desperate and likely wounded state. Whoever had left both sets of prints had perhaps sought refuge within the lighthouse's sturdy walls, discovering nothing remained of its interior.

Beyond the lighthouse, walking for a half-mile, Will came to the outskirts of St. Ives. High up on the ridge, the elevated vantage point offered a panoramic view of the devastation that had consumed the once-thriving town below. The infernos raged on still with relentless fury; thick, black smoke billowed upward, adding to the imposing brown sky hovering over the town and afar. The smoke reached even the high ridge where he stood.

He first scanned the town with his naked eyes, searching for movement among the flattened streets. On his second pass, he activated the camera's zoom feature, inspecting the details. The enhanced view revealed a few random properties barely standing, their structures reduced to their foundations. Slowly, he ranged his scope from right to left until the town met the coast. The sea was heaving, frothing like a pan of soup left on the stove. It had been mostly flat yesterday. But then a lot of things had changed in twenty-four hours.

He scanned back, even slower this time, deciding if it was worth going down there, whether it posed any risks or if any hostile forces lie in wait. He wondered when professional help would arrive, whether in the form of military personnel, Red Cross volunteers, or brave locals forming scouting parties. If the radiation levels in the fallout zones were indeed too high for conventional rescue operations, specialised protective gear would be imperative for anyone attempting to enter the danger hot spots. Not everyone had access to the luxury of a spacesuit. Small mercies. The delay in assistance could also be attributed to the thorough planning and precautions necessary for the safety of those tasked with the rescue mission. Was a rescue party even necessary? Who was left to rescue in the decimated town? With that sobering fact in mind, the notion of a rescue party seemed increasingly improbable. In its place, a salvage party, tasked with recovering remnants of life and resources among the wreckage, a slow and methodical process with no time demands, only a reverence to ensure the deceased were accounted for.

Because no one had survived. No one, that was, except for the man Will's camera lens just landed upon.

FIFTY-SIX

Donavon raised his right foot onto the bench and rested his forearm across his thigh to address the crew. "Listen up. I'm going to say what we all must be thinking. We may be safe here, for now, but we need to put our heads together to survive the coming days." If he was worried, it didn't show. His expression was serious, even grim, but that was it.

Ariane added that if they were expecting a rescue anytime soon, it would be wise not to hold their breaths. Any recovery efforts would inevitably be prolonged and arduous, given the staggering toll of death and injury inflicted by the disaster. The number of volunteers willing to brave the hazardous conditions would likely be limited, as would the amount of protective gear available to shield them.

Donavon agreed, stating the clock was already ticking. He explained why they couldn't leave, not least the radiation that posed an existential threat. There wasn't enough oxygen to stay outside for extended periods and nowhere to go, anyway. They couldn't stay, either, not for long, with current resources likely to last a day or two. And they had no food. Even so, with an optimistic spin, he mentioned they could take solace in the fact their ordeal would be over soon. It would take time, as Ariane had pointed out, that was all. He surmised with a few clichés about being there for each other, the beneficial effects of social interaction, and about keeping positive, making Peta raise her eyebrows in disbelief at his sudden compassion.

Once Donavon had the girls accepting the way out of this hell providing they worked together, he moved onto his next suggestion. "We need to find out what resources we *do* have. Collect your bags and belongings and let's see what we've got between us."

Gathering all they owned, they pooled their resources on the tiled floor beneath the headlamps, silently observing their haul as new items were added.

Donavon grabbed Lloyd's bag and sat with it between his legs on the floor.

"That's Lloyd's," said Peta.

Donavon drew down the zip and peered inside. "I know."

"You can't do that!"

"Like he's coming back."

He glanced up at the girls scowling down on him.

Donavon shrugged. "What? We're all thinking it."

Once all the bags had been emptied, they encircled the pile and studied the contents, spreading them out.

A bottle of peach iced tea. Three water bottles holding two litres in each. An eight-pack of baked vegan doughnuts. Two packs of cigarettes and a lighter. Five mobiles. Will's laptop.

The digital camera. One sachet of sleeping pills. Three sets of music headphones: two earplugs, one large muffler type. The Swiss Army knife and keys Peta found. Yesterday's newspaper. One pair of reading glasses. Anti-fog spray. The Nora Roberts novel. A makeup bag. The gun. A roll of mints.

In the cabinet in the bathroom were various medicines and pills.

Donavon left and returned with a spare parachute pack, adding it to the pile.

With limited items to aid in their survival, they calculated a survival range of between five and ten days.

Peta looked at her crewmates and mentioned they would have to share everything evenly. They had gone thirty-three hours without food, excluding Donavon's binge last night. The food and water, desperately needed by everyone, would have to be rationed until they could guarantee where their next sustenance would come from. They agreed on half a doughnut now, half tomorrow, the same again on Tuesday, and the final half on Wednesday, in the event a rescue had not found them by the fourth day.

Devouring the soft, sugary doughnuts, Donavon's mind circled back to the nuclear attack. Obviously, things had gone on behind the scenes even world media knew nothing about, though he believed the main moguls were somehow complicit. Someone, somewhere, had to have answers. The UK had long lived under the shadows of nuclear-armed rockets, and now the outside was a dust bowl. Was that true of other UK regions and cities? How far did the devastation stretch? How many had died? How far had the radiation spread? His blood boiled just thinking about it. A fervent patriot, he harboured an unyielding resolution, vowing that no perpetrator would evade retribution for such a grievous assault on his nation's sovereignty. No one trampled on their dignity and honour and emerged unscathed.

And what of the capital? Even if London hadn't been hit, the fact a substantial region of the country had would have been sociologically crippling. Modern nuclear warheads were unmatched in their explosive force and ability to cause mass destruction. A few bombs would have inflicted considerable damage. Multiple bombs combined could blow countries to damnation. No country remained out of range from the dozen nuclear-capable nations. Even if they were, radioactive clouds could migrate anywhere in the world with atmospheric winds carrying them to the far corners of the globe. The attack had been the deadliest on record. There would be a reckoning.

Many years of opportunities to mitigate and forestall the development of nuclear arms had been squandered, posing a perpetual threat. Earlier that year, China had put the world on edge when it ran a series of nuclear tests dangerously close to the United States. The news coverage had been nonstop, and security levels had been ramped up everywhere, governments from America to Europe responding. It served as a frightening reminder that forces in the world could render you powerless.

"Who bought the doughnuts?" asked Ariane.

"They were in Lloyd's bag," said Donavon.

Choking down the last bit of the doughnut, Peta sighed. "I could eat ten of those. Even if they are vegan and taste like flour."

Ariane licked the sugar off her lips. "Rationing will buy us time until we are rescued."

FIFTY-SEVEN

Will hurried down the steep path leading from the clifftop into the town. The urgency propelling him was as intense as the previous day when his and Ariane's life had hung by the finest thread. The narrow streets were gridlocked with abandoned cars. Not so much abandoned as obliterated. Driving through the town had always been a pleasant experience for Will; the streets meandered gently along the coastline, offering stunning views of the sea on one side and charming, boutique shops and cafes with welcoming façades on the other. Life in this town had been easy-going, with friendly waves from pedestrians and cyclists and community-minded residents showing him road courtesies whenever he visited.

Relying on his bearings and his gut instincts to locate the building he had spotted from afar, Will weaved through the car wreckage along streets once so familiar to him. The bombs had wrought unimaginable havoc on the tiny seaside town, sowing death and destruction indiscriminately. His heart ached with memories of what had been lost as he passed through the maze of ruins until he stumbled upon the building he was looking for. The man he had seen hung from the gaping window three storeys high, his head on the sill and his arms dangling over the edge. But he wasn't dead. Will had seen movement within the camera's circular scope. The vomit splattered across the cobblestones below was further evidence of his survival and the toll radiation had already taken. It was surely Lloyd. Given the identical hair colour, build, and beige clothes matching the one-piece spandex suits, Will was ninety per cent certain he'd found his missing crew member.

The building's interior was gutted. The staircase creaked under his weight as he made his way up each flight. He moved cautiously, aware of the instability of the structure. On the third floor, the remnants of charred wood and debris littered his path along a corridor that led to the room where the man had taken refuge. But it was not a man. A woman of around fifty was arched over at the window, her beige suit filthy but still dignified. She was holding a portable radio tightly in her right hand. Blood matted her short, greying hair. Her blistered skin was sticky with discharge. Both her hands were covered in wet burns. The copper pipe rising through the floor had impaled in the right side of her lower back, leaving blood saturated on her jacket around the exit wound. She was torn up, between life and death that she now teetered upon.

Will took a knee beside her and gently touched her arm.

The woman slowly twisted her head, drifting in and out of consciousness. The burn marks on her face looked as though someone had cruelly stubbed out cigarettes on her skin. Her eyes were like grey stones, reflecting the shimmering flames of the fire burning in the adjacent building; a vacant emptiness stared at him. Was she blind?

Her calm veneer suddenly shaded into a look of dread. She writhed, a futile struggle against the copper pipe holding her in place.

Will desperately wanted to communicate with her, but he knew raising his visor was the only way, and that could allow dangerous radiation particles to drift into his helmet. The risk was significant, yet the need for communication felt even more pressing. He hesitated, weighing potential consequences, and decided to take the chance. He raised the visor just a fraction, enough to speak through but hopefully not enough to let in a flood of harmful particles.

"It's okay, I'm not here to hurt you. I'm Will. What's your name?"

She took time to answer his question, speaking with a raspy whisper. "Melanie. Mel."

"We have shelter, Mel. I can help you. It's not far."

She shook her head. "I'm done." She paused, as if her own words had dawned an understanding that she was not walking out of here alive. Her head slumped forward. "The country's done."

Will frowned, wondering if he heard her right.

She threw up, her bloodied neck stretching forward like a turtle's reaching from its shell. The awful sound of her retching was deadened when Will closed his visor momentarily. She clutched her chest, struggling to catch her breath, her words trapped behind the sheer effort of inhaling.

Will was reluctant to raise his visor, but when it looked like she had found her voice, he opened it a crack.

"Are you there?" she asked.

"Yes. What can I do?"

Her head rested on the sill. "Your voice sounds muffled."

"I'm wearing… protective gear."

"You can't be part of a rescue."

"No, sorry." He frowned. "Wait, what do you mean?"

She managed a weak smile. "It's doomsday!"

He glanced at the radio in her hand. "What do you know?"

"I knew MS was going to end my life sooner than later. I never knew everyone else in the world would die before me."

"Everyone?"

She coughed loudly. "I can't open my eyes, but you need to open yours."

She sounded delusional and unhinged, unsurprising in her dire state. But before he brushed the conspiracy caveat off as nonsense, he was receptive to her views. "I don't follow."

"You will." She moved her head slightly, wincing in pain.

"Hang in there. Someone will come soon."

"No one's coming."

"Not yet, but soon," said Will, glancing out of the window. He studied the horizon for boats out to sea, planes in the sky, and vehicles within the hills. The wind whistling between the building's holes and cracks sounded ghostly. A large portion of the roof was open to the sky, allowing glowing embers from the fire across the road to rain through the gap. The entire corner of the room had been sliced off, making the floor highly unstable, giving Will nasty flashbacks of the office building in which he had landed yesterday. If it gave way, there was no parachute to break his fall this time. He assumed this was one of the many small hotels in the area, and judging by the broken chairs and tables, this could've been the function room.

"No one's coming," she whispered again, turning her neck slightly in his direction. "There is no one!"

Her eyelids slowly slid down but did not fully close. Her head went slack on her shoulders.

He nudged her. "Stay with me! Hey, stay with me!"

Her eyes stuttered open. "Help me!"

"What can I do?"

She managed another weak smile. "Imagine I'm a zombie. We all know how to dispose of zombies."

"I won't do that. What if I lift you off this metal pipe?"

"What for?"

"I can assist you to our shelter. It's only ten minutes away and we can treat your wounds."

"Who will treat yours?"

"Me? I don't need treatment."

"You're exposed."

"Not exactly."

"How did you survive?"

"Long story. I was in a safe place. Kind of."

She shook her head. "Nowhere was safe."

"What are you trying to tell me?"

"I can no longer see, but I hear everything from up here. There were survivors in the town. I heard them talking. People on the radio, too."

The blood drained from his face, unsure if he wanted to know the answer to his next question. "What did they say?"

She threw up bile and air. She must have been dangerously dehydrated. With radiation exposure, she wouldn't live long.

"I can get you water," said Will. "You need it, but you can't drink it in that position. Let me help you."

"Okay."

"I'm going to lift you off this pipe, okay?" His voice was soft and mild, something people often mistook for shyness on first greeting.

"Okay."

Will closed his visor and stood stiffly over the woman. The copper pipe stuck out of her back by two inches. He probably had to raise her torso about ten to twelve to free her. She was petite and shouldn't weigh a great deal. Eight stone. He could think of no graceful way of liberating her other than raising her as steadily and smoothly as possible.

He opened his visor a fraction and placed his hands around her waist. "Are you ready?"

Mel's face remained placid and difficult to read. "As ready as I was for war."

"I'm not going to lie, this will hurt."

Dropping his visor, he resumed his grip around her hips and pulled her towards him, raising her off the window ledge. The copper pipe slowly retracted into her body like a periscope dipping beneath the sea surface. Will heard no sound from Mel as he lifted her off the pipe and dragged her backwards into the corner, setting her gently against the wall, the radio still clutched in her hand.

He took off her beige suit jacket, wrapped it around her waist, and tied a knot using the sleeves above the entry and exit wounds to staunch the bleeding. Visor slightly raised, he told her to press it against the wound and asked her, "How do you feel?"

"I think the pipe missed my organs."

Will was grateful that his only physical complaints were his hunger and thirst, though his aching heart was another matter entirely.

Crazed with pain, Mel twisted away from Will, who barely registered the large wooden beam sliding down the same wall, one inch from whacking him across the head. It knocked a hole in the adjoining wall, causing it to warp and kicking up plumes of dust that smothered everything, including Mel on the floor, causing her to cough.

Will lowered his visor again as the fine particles swirled around the room, reducing visibility to almost nothing until it settled.

Mel shielded her face, but the dust was relentless, and she couldn't stop coughing, which caused her obvious discomfort.

Will, knowing the risk but needing to communicate, lifted his visor a fraction. "This building's unstable. We need to get out of here."

"This is my first time in St. Ives," she rasped, trying not to laugh. "I'm an event coordinator. We had organised a round-table event for some of the country's top medical professionals. It was for mental health, would you believe? I mean, the irony, you've got to laugh."

"Listen, you need water. You're extremely dehydrated."

"I'm dying here. Help me die peacefully, and I'll tell you what *really* happened."

The lump that materialised in Will's throat was a visceral response to the sudden fear that gripped him. Was it possible this event was not confined to their small corner of the globe? Or was this lady past the point of rational thought?

Refusing to accept that this attack had been replicated on a grander scale, he clung desperately to the fragile pretence of hope. To acknowledge anything different, to entertain the idea their plight was not isolated, would be to open the floodgates to despair.

"I'll help you unconditionally," said Will.

She went to say something but winced in pain, speaking only when it subsided. "You're a good man."

"I'll take you to where we are staying. We have a trained nurse with us."

"I'm not going anywhere."

"Why?"

She coughed, struggling to clear her clogged throat. "Will, is it?"

"Yes."

"You have medical equipment?"

"Yes, but only minimum supplies."

"Unless you can carry me all the way because there is no way I can walk, bring me some painkillers, some water, patch up my wounds, and then *maybe* I can make it to your hideout. I'll tell you everything after that."

Will paused. "Okay. Stay put."

She smiled wearily. "Like I have anywhere to go."

"I'll be back in about half an hour."

Securing his visor with a resolute click, Will turned and left the room, descending the rickety staircase at the end of the corridor. Emerging from the building's darkened interior, he turned left, momentarily disoriented by the abrupt transition from shade to light, and paced along the road.

He didn't hear it fall from within his sound-proofed helmet. He neither saw it. But he felt the ground shudder through the soles of his boots, and when he turned to check, the building was gone, nothing more than a heap of materials billowing palls of thick dust. He ran back, but nothing of the structure remained, leaving Mel buried beneath its ruins, forever lost to the collapse. At least she was out of her pain and misery. The thought of her suffering ending was a small, bitter consolation. At least now she was free from the pain and misery that had tormented her. With a mix of grief and relief, he turned away and slowly walked back to the clifftop.

On his return to the lighthouse, a temporary asylum in a place of tumult, he feared what they had witnessed was the tip of the iceberg, and now they faced a battle unlike any they had ever known.

FIFTY-EIGHT

The White Room door opened, and Will appeared wearing his spandex suit and holding the camera.

Peta was the first to greet him, jumping up from the bench and rushing over. "Did you find him?"

Will had trouble focussing on her in the dim light. "No." He avoided mentioning the foot and handprints, the bodies on the beach, or the woman spinning possible conspiracy theories, rationalising the omissions for obvious reasons. "There's no one out there."

"You okay?" asked Ariane, touching his forearm.

He nodded.

"You saw *no one*?" asked Peta. "Not even a rescue?"

Will paused. "No."

"Lloyd's dead!" said Donavon. "The sooner you can accept that, the lighter your conscience will be."

Will handed the camera back to Peta. "We don't know that. Lloyd could still be alive, and we should do everything in our power to find him."

"Why has no one come to look for survivors?" asked Peta, visibly frustrated. "Surely they would send people as quickly as possible."

Will was hesitant to share anything at this stage because it could not be verified. Mel's lack of hydration had most likely made her delusional. "A rescue will come soon. We just need to be patient."

Donavon picked up the helmet. "I'm going to switch the headlamps off to save battery power."

"Just a moment," said Will, walking to the pile of resources on the floor and picking up the lighter. "Okay."

The headlamps were switched off, transforming the room into complete darkness.

Using the lighter to find his way, Will moved to the other side of the room to perform a series of leg and hip stretches, his movements fluid and familiar. This routine had become a staple for him since his balloon accident, a way to maintain his physical health and flexibility. Despite the absence of light, his body moved with the same fluidity and effort exhibited during his daylight workouts. The rounds of physio had helped, but the rest was down to him. It was no more a necessity than it was a discipline, but he often welcomed any excuse not to do it.

After the routine, he returned to the benches and used the lighter to find the helmet, lying on the floor like an upturned tortoise. Switching the headlamps on, he aimed the beams at Donavon, who sat on the bench with his head in his hands, so rumpled, so still.

Will tapped his shoulder. "Did I see cigarettes somewhere, or was I mistaken?"

Donavon popped up and pointed at the pile of gear on the floor. "Didn't take you for a smoker."

Before. For approximately five years. He missed the taste, the numbing sensation on the tongue and gums and the spike in metabolism.

"What's it going to do, kill me?"

About to exit the room, Will stopped when Ariane came through the door. "Your suit's clean. I decontaminated it for you."

Will smiled. "Thanks, you didn't have to do that."

She smiled, touching his arm affectionately. "I know."

Out in the foyer, Will sat on the floor with his back against the wall, facing the glass locker. The compact space reeked of bleach. He lit the cigarette and closed his eyes as the smoke poured down his throat, bringing instant relief to his troubled mind. He sprawled back, blowing smoke rings into the air. Was it the wrong time to resurrect a taste for nicotine? The perfect time? He enjoyed another long drag and let the smoke ooze through his nostrils. He flicked the striker and a spark ignited, giving birth to a small flame. It grew taller, its light shimmering against the foyer walls. The mundane details of the room were transformed into a scene of mystery straight out of an Indiana Jones flick. He stared at the flame, entranced by its warm hues and natural beauty, drawing him into a silent reverie.

Beyond the flame, the lift doors, what stood between them and the inhospitable environment outside, remained sealed. The irony was not lost on him. The lift had been a real pain point for the crew. Todd had humorously declared it a booby trap. In a strange twist, the lift had saved their lives, a bridge between a safe shelter and the dangerous outdoors—a portal between two worlds.

Turning his attention to the locker, he used the light from the flame to observe the spacesuits, inducing memories of their flight to the edge of space. Happy memories soured by tragedy. Then he saw something that made his blood run cold.

He pulled himself heavily to his feet and approached the locker. He pressed his face against the glass, peering into the gloomy display. As he scrutinised the contents, his eyes landed on the small tear on the thigh of one of the suits. It was a subtle but telling flaw. Someone had roamed about outside in a suit compromised by a puncture, exposing them to untold dangers. The question replayed in his mind with growing concern and curiosity: who?

Will had estimated the crew faced a seventy-five per cent chance of surviving the flight. The media had measured it as low as fifty. Had they known a nuclear attack would occur, both parties would have put that figure at zero.

His mind replayed the harrowing scenes of him plunging through the roofless office, the terrifying descent vivid in his memory. He had been fortunate the landing wasn't harsher; miraculously, he had walked away without broken bones or a ruptured suit. Or had he? He questioned his memory, thinking back to the immediate aftermath. His oxygen had shown no irregularities, no obvious signs of a breach in the suit's integrity. The equipment had held up under the stress, keeping him safe despite the perilous fall. But the doubt lingered, a small voice telling him he had been exposed to radiation the whole time he was outside. Determined to find out, he opened the locker and, striking the lighter, used the bright flame to paw through the suits, shoving them aside in search of the one with a tear.

His fingers brushed against the various fabrics until he found the damaged suit. A wave of ice-cold alarm surged through him as he read the name on the sleeve. Staggering back, he closed the door with a trembling hand, then ran his fingers wearily across his shaved head. Should he inform the crew about the breach? They already had so much on their plates. His mind wrestled with the implications of remaining silent versus the potential consequences of speaking up.

Though fortunate to have weathered the biggest disaster in UK history, he appreciated the multi-front challenge they still faced. With no food and very little fresh water between them, they would enter the terminal stages of dehydration within a few days. The procurement of food and water was a critical priority, and the urgency of the situation demanded immediate action to ensure their basic survival. Moreover, the possibility of leaving the country had to be seriously considered if no rescue was forthcoming. His brief encounter with Mel had thrown everything into question. *War. Doomsday.* These were the words she had spoken. The instability and looming threats made it clear that staying was increasingly untenable.

He took a final drag on the cigarette and stubbed it out on the brick wall, grinding the glowing ember until all sparks were extinguished. He held onto the cigarette butt, smelling the tip as a further time-wasting device before heading back inside the white room, relishing the moment alone to gather his thoughts.

A violent coughing fit seized him, doubling him over with its force. Desperately, he used the lighter's flame to inspect his hand, dreading the sight of blood. It didn't seem like a cough related to smoking. It felt different, as if he were losing control of his body. He glanced at his clean palm, finding momentary relief.

Returning to the white room, he stood framed within the doorway, staring at his crew with concern and empathy in his eyes. They were bound together now for the foreseeable future, facing difficult times ahead, stripped of all hope and purpose. Crushed and crestfallen, they were now holding on in the face of cumulative and unrelenting loss. The crew had handled the traumatising events of the weekend as well as humanly possible. Their confusion and shock overrode any feelings of anger. He knew at some point his own shock would give way to terrible grief.

Eager to learn more, he picked up yesterday's newspaper and searched for an article that might shed some light on what had happened. He found a story he had started earlier that day. It concerned the uranium discovered on board a ship bound for Yemen. It had come from North Korea, one of the world's most militarised countries with a million-man army and twenty-two nuclear facilities in eighteen locations, including a Soviet-supplied reactor at Yongbyon, the centre of its atomic science.

"What's this?" Peta held up her camera, showing everyone the display screen. "Did you take this, Will?"

Will's stomach dropped when he approached and saw the body-strewn beach near the lighthouse on the screen. "I was supposed to erase that. My apologies."

"Where is it?"

"Just outside. I'm sorry, I didn't mean to take a picture."

Peta switched the camera off and placed it on the bench.

"Sorry," Will said again. He returned to the bench and read his newspaper. Before long, his eyelids drooped, and he caught the scent of the newspaper as his face landed on it.

The thunderous crack of a gunshot that reverberated in the compact space startled him awake.

A bullet blazed across the room like a firework, striking one of the pillars and causing concrete fragments to rain to the floor.

In the silence and confusion that followed, Will turned to see Peta holding the gun.

Donavon charged towards her and snatched it out of her hand.

She raised her palms as if under arrest. "It just went off."

Donavon turned the safety on. "Why are you touching my gun?"

"I just wanted to see what it was like."

"Fucking idiot!"

Peta's mouth opened. For a moment, no words came out. "Don't call me an idiot! It wasn't my fault. It just went off."

He wedged the gun in his waistbelt.

They headed in opposite directions as calm settled over the white room again.

The calm before the storm.

A storm that was about to batter the crew.

Dong… dong.

When the faint knock sounded at the door, Ariane was on the bench next to Peta, staring at her St. Christopher necklace, looking tired and troubled, her mouth curled down.

Peta had her back against the middle pillar, resting her chin on her updrawn knees and spinning her diamond ring around her finger, just keeping herself to herself after the shooting incident five minutes ago.

Donavon crouched in front of her and gently lifted her chin, forcing her to look at him. He whispered something, perhaps uttering an apology for calling her an idiot, reaching out to find her hand.

The knock was so faint Will hadn't been altogether certain it had even happened. No one else had heard anything, so he dismissed it. He ran his eyes over the crew once more, each of them hurting. Not in a physical sense, but not all wounds were visible. What Mel had told him played on his mind. Had it been a barrage of bullshit, or had she spoken a truth that was hard to accept and even harder to admit?

Had fail-safes failed and communication broken down?

Had this human-made catastrophe occurred on a broader scale?

He could call the sky blue, and maybe it still was. He could convince himself they were safe, and they might be rescued. But they could soon be dead. And perhaps the sky would never be blue again.

The attack had ripped a hole in their mission, leaving their plans in shambles and hopes dashed. But the true challenges and deepest grief still lay ahead, and the first harbinger of these trials came with a second, much louder knock at the door.

Dong… dong… dong… dong…

BALLOON: SOLITUDE

Hope begins in the dark. But what if the dark holds a horrifying reality no one is prepared to face?

In the aftermath of a cataclysm that has reshaped society forever, the surviving crew members find themselves cut off from the outside world. Faced with a grim choice — sitting tight and waiting for a rescue that may never come or forging their own path — they look to Will, their balloon captain, and Ariane, the pragmatic NASA research pilot, to lead them forward.

Driven by a shared determination to survive, the crew encounters multiple obstacles and ruthless marauders in their desperate search for a rescue and vital resources. Each member's unique skills and diverse backgrounds prove invaluable and become their greatest assets in this harsh new reality.

Amid escalating tensions, they grapple with the limits of human endurance and the ethical dilemmas that test their humanity. As alliances are strained and trust is questioned, they confront the haunting question: are the greatest threats lurking beyond their shelter, or do dangers lie much closer to home, buried beneath the rubble of their shattered world?

BALLOON unveils a world beyond imagination. Get ready for a journey where crises collide, and the stakes reach new heights.

BALLOON: LATITUDE

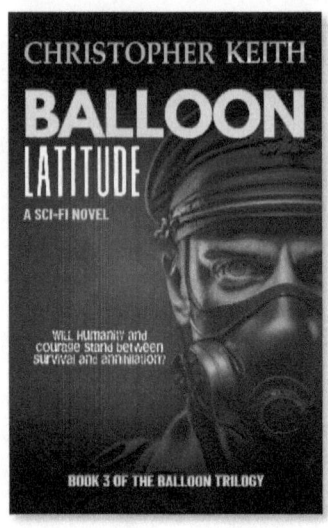

In this third and final instalment, will humanity and courage stand between survival and annihilation?

As rations dwindle and graves are hastily dug, time has run out for the remaining crew. Traumatised by recent events but still alive, they must venture out into the unforgiving environment in one last desperate push to survive.

As they journey across the bleak and hostile landscape, they encounter natural phenomena and the constant threat of dwindling supplies. A land of promise awaits, but first impossible decisions must be made, and the crew must be prepared to pay the ultimate price.

At the critical moment, as the line between triumph and catastrophe blurs and the stakes have never been higher, Will must rely on instinct, devise innovative solutions to their dire predicament, and chart their course in a desperate bid for survival as he once again finds himself on a dangerous high-altitude mission. Will they find the freedom they seek? Or will the shadows of deceit consume them before they can soar to safety?

The genre-bending BALLOON trilogy series concludes with high altitudes, high hopes, and high-octane action adventure.

LIFELINE

A revolutionary breakthrough in human biophysics is poised to redefine the field of medicine.

Dr. Bryan Morgan, a brilliant medic and award-winning clinical psychologist, is struggling with unemployment amid marital and financial strain. That is until the Extended Life Foundation (ELF), a visionary institute at the forefront of scientific innovation, comes knocking on his door.

Using state-of-the-art laboratories, cutting-edge research, and healthcare delivery that prompts both awe and ethical debate, ELF invites Bryan to join the top-secret institute. It's a dream job, but life is never that straightforward, and even the simplest discoveries can have deadly repercussions.

Doubts soon emerge about the consequences of tampering with the natural order. What sacrifices are made in the pursuit of extended life? Is immortality a gift or a curse? And when the lines between scientific progress and ethical obligation blur, who ultimately holds the power to decide?

Ahead lies a frightening and dangerous mission into the unknown, putting Bryan's life, and his sanity, at risk, as the choices he makes will have profound implications. Trapped in a loop of increasing danger, he'll go to any lengths to protect his family and expose the truth before it's too late.

If you're a fan of fast-paced tech-thrillers with mind-blowing medical science, unexpected twists, and a desperate fight for survival, you'll love this science fiction thrill ride.

CLOTHO

For those who read between the lines, the new technology was terrifying.

Following a catastrophic terrorist attack that obliterates a prominent transport hub, Nova becomes an unwitting victim, shattering her memory into fragments. The exact circumstances behind the blast remain a mystery, but it has the radical Anti-Tech Movement written all over it.

As she struggles to piece together the remnants of her past, she becomes entangled in a dangerous pursuit against powerful forces that will stop at nothing to suppress the knowledge she possesses, catapulting her into a confused and lonely downward spiral.

When she crosses paths with Arthur, a middle-aged man still reeling from losing his family in the attack, and a homeless boy, Owen, she forms an unlikely bond, and their lives are irrevocably changed. But can she trust them?

Driven by a voracious desire for answers, Nova embarks on a dangerous quest with her unexpected alliances to unravel the truth that lies at the heart of her lost memories. With every step closer to the truth, she realises her forgotten past is entwined with the fate of the entire world, making her a girl who knows too much.

A journey into how technology and best intentions collide, reminding us that some truths are worth risking everything to uncover. Experience this electrifying tech-thriller crammed with mind-bending twists.

Join the community on
Facebook or subscribe on the
website for the latest news

@christopherkeithauthor
www.christopherkeithauthor.com